D1528224

The Games of Supervillainy

by

C. T. Phipps

Copyright © 2015 by Charles T. Phipps

Published by

Amber Cove Publishing

PO Box 9605

Chesapeake, VA 23321

Cover design by Raffaele Marinetti

Visit his online gallery at http://www.raffaelemarinetti.it/

Cover lettering by Terry Stewart

Book design by Jim Bernheimer

Edited by Tara Ellis and Jim Bernheimer

Visit the author's website at
http://unitedfederationofcharles.blogspot.com/

Printed by Createspace

First Publication: December 2015

ISBN-13: 978-1522874522

ISBN-10: 1522874526

Dedication and Acknowledgements

This novel is dedicated to my lovely wife, Kat, and the many other wonderful people who made this book possible. Special thanks to Jim, Shana, Rakie, Matthew, Sonja, Bobbie, Devan, Tim, Joe, Thom, and everyone else.

C.T. Phipps

Table of Contents

Chapter One 1

Chapter Two...9

Chapter Three 17

Chapter Four 25

Chapter Five 31

Chapter Six..39

Chapter Seven..47

Chapter Eight...55

Chapter Nine..61

Chapter Ten..69

Chapter Eleven 77

Chapter Twelve 85

Chapter Thirteen 89

Chapter Fourteen..93

Chapter Fifteen...101

Chapter Sixteen 109

Chapter Seventeen 117

Chapter Eighteen 125

Chapter Nineteen 131

Chapter Twenty 139

Chapter Twenty-One 147

Chapter Twenty-Two..155

Chapter Twenty-Three 163

Chapter Twenty-Four 171

Chapter Twenty-Five 177

Chapter Twenty-Six..185

Chapter Twenty-Seven..193

Chapter Twenty-Eight..197

Chapter Twenty-Nine..205

Epilogue 213

About the Author 219

The Rules of Supervillainy

Foreword

The response to *The Rules of Supervillainy* has been overwhelming and I'm very glad to have reached so many fans.

A lot of reapers asked me what sort of genre I write in and I say, I write in the *capepunk* genre. Just as William Gibson used cyberpunk to talk about technology as a means of furthering the power of the establishment, I write in a world where superhuman abilities are threats to the status quo of the world. Or so I like to think. Mostly, I just tell bad jokes and write about characters I like.

Our supervillain protagonist, Gary Karkofsky a.k.a Merciless, likes to think of himself as inhabiting a world where conservative superheroes preserve the status quo while supervillains upend it. He's a very angry man, obsessed with changing things to be better and has a lot of misdirected energy. People have asked me if Gary is right and whether or not superheroes are inhibiting progress and social change. I'd argue my anti-hero is misreading the situation.

I think of superheroes as fundamentally anti-establishment, Comic Book Code or not. I can think of nothing more reactionary than trying to change the world for the better and dreaming of a better one. It falls to the hardliners amongst us who believe the current world is the best we can achieve. Supervillains may want to change things but they are harbingers of the oldest status quo of all: tyranny over overs with no regard to their feelings or desires.

Last book, Gary came face-to-face with how badly he misread the world's heroes by facing individuals willing to work against the world's rules for the greater good and just how horrible supervillains could truly be. For a man who romanticized his supervillain brother as a Robin Hood in a world of caped Sheriffs, it was a bitter pill.

We pick up in *The Games of Supervillainy* with him being teleported to Falconcrest City a month after *The Rules of Supervillainy*, time and space bent to give him a look at what his hometown looks like without heroes. Well, at least, very few. Fans of the zombie genre may be pleased with the fact it is a city overrun with the living dead while others may think I'm going slightly off-genre. I could think of no better metaphor for a people stripped of agency and forced to go through the motions of life by a ruthless power above them. Also, intelligent zombie supervillains are cool.

My (anti)hero is a product of a lot of supervillains and heroes thrown together. He's Spiderman, Batman, Jimmy Olsen, the Wrath, Anarky, Kyle

Rayner, and the Hood all thrown together. A figure whom has been given that dual-gut punch of tragedy and unexpected power in the same breath as so many other heroes and villains. I find he's a character who walks a path of unexpected twists and turns, unwilling to admit he's wrong when he should yet capable of great good when he's sworn it off.

I hope you'll enjoy the next installment of his adventures as much as I've enjoyed writing it.

Chapter One

Where the City Goes to Hell (Literally)

I am Merciless.

Gary Karkofsky a.k.a The Supervillain without Mercy.

He of the redundant codename.

I haven't been a supervillain long, the better part of a month from the perspective of the world and less than a week from mine due to a teleporter accident from the moon (don't you just love this world?). I was presently surrounded by at least three hundred or more zombies. We were in the middle of the city's suburbs a few blocks away from my house. There were about a hundred or so burned beyond recognition members of their species already at my feet.

The zombies, themselves, were in various states of decay with many of them showing signs they'd been dead far longer than the month I'd been absent from the city due to the aforementioned teleporter accident. They were mostly wearing formal attire like suits or Sabbath dresses which were probably the outfits they'd been buried in.

The smell was horrifying, with a distinct odor of formaldehyde in the air. Which. to me, said these guys were less likely my former neighbors than the poor bastards the citizens had been burying for the past decade.

And they kept coming, no matter how many I incinerated.

"I don't think they're getting the message," I said, creating a flaming circle around myself which was so hot any of the undead who charged forward not only caught fire but burning to ashes when they tried to cross.

"Zombies are an abomination caught between life and death. They hate their current existence and seek to destroy those who do not suffer from it or some means of ending their torment. They may be coming after you as much because you're capable of killing them than in fear of avoiding death," a reverberating Christopher Lee-esque voice said in my head.

It was Cloak, the ghost of the late superhero Lancelot Warren a.k.a. The Nightwalker. Due to, I kid you not, a shipping error, I'd gotten his magical hooded cloak and costume rather than my infinitely-more-deserving wife Mandy. It was the reason I could levitate, shoot fire from my hands, create ice, talk to the dead, and take all the punches which left most people permanently injured.

"Great," I muttered. "Just what I need, the Walking Dead wanting to usher off their mortal coil."

"*It is what the Reaper's Cloak was designed to do,*" Cloak said, reminding me my powers weren't there to satisfy my ego.

What a crock.

"Death to the living!" one of the zombies let forth a hideous groan.

"Death to the living!" all of them still capable of speech let forth similar monstrous wails. "All glory to the coming darkness!"

"Praise Sylvanas, yeah, yeah," I muttered, levitating upward about ten feet. I could have just floated over these guys but they made the mistake of pissing me off. Summoning forth the ambient necromantic energy in the air, and there was a lot of it, I drew it into myself and then unleashed it in a massive tidal wave of fire which spread over the surrounding crowd in a perfect circle. It left nothing but ashes and melted asphalt across the street and two lawns. There were a couple of straggles left but making finger guns with my hands, I caused them to explode one-by-one.

"Pew! Pew!" I said, watching them go down.

"*Gary, this isn't the time for jokes,*" Cloak muttered. "*We need to find out what's happened to the city.*"

"It's always time for jokes," I said, cheerfully. "Sometimes you need to laugh instead of cry."

Really, I was less upset about the fact someone had overrun my neighborhood with soulless monsters aping life than the fact I'd lost a month out of my life. From my perspective, I'd been on the Society of Superheroes' moon base less than an hour ago. The goody-two-shoes superhumans of the world had locked me up in the Archvillain Wing on trumped up charges only for me to escape during a riot engineered by evil genius Tom Terror.

If I was being honest, and I rarely was, I'd only gotten away because I'd made sure Tom and the absolute worst of the prisoners hadn't gotten away. Honor amongst thieves? Sure. Honor amongst mass-murdering psychos, terrorists, and world-destroying monsters? Not a chance.

"*We will find your wife,*" Cloak said, sounding surprisingly sympathetic. "*Mandy is a resourceful woman.*"

"More resourceful than me," I said, not afraid to say my wife was a better person than me in every conceivable way. I had a tendency to fall in love with women who were way too good for me. "Okay, let's find a zombie we haven't killed."

"Why's that?"

"Because these guys are more like Deadites than Romero shamblers. If they can shout slogans, it's possible they can hold a coherent conversation."

"That's a dubious assumption."

I wasn't so sure. Earlier today, or a month ago depending on your perspective, I'd gotten caught after fighting the resurrected corpse of serial-killer/bank robber the Ice Cream Man. He'd been the second man I'd ever killed and the first I'd done in as a supervillain. The fact he'd come back for some payback as well as to continue his criminal career said to me someone wanted smart zombies.

Albeit, he seemed smarter than most.

"Zombie intelligence varies by level of decay before animation as well as the evil of the spirit within," Cloak replied.

"What do you mean?"

"The souls of the truly damned tend to stick with their bodies as opposed to go on to a proper afterlife. Hence, the Ice Cream Man and other dead supervillains are likely to come back with their minds intact versus these poor wretches."

"That's...horrible," I said, disgusted. "Who designed that system?"

"God, I assume, or one of them."

Cloak had been a polytheist sorcerer in life.

I was Jewish.

Albeit, extremely unorthodox.

I didn't have to wait long before I got my answer. A throaty rasp shouted in the air from nearby. "Merciless! The Great Beast Zul-Barbas demands your death! I'm more than happy to give it to him!"

Zul-what now?

"Zul-Barbas," Cloak explained. *"One of the seven Great Beasts. They are the eldritch gods which were left over from the Pre-Creation Darkness when the Primals made the universe."*

"Uh-huh," I said. "I must have missed that part in Genesis."

I turned around to see what sort of whacked out zombie, weirdo cultist, or some combination of the two was coming toward me. Much to my surprise, I saw a large flannel-wearing man with a black beard, furry hat, and blue jeans hacking away at a horde of colorful-costumed undead with a glowing silver ax. He had a vague resemblance to the guy on the paper towels and it took me a second to realize who he was.

"The Backwoodsman!" Cloak explained, sounding way-way too enthusiastic. *"The Fearless Friend of the Forests! The Rural Renegade! Commander of Canada's Clearest Climate Commandoes!"*

"Please tell me that last one isn't a real thing," I said, appalled.

"They're an ecology themed group," Cloak said. *"Nice bunch if a bit a preachy."*

"Are you part of his fan-club or something?"

"He's one of the oldest continuously active heroes around, Gary. I admit to having a fondness for the fellow. He's just so...sunny."

I knew who the Backwoodsman was. Ironically, I knew him for his association with various Pro-Supers groups like the Tomorrow Society, the Genetix, and the Transhumans. One of the increasingly common "born" supers, he'd hit the proverbial superpowered lottery with immortality, super-strength, and invulnerability. In the Eighties, a group of renegade scientists working for P.H.A.N.T.O.M. had tried to extract his powers and ended up grafting a cybernetic ax into his arm. It appeared whenever he wanted it to and disappeared otherwise.

I didn't think he needed my help.

That was right before one of the zombies; a fresh-looking thing dressed in a pink dress with a double M on the chest area, hit him across the face and sent him flying thirty yards back in the air. I had to turn insubstantial to avoid getting hit with his three-hundred-pounds-of-muscle frame.

"Okay," I said, looking between the two figures. "That was unexpected."

"The pink one is Mary Martian," Cloak said, sounding horrified. *"A superheroine from the Sixties who retired here in Falconcrest."*

The pink-wearing zombie hissed at us, half of its jaw hanging down and then charged along with the ones beside her. They were all dressed like superheroes but ones I didn't recognize, which was a fairly rare occurrence.

Cloak, obviously, did recognize them. *"The Heroes of Today. All murdered. The Brotherhood of Infamy will pay for this."*

"The Brotherhood's the generic doomsday cult you used to hang with before you became a superhero, right? The one that built this city to be a giant summoning circle for evil?"

"Yes."

"Just checking."

I remembered the Heroes of Today now that Cloak mentioned them. They'd been Fifties to Sixties Falconcrest City do-gooders without much in the way of powers. Mary Martian had been the exception, possessing the standard "flying brick" power set from her Venusian heritage. She wasn't flying right now, though, and I wondered if she'd forgotten she could with all the brain rot having set in. Smart zombies tended to be assholes in real life, something about the evil magic preserving only the very wicked. Either way, it didn't matter much because I set the entirety of the group on fire with my mind.

The zombies hissed and screamed as the group stopped in its tracks and began a brilliant bonfire. The Reaper's Cloaks were designed to aid the wearers in serving as psychopomps for the souls of the restless dead. As such, the magic seemed particularly effective against the various tin-hat, colored jumpsuit, and long cape crowd ahead of me. They'd been heroes in life so watching them go up like dried paper was oddly comforting. They no longer would have their bodies defiled to harm the innocent.

"Requiescat in pace," I said, seeing only one single corpse remain in the glowing orange and yellow flames.

"Hiss!" Mary Martian said, turning to growl at me.

"Ah crap," I said, watching the now-flaming superpowered monster crouch down and fly at me with the speed of a car.

So much for that theory.

I tried to shift to insubstantiality but realized I wasn't going to be able to do it in time. As such, I was hit square in the chest and sent spiraling on the ground. If not for the Reaper's Cloak giving me very-very limited invulnerability, I would have had my organs liquefied. Instead, I just felt like I'd had the crap kicked out of me. Mary Martian then grabbed me by the front of my costume, the flames on her wrist licking my neck before pulling back her fist to smash my face in.

That was when an ax buried itself in her head.

The superheroine fell to her knees then over.

Destroyed.

"Rest in peace, indeed, eh?" The Backwoodsman said, standing above me. "Oh, hey, Merciless. Whatcha doing here?"

The Backwoodsman was a stunningly handsome example of masculinity in that slightly-outdated way with muscles, a hairy chest visible from his slightly unbuttoned shirt, and the broad smile on his face.

"Uh, hey?" I said, shaking my head and climbing to my feet. I was still a bit winded from Mary Martian's attack. "You know who I am?"

"Oh yeah," the Backwoodsman said. "I was there when you escaped from the Society of Superheroes' prison on the moon. I heard about all those lives you saved during the riot."

I grimaced. That was going to kill my rep. "Yeah, well, I only just got back. Do you mind filling me in on some details as to what the hell has been going on?"

The Backwoodsman checked his watch. "Okay-dokey. Just know I can't spare too much time. There's a lot zombies out and aboot."

I stared at him. "Canada is literally just across Falconcrest Lake. Half our population is Canadian. They do not talk like that."

The Backwoodsman dropped the accent and spoke with a deeper more gravelly accent. "Eh, I just do it to fuck with people. Be glad I hadn't gotten to randomly inserting maple syrup and hockey into the conversation. How can I help?"

I had plenty of questions, most of which the Backwoodsman probably couldn't answer. How was my wife? How were my henchmen, Cindy and Diabloman? How was my family which lived in the city? How were, ugh, my in-laws? Instead, I just settled on asking a very simple question. "How the hell did the city start to look like a *Resident Evil* level?"

"Wow, you have been gone awhile." The Backwoodsman looked over to the Falconcrest City skyline visible from our current position in the suburbs. "It started a couple of days before the big moon breakout. Supervillains killed in the fight to see who would own the city after the Nightwalker's death started rising from the grave and taking revenge on those that killed them. Then those supervillains started rising from the grave. It became more than the police could handle."

"Can they handle anything?" I asked, sarcastically.

The Backwoodsman snorted. "No. They don't even try. Probably why they're still alive. A few people started to put up a token resistance when they realized the authorities wouldn't help. That rich girl, Amanda Douglas, started organizing citizen's militias with that old fart Sunlight while a new heroine called Nighthuntress took down several of the more powerful zombies. She was accompanied by some new heroes in masks, a strong man and a sexy woman in a red hood."

My heart seized up at the mention of Nighthuntress. That had been the name my wife had chosen for herself when she decided to become a superheroine. It seemed Mandy had decided to begin her career when the city needed her most. The others were probably Diabloman and Cindy, disguising the fact they were helping a hero. "Go on."

"That was when the Brotherhood revealed itself. Hundreds of the city's rich, famous, and powerful proclaimed they were in service to Zul-Barbas and cast rituals which raised all of the city's dead in graveyards across town. Thousands of dead, including bodies they'd been stockpiling from P.H.A.N.T.O.M attacks and the last couple of alien invasions. Many of the police chose to join the cult for protection and those that didn't joined the ranks of the dead. Millions evacuated the city as fast as they could."

"What about Nighthuntress?"

"No idea. She's hot, though."

"That she is." I nodded, holding the bottom of my chin as I thought about what this could all mean. "Go on."

"President Omega and the government declared a state of emergency and helped with the evacuation. They forbid the Society of Superheroes from sending in reinforcements, claiming the government would send in a military response to deal with the zombie threat. The Society was then distracted by Pyronnus and Entropicus waging a war over the Cosmic Starchild. It's only us second-stringers left over to help."

"You're not a second-stringer!" Cloak shouted in my head. *"You are an inspiration to children everywhere!"*

"Merciful Moses, dial it down," I said to Cloak. *"You're going to give me brain cancer."*

"Sorry," Cloak said. *"I read his Junior Adventure Novels as a boy. They were a great inspiration to me. Did you know the Backwoodsman killed a bear when he was only three?"*

"I'm pretty sure that was Davy Crockett," I said.

"Maybe they both did."

I sighed, disregarding Cloak's statement. "Stupid team-wide crossovers. The Society of Superheroes will be gone for months. What about the government response? If President Omega is trying to show off by handling this, what has he done?"

"Not a damn thing. I believe he's keeping Congress deadlocked while looking like he's trying to get them to move in order to increase his political power. The bigger the disaster, the more it makes him look heroics when he resolves it. Pfft, politicians. A few heroes like me have broken the Foundation for World Harmony blockade of the city, though. Ultragoddess and a team of renegades have been fighting the monsters left and right. A real hell-cat that one but magic is one of the Ultra-types weaknesses so they haven't been able to sort things out."

"No one could do a better job under these circumstances." I had a lot of faith in Ultragoddess, real name Gabrielle Anders, who, I shit you not, had been my girlfriend in college. Back on the moon, she'd confessed she'd broken up with me to protect me from her enemies. The oldest excuse in the book. She'd indicated she still loved me but I wasn't going to leave my wife and she wasn't a home-wrecker. It was good to know Gabby was out there, though, fighting the good fight.

"I don't doubt that," the Backwoodsman said, sharing my opinion of Gabby.

"Any idea why the Brotherhood is doing this?" I asked.

"To be evil?" The Backwoodsman suggested. "Supervillains aren't complex."

I glared at him. "I'll pretend I didn't hear that. Thank you."

"You're welcome. Gotta run, though! My cybernetic receiver says there's more folk needin' rescuing." He then turned around and started running like a speeding locomotive, leaping onto one of the nearby houses and then leapfrogging to the next a street over, heading toward the city.

I sighed, taking in everything he'd told me.

"What now?" Cloak asked.

I took a deep breath. "Now I go to my house to see if my wife is there."

Chapter Two

Where I Find Out What My Henchmen have been Doing

Within minutes, I was in front of my home. Not much had changed, though the Nightcar was parked in front of the driveway.

The Nightcar was a futuristic looking tank-car hybrid created by the late billionaire Arthur Warren, reclusive scientist and philanthropist, for his brother the Nightwalker. The vehicle was black with armored plating and stealth technology plus god knows how many upgrades from alien tech as well as Society of Superheroes super-science.

Ironically, Cloak said the Nightwalker never used it for anything but public gatherings since he preferred to travel around the city in an innocuous white van or with magic. Being more theatrical, I'd retrieved the Nightcar from the Nightwalker's former base a month ago, hoping to use it in my crime sprees. The only concession to its new identity was the big Red M spray-painted on the front hood.

Aside from the oddity of leaving such a machine right outside of my house, which kind of defeated the purpose of a secret identity, there was also the fact the rest of the block seemed to have been fortified. All of the houses had been boarded up, automatic sentry gun emplacements put down in their lawns, and "M" graffiti placed over everything as if to announce to the world that Merciless lived here.

The sentry guns followed me, but didn't fire, for which I was grateful. Taking a moment to look through the cracks of one of the boarded up windows, I saw my neighbor's homes had been converted into makeshift bank vaults. There was art, cash, weapons, and food all stored inside. Someone had been busy during the past month and I hoped my neighbors weren't too pissed off at what my henchmen had done.

"Go ahead and say it," I muttered.

"*What?*"

"Say I told you so. Everyone will know who I am." Cloak had warned me Diabloman and Cindy were trouble.

"*Are you maintaining a secret identity? I wasn't sure. Everyone in the Society already knows who you are. You were just in prison after all.*"

Turning back to my house, I started up the front walkway. I lived in a two story white-house with a tiny front lawn, garage, and moderate sized backyard. It was more than I could have afforded as a bank teller (my previous occupation) but something Mandy had been able to pay for with her family's inheritance. The lawn hadn't been mowed in a while and the cherry tree to the side was dead, a sight which bothered me.

I walked up to my front door and rang the doorbell. It was my hope Mandy would meet me at the front door, we'd have a tearful reunion, and go on to make love. I had a feeling it wasn't going to be that simple. To only my mild surprise, the door mat collapsed under me and I fell through a trapdoor down a funhouse-like chute.

Seconds later, I landed in a steel cage against the wall of a house-sized cavernous lair. There were stacks of money, gold bullion, jewelry, food, weapons, and supplies next to a large number of warehouse crates. A big "M" hung over the back of the wall and it overlooked the Nightcomputer. Apparently, my henchmen had relocated it from the Nightwalker's former base in the Falconcrest City Clock Tower.

A staircase led up from a spot a few feet away from me to the old basement entrance which connected to my kitchen. The strangest thing? The fact my washing machine and dryer was still present. It seemed my henchmen had expanded my basement to house their equipment and loot only to start filling up the neighbor's houses when they were full up.

"Alright, this is new," I muttered.

"*You've added a Merciless Lair, I see.*"

"So I have."

"*The words 'low profile' really aren't in your vocabulary, are they?*"

"Hey, this wasn't my idea!" I snapped back. "I would have gone with a big M-shaped nightclub."

Moments later, the door opened up to the kitchen and Cindy started down the stairs in pair of jeans and a t-shirt. She was carrying an empty laundry basket and seemed to do a double take at my presence. Cindy Wakowski was, if you'll forgive a married man saying so, gorgeous. She was a pale-skinned redhead with a body to die for, and a tendency to flaunt it.

We'd been boyfriend and girlfriend in high school before I'd realized there were some girls who were a lot of fun but not quite what you wanted from a relationship. I think our breakup had been over a threesome, happy gas, an exploding abandoned gas station, and a stolen bowling ball trophy. It bothered me on some level we'd remained friends after that. There was something seriously wrong with me.

"*On that we'll agree,*" Cloak said.

Before I'd been whisked away to the moon by Ultragod, Cindy had been my first recruit to the Merciless Gang ™. Yet another ex-girlfriend, Cindy was also a medical doctor who had decided to pursue a life of crime both for kicks as well as to pay her expansive medical school bills. Mandy had been less than pleased at Cindy's recruitment but, honestly, I don't think I could have done it without her. It also helped she really brightened the room.

"Oh my God." Cindy's mouth hung open. "Gary!"

"Ahem." I cleared my throat." When I'm in the cape, it's *Merciless*. You don't want to spoil my secret identity do you?"

"*You have the Nightcar parked out in front of your house. I'm not sure you have one left.*"

"That was sarcasm, Cloak," I said, rolling my eyes. "You'd think you'd be used to it since every other sentence I say is it."

"*Only every other?*" Cloak said.

I smiled and turned insubstantial before passing through the bars. I didn't really want to risk that one-out-of-ten chance. "It's good to see you, Cindy. I escaped certain death and life imprisonment on the moon. I killed a few bad guys, destroyed Magog the Nephilim, reunited with an old friend, defeated the world's greatest superhero, and claimed a million dollar ransom. *Now, where the hell is my wife?*"

Cindy winced as she walked up to me, laundry basket in hand. "Uh, wouldn't you rather hear about the nifty new lair we built for you? Hey, maybe we could tell you about all the money we've made extorting protection from the people of Falconcrest! Saving people from zombies in exchange for wealth! It's like heroism only *better!*"

I narrowed my eyes. "As happy as I am with your criminal initiative, no, no I don't. Where is Mandy and I'm not going to ask for a third time?"

"Would you like me to put on some music? I've just added Powerman 5000's 'Super Villain' to our playlist."

I stared at her, my gaze capable of cutting through steel.

"I... I don't know," Cindy admitted. She slowly walked down the steps, putting the laundry basket on the ground beside her.

I paused a second, my heart skipping a beat. "Explain."

Cindy tapped the ends of her fingers together. "Well, Gary, she was mad at you."

I felt sick, thinking about my month-long absence. "I can't imagine why."

Cindy nodded, apparently missing my sarcasm. "*Very* mad at you. There was also the fact we were using your house to conduct criminal mayhem. I think she got fed up with us and moved out."

I looked at the piles of cash nearby. "I don't suppose it occurred to you *to find a hotel?*" I wasn't going to set fire to her or strangle her. However, the fact she'd kicked my wife out of her own home made me sorely tempted.

Cindy followed my gaze to the piles. "But your house is so nice! You have a flat screen television and such cute doggies."

"Yes well... "I stopped cold. "Wait, the dogs are still here?"

"Yeah, why?" Cindy asked.

"Oh my God." I couldn't breathe. "She's been kidnapped."

Cindy suddenly looked alert. "Wait, what?"

My heart pounded as I realized the full terrible implications of this. I needed to sit down. Walking over to the Night Computer, I plopped myself down in the leather seat in front of it. "Do you own any pets?"

"No," Cindy admitted.

"Trust me; *under no circumstances* would she leave our dogs. Is Diabloman here?"

Cindy nodded, shouting up the stairs. "D! The Boss is back!"

A few seconds later, Diabloman came down the stairs wearing a fresh set of wrestler's trunks with a big 'M' on the front. His chest, arms, and neck were covered in tattoos of demons now visible thanks to his attire. In his hands was a small action figure of me and a cell phone. "Is this important, Cindy? I'm on the phone with the Evil Promoter. He's interested in bringing us in as a stable of Heel wrestlers for the next Slaughtermania."

Diabloman was one of the sadder stories of Falconcrest City's underworld. A former A-lister from the Eighties, he'd become a B then C and finally D-Lister henching for losers like the late unlamented Typewriter. As I understood it, he was a practitioner of tattoo magic and a worshiper of demonic forces raised by a Satanic cult to destroy the world.

Despite this, Diabloman was an extremely affable man who'd seemingly abandoned his plans to take over the world after getting married and having a kid. While he claimed this had nothing to do with his fall from grace, I couldn't help but suspect there was a link to his status as a devoted family man and his lost favor with the Lords of Hell. D had taken to henching for me with gusto, mostly because my plans seemed to actually work. He was a great deal smarter than either Cindy or me and would probably be able to find where Mandy had been taken far quicker.

While possessed of an above-average IQ, this comic book nerd/anarchist/ex-bank teller/*Star Wars* fan wasn't exactly up there with Tom Terror for supervillainous genius.

"My wife has been abducted!" I shouted at Diabloman. "I want the National Guard, Marines, Foundation for World Harmony, Society of Superheroes, and Detective Duck on the case!" I shook my fist in the air, standing up. "Get to it."

"*You realize she could be de—*" Cloak started to say.

"Do not finish that sentence," I threatened.

Cloak, surprisingly, didn't.

Diabloman did a double take at my appearance. "Boss?"

"Yeah. He's alive," Cindy said, crossing her arms. "That means we have to split the loot. So it's both good and bad. Mostly good."

"Cindy..."

Cindy winced, shrugging her shoulders. "Sorry, sorry. Old habits die hard. I keep forgetting you're a touchy-feely kind super-criminal."

"Not to mention the whole ex-lovers thing," I said, annoyed. "But who are we to quibble on relationships?"

Diabloman rushed down the stairs and grabbed me in a hug. "It is a glorious thing to discover you have managed to escape the custody of the Society. I have tried to oversee your empire well in your absence."

"Watch me not care." I rolled my eyes. "What do you know about Mandy's disappearance?"

"I'm sorry, Boss. I have failed you. I do not know what has befallen her. You may take my life if you wish," Diabloman said, ending our embrace. Taking a step back, he knelt down and offered his throat to me. If I wanted to, I could have killed him then and there.

I shook my head and crossed my arms. "This isn't feudal Japan and I am not Darth Vader. You will live to fail me many more times, I hope. I need to find out where she is and who has her."

"I may have an idea." Cindy walked over to a nearby pile of mail which had been put together with a rubber band, reaching in she pulled out a long golden envelope with glitter on it. It was, quite frank, ridiculous looking. I could also smell it from here as it was covered in a thick perfume. "This could be a clue."

"Do we often get letters from David Bowie?" I asked, raising an eyebrow. I also wondered why the hell the mail was still being delivered and why they were just tossing it down here. Maybe they'd rigged the mailbox with a trapdoor too. Nah, that was ridiculous. You know, unlike the trapdoor tied to the door buzzer.

"It says *If you ever want to see your wife again* on the front," Cindy said, pointing to the red lettering on the front.

I walked over and snatched it from her hands, mentally revisiting the question of killing her. No, I wasn't that sort of guy. Especially not a friend, even if she drove me crazy. I would do anything to protect Mandy, though. If someone had abducted her, I was entirely willing to tear this city down to its foundations.

The letter read:

Merciless,

I have watched your activities with great interest. Not many people can make a fool out of Tom Terror, destroy a team of superheroes, and eliminate three of Falconcrest City's worst criminals in their first week of activity.

There can be only one Boss of Bosses, however, so I challenge you to a gentleman's contest. Come alone to the Falconcrest City Opera House and we shall see who is the superior criminal mastermind.

You have my word of honor no harm shall befall her until your arrival. However, if you try and double cross me I shall be forced to do something unmentionable to her.

Sincerely yours,

Angel Eyes.

"Just when I thought the criminals in this town couldn't get any stranger," I muttered. "Who calls themselves a criminal mastermind?"

"*You've done so several dozen times in the week I've known you.*"

I didn't bother responding to Cloak, looking between my two henchmen. "When did this letter arrive?"

"I am fairly sure it's new," Diabloman said.

"I'm one-hundred-percent sure that it was within the last twenty-four hours," Cindy said.

"You have no idea, do you?" I asked.

"She only vanished a few nights ago," Diabloman said. "Nighthuntress worked us ragged protecting the city in your absence."

"She was very mad, though," Cindy said. "Mandy was getting really frustrated waiting for you to get back from your teleportation whatchamacallit."

I tried to remember what I knew about this Angel Eyes character. I didn't remember much about the guy. Falconcrest City had over four hundred supervillains alone and even an amateur enthusiast like myself couldn't remember them all. I did recall, however, he was one of the

Nightwalker's more powerful foes and one of his occult rather than street crime villains.

"*He was both, actually,*" Cloak corrected.

I have to ask Cloak for more information in a minute. "Okay. We need to form a posse to take this Angel Eyes guy down."

"You're not going alone?" Diabloman asked.

"Don't be ridiculous," I said. "The very fact the guy said I should come alone is a good reason I should come with a small army."

"*Occasionally, you surprise me with a bit of cleverness.*"

"Thank you, Cloak," I said. "Okay, everyone, what do we know about this Angel Eyes guy?"

Cindy raised her hand as if she were in grade school. "Oooh! Pick me, I know all about him."

"I know much as well," Diabloman said.

"*I'll fill in any blanks they miss,*" Cloak said.

"I'll go to the greatest resource in the world first." I went to the Night Computer and pulled up Angel Eyes' Superpedia page. Most of it consisted of listing his crimes, which were considerable. Angel Eyes a pretty heavy hitter, which surprised me because I only recalled a few facts about him. Memorizing everything I could, I decided to let the others speak anyway. "Go ahead, Cindy, I'm all ears."

"I used to hench for him." Cindy sighed dreamily. "He's gorgeous. Like the most beautiful supervillain in the world."

"That... doesn't help." I wrinkled my nose.

Diabloman had more information. "He was once an actor, stage as opposed to screen. Supposedly named Thomas Star, no one knows where he came from. Star was disfigured by an obsessive fan after rebuffing her advances. He started wearing elaborate masks to cover his scarring. Later, he started adopting the persona of the roles he used to play. In the end, his obsessions turned to murder."

"Wow, that's...incredibly unoriginal. It's a half-dozen literary and movie clichés strung together. All you need is a dead girlfriend." It was, unfortunately, more or less what his webpage said along with the fact he was a really powerful wizard who ran an upscale criminal organization in Uptown.

"*All of that is misinformation,*" Cloak said. "*You shouldn't trust everything you read on the internet. Supervillains change their pages all the time.*"

"Those fiends!" I said, in mock horror, trying to distract myself from the fact my wife had been taken. I wasn't succeeding. Even so, I checked out my Superpedia page to see what it said about me. Much to my disgust, I found out I was still a stub entry.

"Angel Eyes is just *sort of* disfigured. You know, like the Phantom of the Opera in the musical," Cindy said, defensively. "He's *wonderful.*"

I snapped my fingers in front of her face. "Stop admiring the guy I'm going to kill."

"Sorry." Cindy looked down at the ground in shame.

"*Angel Eyes is the mortal avatar of the Greek god Adonis. Aphrodite him restored him to life after his first death and fed him ambrosia only to cast him away due to damage sustained to his face from Hephaestus' hammer. Blessed with her favor despite his minor disfigurement, Adonis has spent the past few thousand years engaged in self-improvement. He's a staggeringly powerful magician, hedonistic and amoral, limited only by his melancholy. I suggest caution since he's as likely to destroy a man as give him a present and vice versa.*"

Great. I was going to have to fight *another* god. Worse, a *Greek* god. I hated the Olympians. It was a Jewish thing. "Is he dangerous to Mandy?"

"*No. He doesn't harm beautiful things and, for all of her skill and foul temperament, Mrs. Karkofsky is a very beautiful woman.*"

"That's good news." I breathed a sigh of relief.

"*The problem is he's probably not working alone.*"

"What?" I asked.

"Don't you hate it when he talks to his cape like that?" Cindy said. "I always worry it's talking about me."

Diabloman made a 'shh' gesture.

"*Angel Eyes does not like to work alone. He demands an audience and routinely teams up with other archcriminals. If any of the city's other supervillains are involved, I do not know if we can guarantee your wife's safety.*"

"Well, crap," I said, breathing in. I had to trust in Mandy's ability to protect herself. She'd been trained to be an agent of the Foundation for World Harmony by her father since near-birth and was the original candidate chosen by Sunlight to replace the then-recently-deceased Nightwalker. While I didn't give her even odds against a demigod since she didn't have any powers, I didn't think she was the helpless damsel-in-distress either. As much as it went against my every instinct, I needed to handle this cautiously and not go off half-cocked.

Aw, who was I kidding?

"Get in your uniforms and get the car," I said, looking between them. "We're getting my wife back."

Chapter Three

Where I Go to Confront Angel Eyes

Time had called the Nightcar the most advanced car ever made. It could move like a jet and possessed an arsenal equal to a military helicopter. It was the perfect vehicle to get me to Angel Eyes as fast as possible. Only one small problem: I had no idea how to drive it. Thirty minutes after taking it out I'd smashed into three cars, nearly sideswiped a still-human grandmother, and set fire to an abandoned building trying to turn on the radio. Thankfully, no one was hurt...too badly.

"Are you sure you want to drive? I can do it just fine." Cindy asked, reading *Esoterrorism* in the back. She'd changed out of her previous outfit to her sultry Red Riding Hood costume with corset, scarlet hood, fishnets, and all-too-short skirt. I doubted it was very good for fighting but it certainly was an attention grabber. Too bad I couldn't appreciate it in my concern for Mandy.

"Everything I'm doing is intentional," I said, keeping my eyes on the road and hoping I didn't accidentally kill us all.

"Even the stupid stuff?" Cindy asked.

"*Especially* the stupid stuff," I said, slowing down to a more reasonable speed. The streets were hazards of abandoned cars, dead bodies, debris, and worse.

Falconcrest City's downtown was like no other city in the world. Whereas the rest of the world's architecture had moved on, Falconcrest had kept to a 1940s art deco style which seemed designed to emphasize the city's power and majesty. There were huge towering buildings with statues of Atlas holding up the world, faceless figures holding swords, and gargoyles aplenty. There were a few modern buildings but they were the exception rather than the rule.

The damage from the recent events, not just the zombies but the rise in superhuman violence following the Nightwalker's death, had left many of these buildings damaged. Some were burnt out remnants of their former selves and others had whole sections blown up by forces unknown. Others had been decorated in Satanic graffiti or bodies chained to the side by the Brotherhood. Large banners proclaimed Zul-Barabas' imminent return and a few had cheesy slogans written in red paint. At least, I hoped it was red paint. One of the most effective was a simple one: "Where are your heroes now?"

It hurt me to see Falconcrest City this way. While I'd grown up in New Angeles for most of my formative years, I'd moved to this city in my late adolescence. Life had come down hard on my family and, for better or worse, Falconcrest City had taught me how to be mean enough to survive. Despite all the problems the city had with poverty, supercriminals, and corruption, there were good people here. People who were being abused by individuals who had the exact same sort of powers I did.

I wanted to help them.

I just didn't know now.

"Anyway, let's focus on figuring out how we're going to take out Angel Eyes. He's vastly stronger than anything you guys are used to facing. Well, maybe not your earlier career, D, but recently."

"Ours is not to reason why, ours is but to do and die," Diabloman quoted Tennyson.

"Let's avoid the dying part."

"Agreed," Cindy said. "Also, let's avoid anything too hard or dangerous too. What's the point if you have to work to be a criminal?"

"I like your philosophy." I slowed down the car in hopes of getting better control over it. "But we're saving Mandy first."

"Agreed," Cindy said. "I like her and you'd be insufferable if she died."

Sometimes I wondered why we were friends.

"So tell me about these 'zombie outbreaks' affecting the city. I'm not going to have flesh-eating undead as the sole occupant of my city soon, am I?" I asked, hating what had happened to my home. I needed more information, though, if I was going to resolve this. What I'd learned from the Backwoodsman was a drop in the bucket to a month's worth of being in the thick of things.

"People didn't panic immediately when the zombies arrived," Diabloman said. "After all, this is Falconcrest City. The dead rising is just another Thursday."

"Oh yes," Cindy said, smiling. "Remember Halloween 2008?"

"Ah yes." I remembered I'd been attending a party at the university. "The Nightwalker versus Dracula. Six vampires came in to the frat looking for victims. We ended up serving them pizza with garlic. Old Drac didn't look for brains in his followers, did he?"

"*For an elder vampire, Vlad III was never very bright,*" Cloak said.

"So are people panicking now?" I asked.

"Most people are gone," Diabloman said. "Spooked or driven from this land by the cult's reign of terror."

"What happened?" I said. "Assuming the ever-rising tide of the dead didn't spook them like lesser, sane, mortals."

"The Mayor was killed by the cult along with a lot of other people," Cindy said, looking up from her book. "That's when people started evacuating the city. Almost two thirds of the population is gone now. The rest are riding it out to see if things get worse before they get better. They're gathered in places like the sports stadiums, hospitals, subway stations, and more in hopes things will get better. Sadly, the Brotherhood is targeting these places in hopes of getting at the survivors."

"I... see," I said, trying to picture that. I was unable to comprehend people who would do such a thing.

"*Perhaps, then, supervillainy may be not be your calling,*" Cloak said.

"You shut up," I muttered. I didn't need his moralizing when the city was falling apart.

Diabloman continued his discussion of Falconcrest's sorry state. "Your wife did her best to work with Amanda Douglas, Sunlight, and the other survivors who chose to resist. As Nighthuntress, she turned the unarmed civilians of this land into a force capable of resisting the slaughter. Many thousands of zombies were sent back to the grave and it seemed the Brotherhood of Infamy would fall beneath her and Ultragoddess' efforts."

"Mandy and she, uh, met did they?" I asked, hesitantly.

"No," Diabloman said. "For some reason, they seemed to be avoiding each other."

I couldn't imagine why that would be the case.

"Mandy did, however, work with several supervillains who weren't of the, 'kill all humans' variety," Cindy said. "Starting with us but also including the Puzzle Family, Jigsaw Jones, the Ice Screamers, the Raincoat Man, and the Flower Power Guru. She did a lot of coordinating with the Black Witch who served as an intermediary between Mandy and Ultragoddess."

I grimaced, trying not to feel jealous. The Black Witch had been Mandy's girlfriend, the woman she loved if I was honest, during college. As much as I felt for Mandy and she for me, we'd joined together after bad breakups. The Black Witch had been hers the same way that Gabrielle had been mine.

"We'll put a stop to these bastards after I rescue Mandy. No one menaces my town but me."

"Freeing this city from the curse of the undead may be easier said than done," Diabloman said, leaning in over my shoulder. "In addition to the zombies and various undead supervillains running around, the Brotherhood of Infamy has begun working all sorts of perverse magical rituals across town. There are many threats here which did not exist before and will be far harder to remove than the zombies."

"How bad could they be?"

We hit a hellhound. It was eight-feet-long, made of stone with cracks leading to a hellfire core, and possessed glowing red eyes. It landed against the windshield and was cracked in several places from the Night Car's armor.

"You did that on purpose!" Cindy shouted.

"No, I didn't! It was just very appropriate timing." I turned on the windshield wipers. They banged the hellhound in the face repeatedly. "How did the Nightwalker ever drive this thing?"

"I took lessons before driving around in a fusion-powered jet on wheels."

The windshield wipers were just annoying our hellish hood ornament so I hit the brakes, sending the monster flying off onto the back of a car in front of us. The injured demon got up as I saw the damaged car held a family of four. It was minivan filled with supplies and two of the people inside were children under the age of twelve.

Letting children die due to negligence was in poor taste for a criminal genius, so I snapped my fingers and caused the monster to become trapped in a block of ice a foot larger than itself. It took much of my remaining energy reserves, which were running low now, but was worth it. The family drove off, hopefully not getting a good look at me. The last thing I needed was the police knowing I was back in town.

"Case in point. There are over twenty-five thousand zombies within the downtown area alone," Diabloman said. "That is not counting the cultists, their hellhounds, tentacle beasts, mercenaries, and intelligent super-powered servants. We've had worse times in the city but not by much."

"Yeah, well, I'll take care of this." I reassured them, not at all confident about our chances. "Okay, we should be seeing the Falconcrest City Opera House any time now. I followed the internet's instructions to the letter. I thought it was on Central and Sixth."

Cindy said, leaning up into the driver's seat. "No, that was the *North* Falconcrest City Opera House. We're looking for the Falconcrest City

Opera House proper. As opposed to the South Falconcrest City Opera House or the Uptown Falconcrest City Opera House."

This city liked opera way too much. "Right, right, I knew that."

"Perhaps I should drive," Diabloman offered.

"No," I replied, raising a hand. "I need to learn how to do this. You'd think there'd be a Night-GPS onboard with all the fancy doohickeys the Nightwalker installed on this thing."

"Third button on the right."

I pressed it. A holographic map appeared over the dashboard, giving directions to the opera house.

"Oh," I muttered. "Okay."

"The car also has autopilot designed to avoid innocent bystanders and road obstacles."

"Uh, take me to the Falconcrest City Opera House?" I asked, hoping this worked.

"Affirmative," the car dashboard said in a feminine voice.

"I meant to do that." I then said to Cloak, *"Why didn't you tell me about that?"*

"I needed you to calm down. You were panicked when you first heard your wife was threatened. If you're going to face Angel Eyes, it should be after you've had some time to cool down."

"Devious. I'm rubbing off on you."

"I hope not."

"So, Cloak, does Angel Eyes have any weaknesses?" I asked, hoping I could figure a way around the wizard demigod should things get dicey.

"None you'd be able to readily exploit. Adonis is more powerful than any Reaper's Cloak wielder and immune to most of your abilities. Bluntly, fire and cold won't affect him nor will you be able to turn him intangible. He, by contrast, will be able to do any number of sorcerous effects. He could turn you to snow, music, dust, or erase you from existence with little more than a few words. Worse, I can't teach you the defenses I learned through years of studying magic to prevent it."

"In short, I'm probably screwed."

"Yes," Cloak said, honestly. *"However, he is possessed of a weak mental core. Like all incredibly vain people, he longs for validation and approval from his peers. Present yourself as a peer or superior and you might be able to charm him over to your side."*

"I'd prefer to just shoot him in the head."

Cloak sighed.

"Do you guys know where Ga...Ultragoddess and her team are working from? Can we get in touch with them?" I asked. If there were superheroes in town, it seemed like a good idea to try to coordinate our efforts.

Of course, neither of my henchmen knew about my past relationship with Gabrielle or the fact while on the moon, I'd coordinated with her off-the-books team, Shadow Seven.

As insane as it sounded, America's sweetheart and the daughter of the world's greatest superhero was doing anti-government covert operations against the worst tyrants and organizations in the world. Her team was composed of repentant criminals and heroes willing to work outside the law.

All of them were willing to fight and die to get the job done. The Society of Superheroes couldn't be seen operating against legitimate civilian authorities but as President Omega's decision to abandon Falconcrest City's citizenry proved, sometimes you needed to do just that. I just never expected the S.O.S to have the balls to do it.

"I'm afraid not," Diabloman said, frowning. "Mandy was our chief contact with them and they've always been on the move throughout the city. They're the chief targets for the Brotherhood of Infamy as you might expect. By comparison, we've only had a dozen or so attacks against our headquarters."

"If by headquarters, you mean my house, I think I may have thwarted one against you. Three hundred and fifty odd zombies plus a bunch of undead superheroes came against me a few blocks away from you."

"Anyone we know?" Cindy asked.

"Mary Martian."

"No!" Cindy said, aghast. "My mom loved her!"

"I should warn you," Diabloman interrupted our digression. "Ultragoddess' team has supervillains on it other than the Black Witch. It's also staying off official channels and mesmerizing many witnesses to have a dim recollection of events. I'm immune to such and keep a hypno-wheel for undoing what was done to Red Riding Hood." He gestured to Cindy. "I do not know what the S.O.S is up to but it is not right."

"Superheroes and supervillains working together just isn't right," Cindy said, disgusted. "It throws the entire dynamic off."

"Leave that to me," I said, not wanting to reveal I considered them friends. "I know how to handle them."

Diabloman and Cindy exchanged a concerned look.

"As you wish," Diabloman said, speaking for both of them.

Five minutes later, we were outside the Falconcrest City Opera House. I'd managed to park the Merciless Mobile in the bushes, having knocked over six parking meters in the process.

Diabloman stared out the window. "Your parking needs a bit of work."

"I insist this was all deliberate," I said, unbuckling and stepping out. "I saw no reason to let the autopilot do all the work."

"I did," Cindy said. "The fact you suck at driving."

I gave a dismissive wave. "Don't cloud the issue with logic."

The opera house was typical architecture for the city, looking more like a cathedral than a place to put on musicals. It made me wish someone would tell the city council colors were not the antithesis of a well-ordered community. Even brown or red would have been a welcome change from the endless black and stone edifices.

"Do you have a plan, Boss?" Diabloman asked.

"Yes, I want you guys to sneak in while I go in guns blazing to distract him," I said. "You take out his henchmen or monitor the situation and report back to me via cellphone. Whichever looks like it would help more."

Diabloman looked guilty. "I don't think that's going to work."

"Why?" I asked.

Diabloman pointed over my shoulder at a group of punks in white plaster masks carrying M16s.

"Ah, that." I held up my arms in surrender.

Chapter Four

Our Confrontation with Angel Eyes

The punks surrounded us in a circle, aiming their M16s at my head. Their leader said, "Don't try anything funny."

My immediate reaction was to be less than impressed. "I'm sorry, but who the hell trained you? When you're carrying guns, *do not* encircle an opponent. You're only going to end up shooting each other."

The punks moved to one side, forming a firing squad. Their leader, a man with a mohawk under his plaster mask, said, "Thanks for the tip."

"You're welcome."

"Gary, what was the point of that?" Cindy asked.

I blanched. "I don't know, I was hoping to think up something in the few seconds that would buy."

"Did you?" Cindy asked, sounding hopeful.

"Nope. I got nothing."

I could turn intangible but in the time it would take me to grab Diabloman and Cindy, all three of us would be gunned down. I couldn't set them all on fire either, at least from what little I knew of my powers.

"Any suggestions, Cloak?"

"Go with them."

"A fat lot of help you are."

"Who are you talking to?" The punk leader asked.

"Santa Claus," I said. "He says you've been a very naughty boy."

The punk looked at me strangely. "Huh?"

"Sorry, my wife has been kidnapped so I'm off my game," I said. "I'm usually much wittier."

"No, you're not."

Lead at gunpoint into the opera house theater, I saw the stage had redecorated as a miniature house. There was a banquet table, expensive paintings, a bedroom, television set, and couch. It was like Angel Eyes lived on the stage.

I tried not to think about where he went to the bathroom.

Moments later, a fog filled the air and it convalesced into a six-foot tall man with blond hair and a well-toned body. He was wearing a white suit looking like it came from the Nineteenth century, complete with cape and shoulder tassels. True to Cindy's depiction, he was gorgeous, Brad Pitt level gorgeous. There was just the small issue of the white plaster mask covering his face.

"Behold the glory of Angel Eyes, mortals!" the criminal said, spreading his arms out. "Gaze upon my visage and know were my face not so tragically deformed, you'd bow before me in reverence."

"Huh. He *is* David Bowie," Diabloman made an uncharacteristic joke.

I snapped my fingers, expecting him to burst into flames. Nothing happened. Staring at my fingers, I snapped them again and again. Angel Eyes just stood there, looking resplendent in his ridiculous outfit.

"*I told you your powers wouldn't work,*" Cloak muttered.

"I didn't believe you," I shot back then made the mistake of looking at him directly. Cindy was right, he was *damn* good looking. Not even the fact he was wearing a plaster mask impeded how flat out sexy the dude was. A fact I was not often inclined to observe about dudes.

Cindy nodded. "I want you to know, I won't betray you for at least ten more minutes."

"Thank you. I appreciate that." I didn't find her joke to be all that funny, if joke it was.

Supernatural beauty was one of the less common superpowers but still in existence. Many people debated it, really, since so much about beauty was in the eye of the beholder. It was a mental effect, though, as much as physical with as many men possessing it as women. Simply put, it was a quality about a person which implanted the idea they were beautiful and you should do anything to impress them. Guinevere and Succubus possessed it and, apparently, so did Angel Eyes. I couldn't help but start questioning my sexuality after just thirty seconds of gazing at him.

He was using it passively, though, so it only took thinking about Mandy being his prisoner to shake me out of it. I had to be wary, though, as using it directly against us might be more dangerous than any spell he could hurl at us. The Black Witch could boost her appearance with spells and that had led to whole teams of trained Foundation for World Harmony willing to turn their guns on themselves.

I myself, made the mistake of accidentally taking a potion which granted me supernatural beauty in college. I'd ended up locking myself in the bathroom for a week out of fear and disgust to its effect on the heterosexual women around me (and a couple of gay male friends).

Angel Eyes might actually be capable of convincing Cindy to betray us.

Or Mandy.

Crap.

"Shut up you two." The mohawk-wearing punk smashed me in the gut with his rifle before aiming his rifle at Cindy.

Before I could react, Angel Eyes lifted up a hand which shot forth glowing lightning. The mohawk-wearing punk was consumed in an instant, disappearing in a shower of light.

"It is not polite to strike guests," Angel Eyes said, his voice solemn. "It had been my hope to settle this honorably but you have violated my request to come alone." Angel Eyes' voice was almost melodic. "I must now deal with you the same way I deal with all dishonorable men."

Angel Eyes lifted his hand again and I grabbed the punk nearest to me, using him as a shield. The lightning washed over the gangster, disintegrating him the same way the previous one had been.

The other punks reacted by pulling their guns up at my face, only for Cindy and Diabloman to grab at their weapons. Diabloman managed to disable two at a time, taking their M16s under his arms and aiming them at the ones Cindy hadn't been able to cover.

"Toss your weapons on the ground," Diabloman said.

Seconds later, the remaining punks tossed their guns on the ground and ran away. I took a step forward and shook my fist in his general direction.

Angel Eyes looked at the sudden reversal with a bored disinterest. At least I think it was bored disinterest. It was hard to tell through his plaster mask. "How very droll. To think I went to all the trouble of immunizing myself to your powers for this."

"Well, you didn't know you were dealing with a criminal mastermind like me," I said.

"Yes, I did." Angel Eyes wrinkled his nose.

"No, you didn't," I replied.

"Yes, I did!" Angel Eyes snapped.

Cindy put two fingers in her mouth and whistled. "Please!"

"Sorry! Okay, Adonis, *where is my wife!?*"

"She is safe," Angel Eyes said, making a dismissive gesture with his hand. "It was she who came to me rather than the reverse. Your wife has been attempting to unite the various gangs and criminal organizations remaining in the city into an alliance against the Brotherhood of Infamy. I found her company charming and foreseeing your return to the city was imminent, decided to make out an invitation for you to come."

I blinked. "So, she's not been kidnapped. You just implied she was because you're a jackass."

"Hold your tongue," Angel Eyes said, waving his hand and removing my mouth. One second it was there, the next there was nothing but a smooth plate of flesh where my lips used to be.

I made a finger gun with my right hand and aimed for the stage lights above his head, causing several to fall by melting the metal holding them up. Angel Eyes was caught by surprise by this, allowing me to generate an anvil made of super-dense packed ice over his head and cause it to fall on his head.

There was a hint of unease as it became clear I wasn't going to be helpless against him. He might be immune to direct use of my powers but didn't appear to be such by use around them. I was about ready to conjure a cube of ice around him then burn away all the oxygen inside when, much to my surprise, he waved his hand and restored my mouth.

"You've made your point," Angel Eyes said, surprising me. "Perhaps you are not a mere jack-a-napes playing at the games of gods."

I felt my lips in order to make sure they were there. "Oh, are we friends now?"

"Gary—" Diabloman started to say. Clearly, he didn't want me picking a fight with this guy. "We are outclassed here."

Cindy then surprised me by pulling out a pocket-sized 1950s looking ray gun from her picnic basket and aiming it at Angel Eyes. "I've got you backed up. This was designed to kill Wrathion Space Vampires and they're magical."

"Where did you get that?" I asked.

"Remember FalconCon 2012?" Cindy asked. "With Captain Galaxy and the Astronomers as the guest speakers? I kind of picked this up after blowing—"

"Eh, eh, eh," I raised my hands in surrender. "I don't need to know the details."

Captain Galaxy and the Astronomers were space explorer superheroes with the latter empowered by the Ultra the same way Ultragod and Ultragoddess were. They were just far weaker. Captain Galaxy had no powers but made due with astronaut training, a jet-pack, and a gun very much like that. He was also known as a relentless horn dog that made use of the constant stream of groupies most superheroes eventually acquired.

"I figured it'd be nice to have some power so I've been picking up toys from the various supervillains you've killed," Cindy said. "It's also amazing what the cops will let you have out of the evidence lockers if you pay them."

I made a mental note of that for future reference. "What do you have in that picnic basket anyway?"

"A lot more than it looks like," Cindy said. "I had Mechani-Carl outfit it with an extra-dimensional space and some magical cross-wiring. Oh and Angel Eyes, he's *way* closer to Venus than you."

Angel Eyes coughed, then looked directly at Cindy. He became slightly indistinct and as beautiful as an angel. "Surely, you don't want to shoot me?"

Cindy blasted his table. "Looking at you is like falling in love but Gary pays me. I know which I choose."

I should have been heartened by that but I wasn't.

Diabloman sighed. "So be it."

The Mexican Marauder proceeded to touch the side of his suit, which I knew covered a huge number of magical tattoos. Spring forth was a huge hellhound which was about the size of a small car. The hellhound was made of fire and shadow and looked like a wolf-shaped Balrog from the Lord of the Rings movies by Peter Jackson. The creature spit little spurts of fire and clawed at the chairs around it, tearing them to pieces.

I suddenly felt a lot better about our chances.

"Please," Angel Face said. "Heel."

The hellhound whimpered and covered its face with a burning paw.

Okay, I was back to feeling awful about them.

Angel Eyes looked down at us. His aura of beauty made me weak in the knees but I refused to buckle. Instead, I concentrated on the words he spoke. Like a commanding god, he said, "I have been researching your team since it debuted a month ago, Mister Karkofsky. I did not like the Nightwalker, he was an arrogant controlling busybody—"

"Also rude, condescending, and irritating," I added.

"*Ha-ha,*" Cloak said.

Angel Eyes didn't stop to acknowledge my words, "—but I respected him. You are an inadequate inheritor. When I saw how much effort your bride was putting in to saving this city while you were off the Twelve knows where, I knew you were unworthy of her too."

"You want to know unworthy?" Cindy said, keeping her ray gun trained on him. "We used to date too."

"I find that perfectly believable," Angel Eyes said.

Cindy looked like she was ready to fire that instant.

"Hold," I said, holding out my hand. I didn't want to kill Angel Eyes just yet. I had his measure now. I'd met plenty of guys like him before who measured themselves by lording over other people. He wanted me to stand there and take it as he lectured me on how much better he was. The problem was, I wasn't the kind of guy to sit around and take it.

"Yeah, yeah," I said, shaking my head. "I get it, you're crushing on my wife and trying to make me feel inferior. This, despite the fact you're living in a frigging opera house with a high-class version of a paper bag over your head. You're right, I don't deserve Mandy and I thank God every day she came into my life. However, if you think you do, that you have any right to lecture me on being the person she fell in love with—you are dreaming."

Angel Eyes looked at me and for a second, I thought he was going to go nuts and start hurling spells like Gandalf.

If so, I was ready to go Balrog on him.

So were Diabloman and Cindy.

That was when we had a surprise visitor. Mandy Karkofsky stepped out from behind a nearby stage set wearing an elegant black dress and high heels. Her hair was up in an Audrey Hepburn style and she looked stunning.

"Okay, I was downstairs looking over the food stores we're about to deliver to the citizenry when I heard all sorts of—" Mandy stopped in mid-step. She seemed stunned at my presence. "Gary?"

I knew my wife well enough to know she was manipulating Angel Eyes. She was a smart and cagey enough woman to play on whatever feelings she perceived from him to get his help to assist the citizens of Falconcrest City. I doubted she was interested in the supervillain. Seriously, at least. My wife might have a type given her history with two previous supervillains of mixed morality but I'd never had cause to doubt her fidelity. It still hurt, however, to see her wearing that sort of outfit for someone else.

"Hey Mandy," I said, waving. "Good to see you."

"My lady." Angel Eyes looked embarrassed. "I was just warning your husband about the fact the zombie forms of the Ice Cream Man and Typewriter, those supervillains he killed last month, are searching out him."

"Oh, is that what you were doing? Because you didn't mention those two losers in your speech about how much I sucked," I said, having well and truly had enough of his shit. "Oh, and, Angel Eyes?"

"Yes?" he turned to me.

"Goodbye," I said, pointing my rifle at him and opening fire.

Chapter Five

Where I Negotiate with Angel Eyes

All of the bullets I fired at Angel Eyes bounced off an invisible force field surrounding him. The shots ricocheted and took out three stage lights and one of Angel Eyes' punks. They screamed and went instantly, bleeding out on the ground. Thankfully, none of the bullets hit Mandy.

Angel Eyes retaliated by pulling out a wand and shooting a blast of pure mystical force at me. I conjured a shield of super-condensed ice in front of it which was shattered to pieces, but dissipated the effects of his spell. Angel Eyes prepared another blast only to be knocked backwards by Diabloman's hellhound slamming into him. Apparently, the demonic poochie had marshaled its courage while everything was going to hell.

"He is vulnerable to my magic," Diabloman said. "We can kill him if we work together."

"Good work!" I said, ready to take advantage of that fact.

Angel Eyes grabbed the hellhound by its throat and proceeded to snap the creature's neck, causing it to disappear in a puff of brimstone and fire. Angel Eyes was, officially, pissed off now.

"Gary!" Mandy shouted.

I waved for her to run to us. "Run away, Mandy! He's a crazed stalker! Who knows what he's capable of!"

Angel Eyes got up, glowing with bright and brilliant energy which caused the entire opera house to shine. "You *dare* strike the Chosen of Aphrodite?!"

"When they tell me they kidnap my wife and hold her prisoner?" I said, snapping. "Yes. Prepare to die, pretty boy!"

Mandy pulled out a pistol attached to a holster hidden against her leg and fired it in the air. "Please!"

Everyone stopped.

"Gary, I'm not a prisoner," Mandy said, staring between me and Angel Eyes.

"You're not?" I asked.

"I said she wasn't!" Angel Eyes snapped.

One of the surviving punks said, "Hell no, she's not a prisoner. When we tried to bring her in, she killed two of us! She forced Barry to bring her to the Boss at gunpoint."

Mandy looked annoyed. "I was hijacking a food truck for refugees when they tried to ambush me. How the hell would you react?"

The punk looked down. "Sorry."

I stared at Angel Eyes. "So you did try to kidnap her but you failed."

"She did, technically, come to me rather than the reverse," Angel Eyes said, looking embarrassed. "She came to me, this brown-haired warrior goddess, holding my men at gun point." Angel Eyes placed his hands over his heart. "I was smitten and it took it upon myself to woo her. I would never have sent my challenge to you if I'd known what a charming creature she was."

"Okay, Angel Eyes, you're going to die," I said. "I don't know how I'm going to do it but it's going to happen."

"Gary!" Mandy shouted. "You are *not* killing him."

"I'm not?" I said, really wanting to teach this guy a lesson.

Mandy explained her reasoning for coming here. "Angel Eyes is the leader of the most powerful gang left in the city. He controls territory, weapons, magic, and supplies. I came to him to negotiate a truce for the good of the refugees. I was just about to seal the deal when you guys came barging in."

"What's with the evening dress then?" Cindy asked, staring.

Mandy looked at her next. It was a death-glare worse than the one she'd given Angel Eyes. She didn't have to justify it to me, even if I found the implications she'd use whatever method she could to influence him...disquieting.

Cindy then looked to me, only to see a similar expression. "Right, this is none of my business. I'll be shutting up now."

Cindy put away her ray gun, which she hadn't fired anyway. Maybe it was harder for her to strike Angel Eyes than she let on.

"Wise idea," Diabloman said.

I sighed, putting my hands on my hips. "Fine. D, stand down. Punks? Know I could kill you all with my brain. As I'm enjoying this insanity. I need a few moments alone with my wife. Can we call a ten minute truce?"

Angel Eyes bowed his head, placing his hand over his heart. "As you wish."

"That works?" Diabloman sounded surprised. "Dammit, I could have done that with the Nightwalker."

Climbing up on the stage, I walked over to my wife and took her by the hands. Looking over my shoulders to make sure no one else could hear our conversation, I whispered, "*Please* don't divorce me."

"What?" My wife looked as confused as she'd ever been, which was impressive given she was married to me.

I started to ramble, cupping my hands together. "I know I've been gone a month and it's my own damn fault for being involved in all of this supervillainy stuff. I swear to God, though, I did everything in my power to get back here as fast as I could. It was an accident with the teleporter and I never meant to leave you alone for a day let alone a month. I love you more than life itself and can't bear to imagine life without you."

I was feeling more than a little bit guilty about my missing time, becoming a supervillain, and most of all about the kiss I shared with Gabrielle on the moon. It had been a moment of weakness between the two of us. This whole supervillain thing had spiraled out of control and if I had to choose between it and my marriage, well, my marriage came first.

As hard as it would be.

"Gary, I'm not divorcing you," Mandy said, looking surprised I even thought it was possible.

"Oh thank God." I breathed a sigh of relief.

"I knew you weren't deliberately avoiding me," Mandy said, stared at me. "Ultragod called me within ten minutes of your teleportation and said you were stuck in the fold-space relay's feedback loop. I was pissed off at you for getting involved in a supervillain prison riot but he explained you saved his life. You saved a lot of lives, something about a giant demon, and you killing it."

"Shh!" I put a finger over my mouth. "Don't talk about that. It would destroy my reputation forever."

Cindy shouted over at us. "Gary, we already know you're a VINO. We forgive you."

Apparently, I'd underestimated the distance necessary to not be heard. Either that or she just had really good hearing.

Mandy raised an eyebrow. "Vino?"

"Villain In Name Only," I replied, glaring at Cindy. "It's about the worst label which can be attached to a villain. It's all downhill from there. Hell, you might as well defect to becoming a hero. Thankfully, I'm just beginning my career and can always work my way up to Villain In Actuality."

"*You just are incapable of having an epiphany about yourself, aren't you?*" Cloak muttered.

"Hmm?" I said back.

Mandy sighed and felt her head. "We do need to have a serious talk about your henchmen but otherwise, I'm fine."

"Hench*persons*," Cindy corrected.

"What part of *a few moments alone* did not register with you, Cindy?" I shouted back at her.

"Clearly the entire concept," Cindy said, throwing her hands up. "I'll be over here."

Mandy looked tired of this entire business. "I like Cindy, sort of, but I do think we need to set some boundaries."

"Will do," I said, looking over at Angel Eyes. "What about the Phantom of the Opera?"

"We need to recruit him," Mandy said. "We need more power to fight the zombie infestation and he's a heavy hitter. I also don't think he's evil. I…I think he's mentally ill."

"I never would have guessed!"

"*Remember the old adage about people throwing stones in glass houses?*"

"I think we can help him," Mandy said, diverting the subject. "With the right treatment, he could not only help this city but become a powerful force for good in general. I think he just needs the right encouragement to get help."

"You're kidding, right?" I asked, appalled.

Mandy stared right back. "I've been putting up with your henchpeople for a month. Look what they did to our basement. By the way, I want it put back to the way it was. I don't need to walk two stories to do our laundry."

"Okay." I waved my hand dismissively. "I don't need a lair, anyway."

"Seriously, your henchmen *need* their own place."

"Will do," I answered. "I'll buy them a nightclub or decaying mansion to stay in. I have a small fortune in gold down in the baseme—"

"And you need to return all that stolen money."

"That might be a problem."

"Gary… "

"Can't we donate half of it to charity?"

"Gary, I'm allowing you to be a supervillain. Don't press me on this."

"I'll return all the money which belonged to people who either didn't deserve it being taken away or couldn't afford it," I replied, sighing. "If I can't find them, I'll put it in a generic zombie relief fund. Can we at least keep what we extort from criminals?"

"Fine."

"Thank you," I said. "I'm still not sure about this 'not killing Angel Eyes' thing, though."

"He's a demigod, Gary, how would you even go about killing him?" Mandy pointed out an obvious problem with my plan.

"I'm sure the Society of Superheroes has some hydra blood somewhere. I'll sneak back into New Avalon and take it," I said. Technically, I'd already killed a god during my prison break. I'd destroyed Magog the Nephilim, a being which was just sort of Godzilla in terms of strength and power. I'd done that with Death's help, though, and I wasn't sure what kind of cost I was going to be paying for that down the line. None of that was relevant now.

Mandy glared again.

"No dice?"

"No dice," Mandy repeated. "Now I want you to go over there and make peace with Adonis."

I glanced over at him, taking in the man's majestic presence. "The fact he looks like Brad Pitt's more attractive younger brother isn't influencing your decision, is it?"

"Don't be ridiculous," Mandy said. "You can't even see his face."

"No," I said. "Just his rippling biceps, long flowing hair, and s... I'll stop now."

"Please do. Unless there's something you want to admit to me." Mandy gave me a half-smile.

"No," I said. "I have nothing to admit."

"Are you *sure*?" Mandy teased.

"Absolutely."

Mandy made a little 'go hither' gesture with her fingers. "Then go make peace. Maybe we'll be able to save this city with one of the city's most notorious occultists at our side. Reformed and redeemed."

"Yeah, because that's what I'm all about, redemption," I grumbled.

"Gary... " Mandy trailed off.

"*Fine-fine*, I'll do it." Walking over to Angel Eyes, I said, "Okay, after a long discussion with my wife, I've decided to let you into my gang."

"*Your ability to take refuge in audacity never ceases to amaze me. **This** is how you're going to make peace?*"

"You know, you weren't this snarky when you were the Nightwalker," I mentally said to Cloak.

"*I've got eighty years of dry observations to cut loose with.*"

"*Trust me, though*," I said, prepping my upcoming speech in my head. "*I know how to speak this guy's language.*"

"*Ancient Greek?*"

Angel Eyes reached up to his white plaster mask. Pulling it very off less than an inch, I caught a glimpse of the face underneath. He was beautiful, possibly the handsomest man on Earth. The male Guinevere if you will. I could just make out the *tiny* scar on his right cheek. It was only a slight blemish, almost unnoticeable. I suppose, though, to Adonis it was probably equivalent of having acid thrown in his face.

"I'm thousands of years old, I've made love with goddesses, I know the secret arts of Circe and Medea, and you want to *hire me to be part of your gang?*" Angel Eyes asked. His tone had none of its earlier melodrama. It was clear he was serious.

"That's about the size of it, yeah," I answered, stretching my arms behind my back.

"I will have to decline," Angel Eyes replied, putting his mask back on. "It demeans the Chosen of Aphrodite to subordinate himself to mere mortals."

I clasped my hands behind my back in order to keep myself from strangling the pompous ass. I hadn't been this insulted since high school.

"*I can't believe I'm doing this, but let me help. Angel Eyes is obsessed with his image above all else. Even more than his pseudo-romantic worldview, he's vain. You can use this to direct his actions.*"

"Thanks, Cloak. I forgive you for hiding your true identity for me."

"Hmm?" Angel Eyes said, obviously not able to hear Cloak like some of my companions.

I paused for dramatic effect, ready to get to the meet of my argument. "You need to join me because you're in danger of falling off the radar."

"Excuse me?" Angel Eyes asked, offended.

I gestured to myself. "I'm the new hotness. Everyone is talking about Merciless. The whole doomed tragic lover thing you've got is last Thursday. You're not even a vampire, so you can't attract the supernatural romance crowd. Bluntly, Angel Eyes, you're in danger of going stale."

Angel Eyes was the Chosen of Aphrodite and a demigod. While I wasn't exactly boned up on my *Bulfinch's Mythology*, I knew enough about the Greek Gods to know they were all vain as hell. I figured a supervillain Olympian had to be even more so, especially one whose story has gone down in history as an example of self-love. Maybe playing to his ego wasn't the most original plan in the world but I suspected it would work.

Angel Eyes looked at me for several seconds then lowered his gaze. "It bothers me I'm listening to you despite your transparent attempts at manipulation."

"It's because you know I'm right." I waved my hands around as I talked for emphasis. "Like every actor and musician, you need regular re-invention. I mean, an opera house and a plaster mask? You're not doing yourself any favors by ripping off Andrew Lloyd Weber."

"Gaston Leroux wrote the *Phantom of the Opera*," Angel Eyes corrected me. Looking at me for a moment, his shoulders slumped and he turned away. "I have noticed a drop in media attention relating to my crimes. What do you suggest?"

I decided not to mention that was probably because of the apocalypse going on outside. "You need to think big." I gestured to the ceiling. "Start by getting some cross-promotion. Do some team-ups and work outside of Falconcrest City. Utilize social-media marketing. You also need some new material."

"New material?" Angel Eyes asked, bewildered.

"Take this whole, 'kidnapping super-people's wives to threaten them' thing. It's so old-fashioned it might as well be fossilized. I mean, what were you going to do for a grand finale? Tie Mandy to a set of train tracks? Angel Eyes, you need me." I put my left hand over my heart.

"Tying someone to train tracks is actually terrifying," Angel Eyes said, looking thoughtful. "Clearly, you have never seen the aftereffects."

I made finger guns at his chest. "Trust me. Together, we will *go places*."

Cindy leaned over to Diabloman. "Is he arguing he should be his boss or his agent?"

"Be quiet!" Diabloman snapped. "The Boss is working."

Cindy snorted and looked away.

Angel Eyes was silent before answering. "I suppose I could agree to an *alliance*."

"That's the spirit." I put my right arm over his shoulder. I was almost overpowered by the strength of his cologne and immense beauty at this close of a range.

Angel Eyes glared at me. "No touching, please."

His words shook me out of my gaze and I pulled away as if electrified. "Not like I want to touch you anyway." I cleaned my hand off on my cloak.

"*There's nothing to be ashamed of, Gary. Just because you're attracted to the most beautiful man in the world doesn't mean...*"

"Never speak of that again."

I noticed Angel Eyes was talking to me. "It is wrong for me to not receive the highest amount of attention in the city and you might be onto something I need to update myself. I will spare your life and allow you to have Mrs. Karkofsky."

"What was that? *Allow?*" Mandy said, looking over at him.

Oooo! He was going to pay for that.

Angel Eyes didn't seem to notice Mandy's reaction. "Of course, now I'll have to break it off with my other partner."

"Other partner?" I asked.

Angel Eyes looked to one side. "Yes, I may have sold your location to another supervillain in hopes of getting rid of you."

Mandy stared at him.

"Who?" Then the answer hit me. "Oh crap."

Seconds later, as if God himself was trying to make sure the humor potential was maximized, the Ice Cream Man drove a gigantic brown, white, and pink steamroller through the wall. The undead supervillain had become even more hideous, his face having mostly rotted off by now.

"Hey, Merciless! Glad you could make it!" The Ice Cream Man shouted, standing up on top of the steam-roller with another bazooka shaped like an ice cream cone.

The Ice Cream Man was the former leader of the Malt Shop Gang and the third-most famous supervillain in the Midwest. He was dressed in a pink button-down shirt, white pants, suspenders, and a little paper hat. The Ice Cream Man also had cut off his lips and sharpened his teeth to shark-like levels. The Ice Cream Man would have looked terrifying even without the fact he was bloated from decay. A foul stench wafted from his hideously diseased undead frame even from across the hall. I'd killed him last month but he hadn't stayed dead, being the first of Falconcrest City's supervillains to rise. Apparently, he was still sore at me for the whole murdering him thing.

Before I could react, he fired his bazooka and a shell of some kind landed at my feet. I managed to grab Mandy and turn intangible but it wasn't acidic or explosive like I expected. Instead, a weird Neapolitan-colored smoke filled the room. Despite being intangible, I felt the gas enter my lungs and blackness claimed me.

Dammit.

Chapter Six

Floating in the Seas of Days Gone by

I had a troubled mind.

I know, what a *shocking* revelation.

Seriously, though, I had always struggled with my inner demons. Even as a child, I'd been separated from others by my intelligence and a vague disquiet there was something terribly wrong with the universe. It wasn't my parents' fault. They did everything in their power to make sure I'd grown up loved and safe but there are some things you're never prepared for.

My brother's murder.

My revenge.

Lost friends.

One consequence of this was the fact I often had dreams. Sometimes awake, most times asleep. These dreams which took me out of my head to the past. Psychotherapists said I just had an incredibly vivid imagination but I sometimes wondered if it wasn't something more. Either way, I'd been drugged by the Ice Cream Man and very possibly was going to die while unconscious. If I survived, it would only be because the Ice Cream Man was known to draw out his murders in order to save his victims' pain.

Victims which now included Mandy.

Crap.

Floating through the endless void of my subconscious I found myself thinking back to the days which had set me on my current path. I didn't think of anytime in specific but just let my impulses drown me in a sea of memories.

There was comfort in those.

One of those memories took me to around two o'clock in the afternoon on a Tuesday of the year before my marriage to Mandy. I wasn't dating her yet, was in a committed relationship already, and was twenty-four and pursuing my masters in Unusual Criminology.

Staring out the window of a finely appointed office, I took in the sights of Falconcrest City University and its myriad Gothic buildings with thousands of students scurrying about. The office behind me had hundreds of psychological, mystical, and philosophical textbooks with oddball Eastern statues and mandalas. There was also a map on the wall of Atlantis, the mythical one versus the one which hosted the Summer Olympics last year.

I was undergoing therapy with one of my professors.

Which was probably a conflict of interests.

"So, your brother was the supervillain Stingray and killed by the antihero vigilante Shoot-Em-Up, yes?" Doctor Thule said, sitting in his chair with his notepad.

Doctor Thaddeus Thule was an elegant Austrian man in his mid-fifties with a body-builder's physique hidden underneath his custom-tailored pin-striped suit, thin square reflective glasses, and curly black beard. Both hands were covered in rings bearing mystical symbols. I've often described him as what would happen if you shaved Arnold Schwarzenegger bald, upped his IQ to 180, and tried to pass him off as an occult healer.

Doctor Thule was a double-holder of P.H.D's in both Psychology as well as Unusual Criminology. He was the key attraction of Falconcrest City University to serious students of both. Thaddeus had invented numerous techniques both magical and science-based for the treatment of sick minds with a specialty in the psychosis of supervillains. He also offered free psychological therapy to his students and quite a few of us had taken up his offer of it.

Later, of course, it would be discovered Doctor Thule was an agent of P.H.A.N.T.O.M and charged with locating extreme personalities with a gift for planning. Called the Super-Villain Maker, he crafted forty-two troubled souls into costumed criminals and terrorists for the sole purpose of distracting superheroes from his employer's evil schemes. Needless to say, the University's reputation took a serious hit after the Nightwalker exposed him.

Oh, and by the way, he had nothing to do with my decision to become a supervillain. I chose to do that *before* I met him.

"We've covered that, Doc, yes," I said, looking back.

"How did that make you feel?" Doctor Thule asked, his voice vaguely mesmerizing.

"Angry," I said, growling. "How do you think it made me feel?"

"And at fourteen you hunted him down and killed him," Doctor Thule said.

I did a double take. "What did you say?"

"I said that must have been troubling for a boy your age," Doctor Thule replied, smiling.

I blinked. "Yeah, yeah it was."

"Do you think this resulted in your obsession with following in your brothers footsteps?" Doctor Thule asked.

"I wouldn't call it an obsession," I said, sighing. "My brother wasn't a monster. He never killed anyone in his entire career. Sure, people died when he tried to take over Atlantis and during heists but that wasn't his fault."

"Of course it wasn't," Doctor Thule said. "I think your brother would be proud of your decision to do so."

I looked at him. "You really think so?"

"Yes," Doctor Thule said, putting his hand over his heart.

I wasn't so sure and even if I was sure, I wasn't so sure I was willing to do it anymore. Killing Shoot-Em-Up hadn't been enough to calm the raging beast inside me. I'd spent my high school years constantly getting into fights, trouble, and only pulled myself out of a downward spiral because I thought I might have a chance of redeeming my brother's legacy.

Lately, the anger wasn't there anymore, though. I'd started to think about other ways I could honor Keith. Had he just been a supervillain? No, he'd been other things. My brother had been a family man and a provider. I wanted a family for myself. For the first time, in a long time, I was starting to think maybe I could lay his ghosts to rest.

That was when I saw a yellow and gold streak across the sky.

Ultragoddess.

Seconds later, there was a knocking on the professor's door. Checking my cellphone, I saw it was time for my lunch date with Gabrielle Anders. "Oh sorry, I got lost in my reminiscing."

Professor Thule looked annoyed. "A pity since I think you were close to a breakthrough. You've been backsliding a lot and losing your focus. Too many distractions, I think, from other quarters." His gaze moved to the door. "But I'm sure we can discuss your justifiable antipathy to superheroes next week. Ja?"

"Ja," I said, grimacing for reasons I didn't entire comprehend. "Heroes are a courageous and rational lot and all that." I turned to the door. "I'll be right out, Gabrielle!"

I knew it was her.

I could feel her presence.

"Awesome!" Gabrielle said, cheerfully popping her head through the door. "Hi, Professor Thule."

Gabrielle Anders was a beautiful Afro-Hispanic woman with beautiful brown eyes, olive-skin, and a smile which could burn away the dark in a man's heart. Today, she was wearing her hair in a ponytail and had a pair of upside-down horseshoe earrings. On her face were a pair of surprisingly thick glasses which, really, should have been smaller given today's fashions.

I loved her, though, and found every part of her sexy.

"Hello, Ms. Anders," Professor Thule said, sounding not at all pleased to have her around.

Professor Thule had tried to get her into one of his therapy courses but she'd politely refused on multiple occasions as well as rejected his attempts to get her to private studies. Frankly, sometimes I wondered if she was really serious about Unusual Criminology.

Professor got up and walked to a nearby shelf before removing a black leather book off the shelf and handing it to me. "We'll discuss your situation in-depth once we're in private again. In the meantime, I suggest you read this book. It will provide, I suspect, fascinating insights into your situation."

I read the title: *The Absence of Mercy* by Doctor Isaac Bedlam.

I tapped the title of the book. "This is the book by the Jewish supervillain who stalked and murdered a bunch of anti-Semites in the 1920s and 30s. The one Fritz Lang did a bunch of films on."

Professor Thule smiled. "An interesting figure for discussing the situational nature of ethics."

He stared into my eyes.

I stared back, then blinked, a little uncomfortable. "Uh, Professor, are you okay?"

Professor Thule frowned, confused, and looked over Gabrielle who was giving him a dirty look.

"Oh, it's nothing," the Professor patted me on the shoulder. "Go, play."

"Okay," I said, putting the book into my backpack then heading to the door to join Gabrielle.

Gabrielle shut the door behind me. She was wearing a white sweater over a golden dress. "I do not like that creep."

Gabrielle looked at me in disbelief. "He's named *Professor Thule*."

"Hey, he can't help his parents' last name," I said, shrugging. I then gave her a long kiss on the lips.

Gabrielle smiled, adjusting her glasses. "Are you ready to meet my father?"

"I'm not sure rescuing dolphins in Japan is a good family-bonding exercise," I said, grimacing. "Still, what's the worst he could do?"

"Come in-between our relationship, disown me, and ruin a lifetime of loving father-daughter interaction?"

I gave her an annoyed look. "You are cruel."

"Just be nice," Gabrielle said, smiling.

"You still haven't introduced me to your mother," I said, starting to walk to the elevators.

"That's because she's Polly Pratchett."

"Ha-ha," I said, chuckling. "Ultragod's girlfriend? Please. But if you don't want to talk about her, that's fine."

"I'll introduce you after I reveal all my secrets," Gabrielle said, adjusting her glasses. "You know, I'm not used to relationships lasting this long."

"Neither am I," I said.

"Yeah," Gabrielle said, wrinkling her nose. "Some of us more than others. Did you *have* to sleep with Jessica and Wendy?" They were Gabrielle's best friends at college.

I grimaced. I'd had a lot of one-night or multiple one-night 'relationships' before I'd met someone who was really worth fighting for. "That was before I met you!"

"A likely excuse!" Gabrielle said, rolling her eyes then bursting out laughing. I'd actually met Gabrielle through Wendy, who was helping her at the school paper where Ms. Anders was journalist. "I'm in this for the long haul, though."

"Me too." I took her hand. I decided after this trip, I'd propose to her.

The memory faded away and I was once more in the void of unconsciousness. Cloak, as a disembodied voice, was there with me.

"*You were very blessed to have two kind, generous women to love you,*" Cloak said. "*Most men do not even get one such opportunity.*"

"Yeah," I said, my voice echoing through the darkness. "It didn't work out between me and Gabrielle and I won't lie and say I haven't played the 'What If' game."

Moses Anders had warmed to me, eventually, even if I didn't realize he was Ultragod until years later. When we got back, though, I'd been kidnapped by murderous serial-killer the Cackler. He'd deduced Gabrielle was Ultragoddess and decided to target the person she loved the most. Gabrielle had come within inches of killing him while rescuing me. Later that week, she'd confessed her true identity to me and that she couldn't risk putting me in danger. I'd tried to fight for our relationship but she'd rather have me alive and away from her than hold me in her arms as I bled to death.

Then she'd erased my memory of her identity and implanted a new memory of our breakup. I'd only found out the truth on the moon.

I would never get over that.

"*I sensed you wanted children,*" Cloak said. "*Why did you and Mandy never have them?*"

That brought back its own memories.

It was a year after my marriage to Mandy and things were going well in my life. I admit, we'd probably gotten married a little too soon given we'd only known each other a couple of months. We'd both been recovering from badly-ended relationships but we were in love and I was determined to change for her benefit. I had cast aside my dreams of being a supervillain and embraced my new life as Gary Karkofsky, bank teller.

Yeah, I was going crazy but I could live with it.

I had her.

It was early in the morning and we were gathered around the kitchen table. Our rescue dogs, Galadriel and Arwen, were gathered at our feet while I was making breakfast for my wife. She was wearing a shirt with Princess Leia on it and looking sleepless. She was still getting used to my frequent bouts of nightmares, one of the reasons why I was making her this. Also, I wanted to butter her up for the conversation.

"So, Mandy—" I started to say, bringing her a second plate of made-from-scratch waffles.

"Yes?" Mandy said, obviously suspecting I wanted to discuss something.

"Kids," I said, laying the plates down.

Mandy looked up, blinking. She put down her fork. "Not hungry."

I grimaced. "Probably should have discussed that before we got married."

"Yeah," Mandy said, giving a face equivalent to being punched in the gut.

"What are your thoughts?" I asked, plopping down into my chair across from her.

Mandy looked at me. "My family is a ticking time bomb of heart-disease, diabetes, Alzheimers, and Parkinsons. Yours also has quite a few problems."

"Medicine is very good at treating those thanks to the efforts of Red Crescent, Red Cross, and the rest of the Parahuman-Medics." They were superheroes who didn't fight crime and God bless them for it.

Mandy picked up her fork again and tapped the waffles a few times. "There's also the fact your sister is a born superhuman and your niece. My uncle was a born superhuman. He could see into microscopic spectrums. That means we both have the recessive super-gene."

I stared at her. "You're superphobic?"

"No!" Mandy said, opening her mouth in horror. "I mean, any children of ours who inherit such powers would be subject to discrimination and have to go to—"

I stared at her, not at all pleased at the way she was choosing to handle this. "Given I grew up with plenty of children who had superpowers and were glad to be alive, including close family, you should probably just admit you don't want to have kids."

Mandy looked down, a guilty expression on her face. "No, I don't."

"Is it because you don't want to go through the process?" I asked, hoping that was the case. "If so, there are countless children out there who need homes of a multitude of races."

I'd actually been hoping to adopt at least one or two children in addition to any she wanted to have. Hopefully, super-ones. I had experience with super-children thanks to my kid sister and babysitting my niece. There was a lot I could do to help them through the worst of their adjustment period.

"Children, are just...not my thing," Mandy said, shrugging. "I'm just not the mothering type."

I was silent after that.

"Is this a problem?" Mandy asked, looking at me. I could tell she was worried our marriage would suffer.

If not disintegrate.

"No," I said, lying. "It's not a big deal at all. I'll just move on."

And I did.

But I would still sometimes dream of a family of my own.

"*I see,*" Cloak said, his voice in my mind as those memories faded away. "*How mundane.*"

"Yeah," I said, feeling myself slowly wake up.

It was time to face the Ice Cream Man.

Chapter Seven

Where I Meet Falconcrest City's Newest Hero

Waking up, my head hurting like someone had hit it with a hammer repeatedly, I contemplated how knock-out gas could affect someone intangible. "Okay, that's complete horse-shit. I was intangible, there's no way that gas should have entered my lungs. It should have just passed through."

"Are you questioning the rules of magic with science?" Cloak asked, sounding like he'd been down this road before.

"It's not a question of magic versus science. It's a simple fact of logic."

"Then how do you breathe when you're tangible?" Cloak pointed out.

Thinking about that, I frowned. "You suck."

"This is partially my fault, I admit," Cloak said. *"I was the Nightwalker for eighty years. That gave villains a very long time to field test their various means of getting past my various powers. Gas was one of my more well-known vulnerabilities."*

"So, because you were one of the world's best superheroes, I'm shit out of luck?" I thought back at him.

"No one ever said being a superhero was easy."

"Thankfully, I'm not a superhero."

"So you keep insisting."

It took a second for my eyes to adjust to the spotlight being shined on me. I had a headache and it only took me a second to realize why, I was suspended upside down. All of the blood in my body had probably rushed to my head an hour ago. Furthermore, my hands were tied behind my back.

On the stage in front of us was some sort of weird high-tech pylon with a crystal that seemed out of place in the opera house. It was plugged into the stage electrical grid and making all sorts of weird noises.

"An M-Wave suppression field inhibitor based on 40th century technology," Cloak muttered. *"Dammit."*

"A what in the who now?" I asked.

"A magic suppression device," Cloak said. *"Very rare. He must have gotten it from one of the higher-tech villains in the city. Possibly the Chillingsworths or Doctor Dinosaur."*

I frowned and tried to turn insubstantial. Nothing. That was going to make things...difficult.

The Ice Cream Man, himself, was eating a hot fudge sundae in front of us with an eyeball and finger inside it. His smell was somewhat disguised with a cologne which smelled of chocolate, sprinkles, and strawberries. Except, now it just made me smell ice cream then rotting corpses then ice cream again, making the two smells co-exist. A remote resembling a television one was attached to his belt and I assumed that was related to my current condition of powerlessness.

Turning my head, I saw Cindy, Diabloman, Angel Eyes, and Mandy. They were similarly suspended and tied up. There was a hissing noise coming from below my head and looking down, I saw a gigantic cauldron of green acid bubbling beneath us. Turning up, I saw a weird mechanism of locks and chains which seemed to lower us all if any of us escaped. The old Prisoner's Dilemma, except this one was designed around the idea they would want to protect each other. While it would probably work on the Nightwalker or most civilians, I wasn't sure it would be so effective in our rather villainously-inclined group. We were still on Angel Eyes' stage, only the Ice Cream Man had cleaned off his miniature house and covered us with a set of spotlights before a red curtain. Apparently, our execution via death-trap was going to be part of a show. A show for one since I didn't see anyone but the mutilated remains of Angel Eyes' gang in the audience.

"Wow," I observed. "I'm suspended over a cauldron of acid. I'm not sure whether I should deride the originality or applaud his revival of a classic death trap."

"Acid tutti-fruity," the Ice Cream Man said. "Flesh-melting ice cream is sort of my signature."

"I confess, though, this is kind of lacking," I said, looking up at him.

"Excuse me?" The Ice Cream Man said, narrowing his gaze.

I shrugged, which was almost impossible upside down. "It's just I've been put in death traps by the best. The Cackler arranged for me to be put in a chamber filled with laughing gas in front of a TV of Bugs Bunny cartoons, only to deliver increasing electrical shocks the more I laughed. This is weak-tea by comparison."

"Weak tea!?" the Ice Cream Man hissed.

"Gary, don't antagonize the supervillain," Mandy said, looking decidedly less than impressed with me. I, on the other hand, was quite impressed her slinky dress was staying down. She must have taped it to her legs.

"Wasn't the Cackler a space god or something?" Cindy asked, her bunches hanging down over her head.

"No, that was the second Cackler who appeared after the first one died. The second Cackler was the son of Entropicus from the planet Abaddon at the End of Time. It turns out the second was psychically possessing the first for most of his crimes," I explained.

Cindy stared at me. "I hate this town so damn much."

Angel Eyes sighed. "We've been awake for a while, Merciless. Frankly, you've been delaying us considerably from our confrontation."

Diabloman said, "It is not right we begin until our leader emerges."

Angel Eyes snorted. "Your leader, not mine."

Cindy shrugged. "Gary's a light-weight. After two beers, he was anybody's in high school."

Mandy snorted in agreement. "It was part of his adorkable nature, though."

"He's no Angel Eyes but yeah," Cindy said, smiling.

"I'm *hanging right here*," I said, appalled.

The Ice Cream Man was still fuming, getting more so the more we bantered. "You are in a death trap! How can you be wise-cracking when I have you all suspended over a cauldron of acid?! This is a life and death situation!"

"Yeah, we noticed," I said, shaking my head. "You're an infamous villain, Ice Cream Man. Dead or not, I expect you to bring your A-game and this just isn't it." I wrinkled my nose. "By the way, you need some air freshener. The zombie thing is not agreeing with you."

"*You realize this is more likely to have him kill you, right?*" Cloak said.

"*Trust me on this,*" I said, mentally.

The Ice Cream Man turned to Mandy and pointed a long bony finger at her face. "You don't think I'm serious? I'll start with your wife!"

"No!" Angel Eyes shouted. "Not her!"

Everyone else looked at him, myself included.

Angel Eyes looked abashed.

Mandy then turned back to the Ice Cream Man. "When I get out of this, I'm going to take that maggot-filled skull of yours and punt it into next week." Mandy said, her voice lowering. I pitied the Ice Cream Man. Mandy was probably the worst person in the group to try and scare.

The Ice Cream Man took a step back.

"She'll do it too." I warned. "You should have seen her in her Goth rock phase."

"Mandy was to die for!" Cindy nodded despite being upside down. "Admittedly, the *Black Furies'* last single could have used some work. *I'm Dating a Dork* just didn't have the same beat as *Die, Girlfriend, Die.*"

"So what's your plan?" Cloak asked.

"Still working on it," I admitted.

"Well, it seems like it's time to demonstrate why it's not a good idea to fuck with the Ice Cream Man!" The supervillain growled, grabbing his remote from his belt and looking between the four of us. "I think I'll start with you, Ms."

He was looking at Mandy.

I had no ideas.

That was when Mandy swung herself upside down into the mechanism right above our heads, smashing it out of place and sending five of us spiraling down behind the cauldron. Mandy fired a strange red laser from her wedding ring, which obviously wasn't the one I'd bought her, got up, and then pulled off one of her high heels before hurling it at the M-Wave Generator. It promptly exploded, leaving me to believe she'd packed her heels with explosives. The Ice Cream Man wailed in frustration, pulling out a candy-cane striped pistol with a Tesla battery on its side. Mandy threw her other high heel, which exploded like a flash bang, allowing her to run up to him and kick him in the chest. The Ice Cream Man went flying off the stage.

"Gary, when did Mandy become James Bond?" Cindy asked.

I shrugged, feeling my powers return, then turned insubstantial and escaped from my bonds. "Well, she did have access to all of the Nightwalker's equipment after his death. I'm just surprised he had an evening dress and explosive high-heels."

"Those appear to be things she's made on her own," Cloak said. *"Albeit, they're minor works of magic and gadgetry. Still impressive, though."*

"Nice work, Gary." Mandy smiled. "You going to help or you want me to handle him?"

"Oh, I think you've earned the right to kick some zombie ass. Besides, I'd love to see you deliver a beat down in that dress."

The Ice Cream Man was already climbing back on the stage, somehow having armed himself with a peppermint handled machete. There was no way in hell for him to be able to beat us all without his gas grenades again, especially now that Angel Eyes and Diabloman had their powers back, but he was refusing to back down. I'd have admired his courage if not for the fact it was so stupid.

"Sounds good, Gary." My wife responded to the Ice Cream Man's return by leaping in the air and giving him a spin-kick to his decaying head. The Ice Cream Man went down like a sack of potatoes, or perhaps empty ice cream tubs. Angel Eyes and Diabloman watched in appreciation, enjoying the show. Mandy proceeded to grab one of the wooden chairs behind the curtain and smashed it, gaining herself a sharpened stake.

I smirked. "I think that's for vampires, Buffy."

"That's why I intend to drive it through his head."

"Ah. Wait, don't you have a laser ring?"

"One charge."

Cindy whistled from where she was still tied up. She, after all, was the only one of us without powers. "Not to interrupt, Boss, but could you maybe help me out here? Some of us don't have magical powers or super-gymnastics."

"One second," I said, heading over to blast away Cindy's bonds. My powers had grown to the point I could use my fire like an instant fusion torch or laser.

"Thank you, God." Cindy breathed out a sigh of relief. I'd been good enough to not burn her in the process. "I will never disrespect you again."

I raised an eyebrow.

Cindy looked guilty. "For the next forty minutes. Thank you, too, Gary."

"You're welcome."

The Ice Cream Man was already getting up, however, producing a chocolate-brownie looking hand grenade with an atomic symbol on the side. "Alright, that's it, no more Mister Confectionary. I underestimated you because you're a bunch of idiots but no more. I'm going to skin you alive and wear your heads for hats."

"Try it, Corpse-Breath." Mandy held up her stake threateningly.

"Corpse breath?" I asked, standing beside her.

"I'm new at this." Mandy glanced back at me. "Cut me some slack."

The Ice Cream Man tried to pull the pin on his atomic grenade before Mandy stabbed him in the arm with her stake. Applying pressure, she tore away the upper end of his limb and sent him tumbling backwards. Being dead, the Ice Cream Man didn't react to losing a limb with pain. Instead, he looked irritated.

"Whore!" the Ice Cream Man screamed.

"Why is it the bad ones always end up going for misogyny?" I asked, appalled.

Mandy pulled her stake out from the Ice Cream Man's arm. "Because guys like him are small-small men."

"Just kill him already! Make it stick this time!" Cindy made a thumbs down in a Roman fashion.

"Working on it." Mandy stabbed out with her stake only for him to just barely dodge it.

Diabloman stepped up behind me, untying his arms. "Your wife is a formidable woman."

No kidding. "Tell me about it. I'd been looking forward to killing the Ice Cream Man myself, but she's earned this one."

The Ice Cream futilely continued to fight despite the fact he was grossly outmatched, Mandy dodging each of his attacks only to continue beating him across the face and chest with a combination of punches and kicks. The Ice Cream Man, being dead, was immune to the worst of them but he still felt them.

Because, hey, magic.

I could tell Mandy was having fun but I hated to see that bastard waste any more of our time. "I think he's had enough."

Mandy got a predatory grin on her face. "Agreed. Time to die for good, Vanilla Boy."

"*I hate vanilla!*" The Ice Cream Man shouted right before a pair of twin superheroes glided down from the rafters onto the back of his head. One was bright gold and white, wearing a very familiar costume. The other was dark and somber but distinctly feminine in shape.

"Of course, my night couldn't end on a high note." I cursed under my breath.

The first of the newcomers was Sunlight, having apparently updated his costume to look like something produced in this decade. It was still ridiculously bright and sunny for a man who was supposed to be a vigilante, but it didn't look half as embarrassing as before. He was still way-too-old to be running wearing that costume, being a man well past retirement age even with the Society of Superheroes rejuvenation treatments, but he looked like an incredibly *fit* man well-past retirement age.

Sunlight a.k.a Robert Warren was the *other* superhero of Falconcrest City, barring the six-year-period where Ultragoddess attended university with me to get her Master's degree in Unusual Criminology. The grandnephew of the Nightwalker, Sunlight had been the bright and cheerful costumed avenger of a city which was permanently in a depression.

Sunlight used holograms, gadgets, and Shambhala martial arts to fight crime in place of sorcery like his more-famous relative. In many ways, he was much more like Ultragod, who he'd modeled his costume than Lancel Warren. Sunlight was indirectly responsible for my getting the Reaper's Cloak but had tried to arrest me twice. I wasn't fond of him.

Following him, standing a foot shorter, was a girl dressed in an outfit nearly identical to mine. She had long blond hair sticking out from the back of her cowl and very familiar looking eyes. There was something familiar about her but I couldn't immediately place what. The woman was shorter than me, of Asian American descent, and looked to be in her early twenties.

"Halt evil doers! It is I, the Nightwalker, here to stop you and your nefarious scheme!" The girl shouted before slapping a pair of handcuffs on the Ice Cream Man's wrist and forearm.

Mandy stared at her then looked over at me. "Is she kidding?"

"Amanda Douglas? What the hell are you doing here!?" I exclaimed, recognizing her voice.

The girl looked horrified. "I, uh... don't know what you mean, citizen."

During my second outing as Merciless, billionaire Amanda Douglas had reacted to her kidnapping with courage and honor. It shouldn't have surprised me she'd decided to take up the superhero mantle as so many rich athletic types had chosen to do. Her career might run into trouble now that I'd revealed her secret identity to a bunch of supervillains, though.

Oops.

"That's Merciless," Sunlight whispered in her ear. "He's the most dangerous villain of them all. He's already defeated Ultragod, escaped the moon prison, and defeated me twice!"

"And don't you forget it!" I pointed at Sunlight. I couldn't believe this guy was still alive. Surely some other supervillain had the nerve to kill him? I mean, he couldn't keep ruining my nights forever, could he?

"*He ruined mine for close to two decades.*"

"You're a pretty horrible friend, Lancel."

"*Family is different from friendship. You're allowed to complain about them.*"

The Ice Cream Man leapt to his feet and tried to bite Sunlight's jugular. I would've welcomed it. Unfortunately, Mandy hurled her wooden stake like a throwing knife. The pointy end passed through one side of the zombie's head and out the other side. In an instant, the Ice Cream Man collapsed on the ground, deader than dead.

"Why do we keep saving this guy's life?" I cursed myself.

"Because we're the good guys." Mandy said, putting her hands on her hips. She was sweaty from her fight with Sunlight and I couldn't help but admire the shimmer it gave her skin.

"You're *half* right."

Diabloman shook his head. "In all my years as a supervillain, I have never met anyone as flippant about the job as you."

"Thank you," I said. "Okay, Sunlight, Amanda—"

"Nightwalker!" Amanda said, holding her cape up in front of her. "I am his heir and successor!"

I blinked, stunned she'd claim that title. "Really?"

"*She can't do a worse job than you.*"

I looked over at Sunlight before turning back to Amanda. "Where did you even meet this guy?"

"Defending the innocent!" Amanda proclaimed, proudly. "I vowed to never be weak again after my kidnapping and he promised to train me."

I held my face. "Oh God."

Sunlight then surprised me. "Merciless, we need your help."

Chapter Eight

Where I Make a Deal with (Shudder) the Good Guys

"Excuse me?" I said, not sure I'd heard that correctly.

"We need you rogues to defend Falconcrest City." Sunlight clarified, pointing at each of us in turn. "The Brotherhood of Infamy, a secret conspiracy of the rich and powerful in Falconcrest City, has been manipulating its history for centuries. Worshipers of the Great Beast Zul-Barbas, they have been attempting to make the city as miserable and corrupt as possible since its foundation. This was so they could gather enough negative energy so they could summon their evil god and remake the world into a paradise according to their whims and desires."

Mandy looked enraptured, Amanda just nodded along, I was still confused, and my fellow villains were as put off as I was.

"This is why I don't trust apocalypse cults," Cindy said, shaking her head. "They're always trying to make the end of the world come faster."

"It's why I don't like Christianity," Angel Eyes said.

Diabloman looked over his shoulder, guilty. "I've only tried to end the world a few times."

"The cult almost succeeded in the Great Depression," Sunlight said, shaking a fist in the air for emphasis. "The cult, led by Lancel Warren, and a team of six other followers used evil magics to penetrate the sanctum of Death in the Underworld and make off with her seven magic cloaks. Ones woven for her seven children with Cain, who would become the original Sorcerer-Kings of Acheron. With the cloaks' powers enhancing their necromancy, the Brotherhood's leaders could summon a host of undead which would give them the power to finish their plans but Arthur Warren persuaded his brother not to end reality. As such, the cult was thwarted and he would spend the rest of his life stopping their plans."

"Wow," Cindy said, eyes widened. "The Nightwalker was *evil* once? I have so much more respect for him now!"

"If only I'd known we'd had so much in common," Diabloman said, looking guilty. "We could have been friends."

"*Oh for Chrissakes,*" Cloak muttered.

"We know all this," I said, sighing. I'd learned most of this from offhand remarks from Cloak as well as encounters with his former foes. Brotherhood of Infamy bad, making zombies, stop them. It wasn't all that complex.

"I didn't know any of this," Cindy said. "Why can't I get a cloak?"

"Mandy is up first," I said.

"Oh," Cindy said, accepting that explanation.

"You may know all this," Amanda interjected, "but what you didn't know the Nightwalker defeated the cult and retrieved all seven cloaks by the late Fifties. He couldn't return them to Death, however, given the magics he'd used to penetrate her sanctum required bloodshed and was afraid of what would happen if they were destroyed. He, instead, rendered them inactive and hoped their curse was ended. But the Brotherhood was not destroyed and merely inactive, waiting for his death so they could steal the cloaks back."

"Which they did," I said, getting bored. "Hence, why they're out there doing all sorts of evil nastiness with the other six cloaks."

"Other five," Amanda corrected, pointing to her attire. "My father was a member of the Brotherhood. After he was killed by the cult for resisting their plans at apocalypse, the Cloak passed to me. I intend to use it for good, unlike the rest of those nutcases."

I blinked, looking at her costume in a new light. "Is she telling the truth, Cloak?"

"Yes," Cloak said, sounding as surprised as anyone. "I do believe that is one of the other Reaper's Cloaks."

"I'd already been training to be a hero but now I will avenge my father and bring peace back to the lands of Falconcrest City!" Amanda said, shaking her fist in the air.

I stared at her. "Please don't do that."

"Do what?" Amanda asked.

"Say that without irony."

"Um, okay."

After the Nightwalker's death via aneurysm, Sunlight had been the only Society of Superheroes member to want to try to carry on his legacy. Unlike many heroes, the Nightwalker had made no proviso for who would take over in the event of his death. Sunlight had used computers to search through a list of probable candidates, found one, and sent the Reaper's Cloak along with some other vital equipment to my house.

He'd been trying to send it to my wife.

Eesh.

Sunlight wagged a finger in my direction. Seriously. "Tut-tut-tut, Merciless, one should never be ashamed of taking pride in *justice*."

"I swear to you," I said, over to my wife. "Most superheroes are not like this. Please do not take him as a role model."

Mandy rolled her eyes. "I know, Gary. Sunlight is... unique."

"But kind of awesome," Cindy said.

I stared at her.

Sunlight punched his left palm as if spoiling for a fight. "The thing is, the Brotherhood of Infamy's efforts have reached the misery saturation point of being able to summon their god. Amanda, due to her knowledge of the cult's inner-workings, has indicated the only way we might possibly stop the arrival of Zul-Barbas is *The Book of Midnight*. A mystical tome of darkness which contains all the black magic in the world, including the spells necessary to summon as well as dismiss Zul-Barbas."

"So, you want us to help get the magic book?" I asked, hoping we'd gotten to his point.

"Indeed!" Sunlight proclaimed. He then frowned, looking a little annoyed. "I would have gone to Ultragoddess for help but she flies and it's rather difficult to catch up to her."

"Maybe you could signal her, like with a big U-spotlight in the air," Cindy suggested.

"That would draw thousands of zombies on us," Sunlight said.

"Ooo, good point."

I felt the bridge of my nose, wondering if I was seriously hearing this right. "Do you know where *The Book of Midnight* is?"

"Oh yes," Amanda said. "It's in my house."

I paused. "And the reason you haven't gotten it is—"

"It's guarded by a horde of cultists, wizards, and death machines."

Good answer. "Okay, we'll go get it. Anyone have any objections?"

"Yes," Angel Eyes, Cindy, and Diabloman said at once.

"No," Mandy said.

"Mandy's vote is the only one which counts," I said. "You've got our aid, Sunlight."

"Splendid!" Sunlight said, giving a heroic thumb's up. "May this help atone for your murder of Shoot-Em-Up."

"What was that?" I said, my voice suddenly dangerous.

"But now I must go," Sunlight said, turning around and posing. "To protect the innocent!"

A glowing flash of light from his hologram projector briefly blinded me and when my vision cleared, he was gone.

"So, he just showed up to give exposition and disappear?" Cindy asked. She searched the stage's remains for her picnic basket and found it under some boxes. "Lame!"

"The Brotherhood of Infamy has access to countless evil magics capable of killing even demigods," Diabloman said, showing concern. "It might be a better idea to lay low rather than attempt to engage them directly."

"Falconcrest City does not deserve my assistance," Angel Eyes said, putting his hand over his chest.

"Am I getting paid?" Cindy asked.

"Double your share," I said.

"I'm in," Cindy said.

"Guys, I think you have forgotten the true meaning of supervillainy," I addressed my henchmen. "It's about getting rich and busting heads. Neither of which is going to happen if the Brotherhood of Infamy succeeds."

Neither Angel Eyes nor Diabloman looked convinced.

"I'll give you first crack at any supernatural loot we scavenge," I added.

"Alright then," Diabloman said.

Angel Eyes nodded. "The Chosen of Aphrodite is pleased."

"Please top calling yourself that," I said, feeling my face.

"Why?"

"You're just coasting on a relationship from a couple thousand years ago."

Angel Eyes blinked, then furrowed his brow thoughtfully.

"Thank you, Mister Karkofsky," Amanda said, walking over and putting her hand on my shoulder. "Now that's two I owe you."

"Just get your checkbook ready after this," I said, staring at the billionaire. "I'm not doing this for free."

Amanda nodded.

"Where did Sunlight go, anyway?" Mandy asked, looking at the self-styled Nightwalker.

"No idea," Amanda said, shaking her head. She then made a circle gesture around the side of her head with her finger. "He's a semi-decent trainer but Coocoo for Cocoa Puffs."

"Obviously," I muttered. Turning back to everyone, I gestured to the door. "Okay, everyone, let's all pile into the Nightcar. We're heading to Stately Douglas Manor."

"It's more of a castle," Amanda said. "And not really very stately. More creepy and weird."

"I have my own transportation," Angel Eyes said.

"Good," I said, not really caring.

I took a moment to look down at the late and unmourned Ice Cream Man's zombie corpse. It had a wooden stake jammed into its brain and didn't look like it was coming back. I proceeded to freeze his body to liquid nitrogen levels then conjured forth a sledgehammer made of ice to start breaking it up to pieces.

"Uh..." Mandy looked a little appalled.

"Just in case," I said, sighing, and wiping my head off. I then dumped the sledgehammer on the ground. I then rubbed my hands together to warm them up. Noticing everyone else had left but my wife, I decided now was as good a time as any to make a confession. "I need to talk to you about something."

"Yeah, so do I," Mandy said, removing her earrings.

"Is this about replacing your wedding ring diamond with a death ray? Because that's actually pretty awesome."

"No."

As we stood there alone on the stage, I heard the cracking of thunder outside and the sound of a gentle rainfall. There were also moans outside, coming in through the giant hole in the wall from the Ice Cream Man's steamroller. I wasn't sure how to explain what I was feeling guilty over but I wasn't going to hide it either.

I took a deep breath. "I kissed Gabrielle."

"Technically, she kissed you," Cloak said.

"I kissed back," I replied in my head.

Mandy popped her head up, staring at me. "I'm feeling both pissed and hypocritical."

"Hypocritical?" I asked, wondering just how far she was willing to go to manipulate Angel Eyes.

"No, not him," Mandy said, sighing. "Never him. I admit, I flirted a little but I didn't intend to go any farther. I, uh, kissed the Black Witch. She was with Ultragoddess' team when they came to help. Twice."

Selena Darkchylde a.k.a. the Black Witch was my wife's ex-girlfriend. She was also a supervillain, which meant my transformation into one had to be messing with my wife's self-esteem. Mandy and Selena had been in love during their college years until Selena's increasing fanaticism led her to become a multiple murderer. Mandy finally turned against her and married me but I'd found out, on my journey to the moon, Selena had gone back to the side of the angels by becoming one of Ultragoddess' Shadow Seven. The world would never forgive Selena for her crimes but she might be able to achieve a measure of personal redemption despite it.

And yes, this meant that the Black Witch, Merciless, Nighthuntress, and Ultragoddess had all gone to school together before their other halves got married or joined the same superhero team.

The world was a strange place.

"Eh, you're all in the same profession. It's not that strange," Cloak said.

"I disagree," I thought, trying to sort through my feelings. To my wife, I said, "I'm angry, jealous, and most of all curious what this means. How...how do you feel about Selena?"

"I love her," Mandy said, causing my heart to sink. "I always will."

She paused.

"But I'm married to you," Mandy said.

I stared at her. "I love you."

"Gary..." It was clear my answer wasn't enough for her.

"Together, until the end," I said, smiling.

Mandy smiled back. It was like the whole room brightened up. "Until the end."

I looked out the hole in the wall. "Let's go save this city before I don't have anything left to conquer."

Mandy snorted.

"I'm serious," I added, walking to the door. "I'm thinking of renaming it Mercilessville or the Kingdom of Mercilessland."

We argued about it all the way to the car.

Chapter Nine

Where I Learn the Power of the Cloak

Amanda, uncomfortably, sat between Diabloman and Cindy in the backseat of the Nightcar. Mandy took the side seat beside me. Angel Eyes decided to follow us in a white and gold limousine straight out of the Disco Era.

I tried to remember my car was cooler.

"You stole the Nightcar?" Amanda asked, after about five minutes of driving.

"We didn't steal it," Mandy said.

"Yes, yes we did," I said, smiling proudly. "Fear the wrath of Merciless!"

"No supervillain actually says stuff like that," Amanda said, looking at me strangely. "Right?"

"A few do," Diabloman corrected. "Mostly lunatics."

While I had the autopilot engaged, I did my best to figure out how we were going to save the city. I also started planning my sudden but inevitable betrayal of Angel Eyes. The Greek God was too dangerous, unstable, powerful, and well, Greek, to tolerate as part of my gang. The fact he was stalking my wife, no matter how capable she was, meant he had to go.

"Maybe I should look up hydra poison," I muttered under my breath. "That kills demigods. Yes."

"Hmm?" Mandy looked over at me. She wasn't exactly dressed for assaulting a bunch of well-entrenched cultists but I figured we could break into a store and get her a practical outfit on the way. "Is something wrong?"

"Nothing." I turned back to watching the road. "Just plotting Angel Eyes' death."

"Ah." Mandy was annoyed. "Surprise, surprise."

"It's within the rights of every husband to plot the death of his rival. It's in the Supervillain Code."

"You're not rivals," Mandy muttered.

No, we weren't. My wife might have a taste for supervillains but I didn't think she was interested in the beautiful blond-haired cologne commercial back there with his expensive suits, fabulous style, chiseled good looks marred only a single scar, as well as ravishing....dammit. I really hated superhuman beauty as a power. Really, my actual rival, wasn't a villain at all anymore. The Black Witch gone legitimate, working for the man now, and was ironically working for my ex-lover. Mandy and I needed to talk more about this situation and I positively dreaded it.

Mandy, thankfully, distracted me. "Also, there is no such thing a Supervillain's Code."

"Yes there is," Cindy piped up in my defense. "I've read it!"

"Then you just made *that* up." Mandy sighed, leaning her head against the passenger side window.

"That is *also* in the code." Diabloman placed his hand over his heart. "It is the province of supervillains to make the rules up as they go along. Also, to ignore any of the rules in the code as they see fit."

"Hence, of course, why we're supervillains," I clarified, smiling. "To be a supervillain is to be free to do anything you want when you want it because you say so."

"It's really not," Cindy said, popping her head between the front seats to look at me. "Otherwise, I wouldn't be stuck hanging around with you hoping you'll pull a job which makes me really-really rich. Not that I don't like you. It's just very few of us are doing the supervillain thing as a philosophical lifestyle choice."

"Or any of us," Diabloman said, crossing his arms in the backseat. "You're rather unique, Boss."

"I am what I am," I quoted Popeye, "and what I am is a supervillain."

"Technically, aren't you an antihero?" Amanda said, not realizing my feelings on them. "I mean, you've killed a bunch of supervillains since your debut. You also killed that big demon on the moon and helped save the Society of Superheroes. Everyone is talking about it."

"Gary! How could you?" Cindy said, sounding betrayed. She was mocking me, I hoped.

"I swear, it was for purely selfish reasons!" I said, crossing my fingers. I then called back to Amanda, "And don't ever say that again."

"Weird," Amanda muttered. "So terribly weird."

"The truth is everyone is a hero in their own mind," Diabloman said, looking out the window into the rainy night outside. "I was raised by the Brujah Circle of the 9th Gate to serve as the champion of the Great Beast Arkon-Gul and defeat my little sister, Spellbinder, after she rejected her destiny to be the Anti-Christ. Even then, I thought it would be better for the world to be ruled by the Dark Powers."

I'd heard of Spellbinder, she'd been a Mexican sorceress member of the Texas Guardians, the team which Ultragoddess had briefly been on during the Nineties while I'd been struggling through high school. Her story hadn't ended well. Like a lot of heroes I'd found. I hadn't realized, until this moment, Diabloman and she had been siblings.

"What happened?" I asked, genuinely interested.

"Spellbinder sacrificed her life to destroy Arkon-Gul," Diabloman said, taking a deep breath. "I realized, in that moment, I was the villain in her story rather than the hero in mine. That is what ruined my career as a supervillain and what set me down on the road of ruination I eventually walked." He paused. "Everything else was just an excuse."

"You actually thought the world being ruled by demons would be better?" Amanda asked, staring at him.

"Humans can convince themselves of anything if they try hard enough," Diabloman said, glancing over. "I have too many sins on my conscience to ever go straight and my family willingly sold themselves to damnation, so I do not wish to worship a god who would separate me from them, but I do not lionize supervillainy. It is simply my chosen path because I know nothing else."

"Well, that's just depressing," I said, shaking my head. "You should embrace your idiom with gusto."

"I am," Diabloman said, mysteriously.

Mandy then surprised me by asking. "Are you thinking of taking *The Book of Midnight* for yourself?"

Amanda looked ready to kick Diabloman out of the car.

Diabloman said, "I was tempted when I heard its location. I could kill you, seize the book, summon Zul-Barbas in place of the Brotherhood, and achieve the undreamt of power the cult promised me since birth."

"But?" I asked, suspecting otherwise.

"I find...I do not want to. I was raised to believe that without the hand of gods, mortals would degenerate into killing, murder, and evil. That they would be like the Great Beasts. Fierce and amoral with a hatred for all life and an endless capacity for cruelty. Instead, I find, like you I am inclined to do what I want and what I want is to protect my family. Perhaps your insane philosophy is not so insane after all."

"No, it's pretty damned crazy," Cindy said. "I'm glad I'm doing something rational by killing people for cash." "Well, if I'm the one calling the shots then I better start codifying my philosophy." I put my hands on the steering wheel.

Mandy glanced at me. Her eyes looked like they were boring into my soul. It was sexy as hell. "Oh?"

I coughed. "Rule number one, of course, being to do what my wife says."

"Nice save," Mandy said. "Maybe you won't be sleeping on the couch for the next thirty years."

"I should hope not. I just got out of prison." I started fiddling with the radio. I needed some music to help me think. We had a long ride to Douglas Manor given all the abandoned cars, debris from damaged buildings, and zombies blocking the way. The Nightcar A.I. was good at navigating around them but was taking a lot of detours.

I took my hands off the wheel. Not touching anything was my new strategy. "Okay, Amanda, why don't you tell us the whole story? We've got time and I, for one, am very curious how you managed to get one of the seven Reaper's Cloaks."

"I don't know this is pretty private. Hold on, my dad's talking." Amanda talked with her cloak for a minute, exchanging short phrases that were meaningless without context. In other words, it was like any normal conversation a girl might have with her father. "Okay, my dad says that it's okay for me to trust you. For now."

"Man, trapped with your Dad in your head for all eternity. That's rough. I only have to deal with a perverted old man in my cloak," I said, sympathetically. "God knows what demented voyeuristic kinks I'll have to learn to live with."

"*I hate you. I really do.*"

"I'm not the one who used to hang around with a bunch of weirdos in tights," I said, shrugging my shoulders. "You do that for forty years and you shouldn't be surprised when people talk."

Mandy looked at me strangely. I'd have to explain to her that Lancel was probably going to be watching us for the rest of our natural lives. Add that to the list of troublesome things supervillainy had brought to our marriage.

"I've spent my entire life trying to be little more than the social construct my parents made for me," Amanda Douglas said, frowning. "They're the ones who created the party-girl persona for me as a way of promoting our hotel brand. I've always hated the fakeness and superficiality of the upper class in this city. I'd like to say that's because the majority of them were being groomed for the Brotherhood of Infamy but it turns out most of them are just that shallow."

"What about the sex tape?" I asked.

Mandy shot me a glare.

Amanda rolled her eyes. "Worst mistake of my life and a creation of my manager. I don't think I've ever actually been with a man who really cared what I thought."

I was surprisingly sympathetic. "I'm sorry."

"The kidnapping was a wake-up call so I suppose I owe Diabloman, Cindy, and the Typewriter. You as well, for rescuing me," Amanda said.

"Please don't say that," I said.

"You did," Amanda corrected. "The Typewriter was going to sell me to the Hypno-Slaver after getting the ransom and all I could think of was I helpless because I'd let myself become this way. I hated myself for a long time but I'd taken gymnastics, dance, and self-defense training in the past. Enough that I was on the list of superhero candidates Sunlight was looking through after his first pick fell through."

Mandy gave me a sideways glance.

"I am so sorry," I whispered back at her.

"The city was going to hell the past month anyway so I didn't have much time to train but experience is its own trainer," Amanda said. "I got to do something meaningful for the first time in my life fighting the zombies out there and rescuing people. I was the Nightwalker even when I was wearing a fake version of the Reaper's Cloak. Someone who helped people. I got to give back the strength I was given by someone coming to my aid when I needed it. So, no, Gary, I will say it. Thank you for saving me. I'm not going to need it again but thank you."

"Well, you can save my life and we'll call it even," I said, shrugging. "Hell, when we save the city we'll do it."

"I'll hold you to that," Amanda said, clearly resenting owing anyone. "You can imagine my surprise, though, when my efforts to find who was responsible led back to my house."

I recalled she'd mentioned she knew her father was an evil cultist during her kidnapping. "Somehow, I don't think you were as surprised as you imply now."

"No," Amanda said, looking down. "I always knew my father used black magic to make himself rich. I just didn't realize how black. My mom's death must have pushed him over the edge. Either way, I came home to find him surrounded by a bunch of cultists he'd killed and more on their way. They were there to seize the mansion, *The Book of Midnight*, and all of my father's collection of curiosities. Dangerous stuff they could use to take over the city. We talked, he gave me the cloak. That's the end of the story, simple."

"Your definition of simple is very different from mine." I was about to say more when I heard Mandy's cellphone ring. It was David Bowie's *Life on Mars*.

Mandy picked it up and put it to her ear. "Yes, Adonis?"

"You have a *specialized ring-tone* for him?"

Mandy waved her hand in my face. Her demeanor became serious. "Yes, Adonis, uh-huh. Okay, that's bad. Thanks for the head's up."

"What's wrong? You look like someone just told you someone is trying to kill us."

"Someone *is* trying to kill us." Mandy confirmed my suspicions. "Angel Eyes just said that the Typewriter is coming after us."

"We knew that," I muttered, wondering if Angel Eyes was just calling to make time with my wife.

"I mean now!" Mandy snapped.

I clenched my teeth. "Is no one staying dead in this town?"

If the Ice Cream Man was a B-Lister then the Typewriter was a B-Lister who should have been a Z-lister. What else can you say about a lunatic who wore a helmet shaped like a giant antique typewriter? He wasn't even that devoted to his concept. No crimes based on the proper spelling or anything. He was just a regular criminal with a costume and a lot of access to advanced technology like an energy-spewing cane. It made me ashamed for Diabloman and Cindy that they'd used to work for the guy and Amanda that she'd been kidnapped by him.

Amanda, meanwhile, turned around in her seat to stare out the rear-view window. "I have dreamt of a chance to get my revenge!"

It wasn't a very superheroic sentiment but I'd never quite been clear on the distinction between justice and revenge.

"That's the spirit, Amanda. Too bad the Typewriter is a complete loser or we could have a big epic—" I was interrupted by a pair of abandoned cars in front of us being hit by a glowing energy ray, which caused them to explode in a massive fireball. Pieces of debris and destroyed road hit our windshield as the Nightcar dodged around the resulting hole, followed by Angel Eyes' car.

"Merciful Moses!" I shouted, falling back into my seat.

"Disengaging Autopilot: Activating Emergency Countermeasures." The car's on-board computer spoke in a soft feminine voice.

The dashboard started popping out a bunch of controls I didn't have the faintest idea how to use. Looking in the side mirrors, I saw Angel Eyes' car had pulled out of the way for a long red typewriter-shaped car.

The thing was built like a tank but was moving like a jet, two flames shooting out of its back. Standing on top of the peculiar vehicle's roof was the undead Typewriter, his previously garish outfit now mostly burned beyond recognition. His theme helmet was half melted, missing keys on one side with a chunk from the other side, exposing bits of his fleshy skull underneath. In the eccentric zombie's hands was an Omega Corporation Fusion Cannon, the kind they marketed to the United States military after the last Thran invasion.

"Oh come on!" I shouted, staring at it in the rearview mirror. "That's not even in theme! It should at least shoot out big exploding light construct letters or something!"

The Typewriter pulled out a bullhorn and shouted. "I'm back, Merciless! Do you know what it's like in hell? Hot! Hot and unpleasant! You'd think they'd reward the bad guys there!"

"Do you have any rear-rocket launchers on this thing, Cloak?" I asked, looking at the various buttons.

"*Yes. Did your henchmen bother to arm them before you stole the car?*" Cloak asked.

I asked Cindy and Diabloman. They grimaced in a way which told me they'd sold the ammunition for the vehicle in my absence.

"*I need new henchmen,*" I muttered.

"*I'll tell you how to use the other defenses,*" Cloak said, quickly. We were, finally, on the same page.

In the end, I settled for caltrops and dropped a horde of them behind me. Shockingly, the Typewriter's unseen driver managed to dodge them all. Meanwhile, the garishly-costumed supervillain above him was reloading his rocket launcher.

"Can this thing take a rocket launcher blast?" I asked Cloak.

"*That depends. Do you mean would we survive it if it hits us?*"

"YES!"

"*Then no,*" Cloak replied, sounding as crazy as the rest of us. "I *suggest you avoid being hit.*"

Steering the car hard to the right, I managed to avoid a second blast from the Typewriter, this one tearing another massive hole in the city pavement.

The Typewriter lifted his bullhorn to giggle maniacally at me. "You're going to die, Merciless! Die with a capital D!"

"Finally!" I snapped. "At least a token nod to your theme!"

I could tell everyone wanted to murder me then.

I didn't entirely blame them.

I said stupid stuff when I was excited.

Which was, admittedly, all the time lately.

"*If it's any consolation, you say stupid stuff when you're bored too,*" Cloak said. "*You need to rely on the Nightcar A.I.'s skill at avoiding his attacks. That cannon's batteries won't last more than a few shots. There's a reason Omega Corp's weaponry is sold to criminals—no soldier wants to rely on it.*"

Mandy stared at me. "Gary, give me the wheel!"

I should have let her have it. I trusted Mandy more than I did the autopilot but pride got in the way. "I've got this under control!"

That was when the Typewriter fired another blast which landed right in front of us, exploding under the Nightcar and sending it flying into the air.

Dammit.

Chapter Ten

Where I Deal with the Typewriter (Again)

I have to give credit to Arthur Warren's engineers. The Nightcar was a remarkably durable piece of machinery. It managed to survive not only a fusion blast exploding underneath its front engine but being propelled in the air by said explosion before landing on its roof. Smashing my head against the steering wheel, I felt like I'd been thrown into a washing machine set on 'spin.'

"Wow." I lifted my head up. "That was bad. It could have been worse, though."

A moment later, the Typewriter's novelty vehicle slammed into the side of the Nightcar and sent it into a spin that bounced several times in the onto the Falconcrest City bridge.

I don't know how many times I banged my head during all this but I managed to stay awake long enough to see that Mandy, Diabloman, Cindy, and even Amanda looked banged up but alive. The safety features of the Nightcar had kept them from being seriously injured. I was a different story since a huge chunk of metal had jabbed through the window and struck me in the shoulder.

"*Gary, Gary... are you alright?*" Cloak asked, his voice ringing in my ear.

"Yeah," I said, glancing over at the piece of metal impaling me. "Swell."

Reaching up to my forehead, I pulled back my hand after touching something sticky. To my surprise, my hand was covered in blood.

"Damn. That's no good." I collapsed on the steering wheel.

"*Try and stay awake.*"

"Yeah, I'll do that." I felt blackness swirling over my consciousness.

"Gary!" Mandy shouted, slapping me across the back of the head.

"I'm up!" I shouted, waking up. "Who slaps an injured person?"

"You're supposed to keep a person from going into shock!" Mandy said. "By keeping them awake. I think."

"Leave the medicine to Cindy!" I snapped. Turning down to the piece of steel imbedded in me, I stared. "Okay, how do I pull this out?"

"You shouldn't be doing that," Cindy said, calling from the back. "You'll bleed out."

"I'll call the refugee centers we've set up." Mandy said, rapidly pulling out her phone. "We've got a healer super there."

"I'll be fine. I'm partially invulnerable," I said, trying to pull myself free and only causing myself massive pain.

"Partially is right," Mandy said, dialing rapidly. "Now shut up and let me do this. Amanda, Diabloman, go kill the zombies. Cindy make sure everyone is taken care of and provide backup."

"I love it when you take charge," I said, smiling as I forced down the pain of my ill-advised wiggling. "You guys okay with that?"

"Not really," Cindy replied, coughing. "I demand overtime for this."

"I don't pay you. You just get a cut out of my profits."

"I want a salary then," Cindy answered, not missing a beat.

"Sure," I said. "Time and a half on weekends. *Now go get to killing the Typewriter.* Protect Amanda while you're doing it. I doubt she's fully mastered her cloak."

"*Like you have?*" Cloak said.

"*Not in the mood,*" I snapped back.

Diabloman coughed in his fist. "That may be a problem, Boss."

"Why's that?" I asked, looking over my non-wounded shoulder.

"We're missing *Senorita* Douglas," Diabloman pointed out. "She seems to have slipped out in the last few seconds"

I did a double take, realizing our hostage was indeed absent. "*How the hell* does she get out of this before the rest of us?"

"I can turn intangible," Amanda said, sticking her head through the door beside me. Literally. "Like you should have done."

"Gah!" I practically jumped out of my seat. Given I was impaled at the time, to say it hurt like hell was an understatement defying words. "New definitions of the word pain! Ow!"

"Oh don't be such a big baby," Amanda said, reaching in and turning the bar intangible. She removed it without issue. "It didn't even hit an artery."

"We can get Angel Eyes to cast a spell on it and you should be fine," Mandy suggested.

"Thanks but no thanks," I replied.

Amanda pulled back out of the Nightcar and ripped off the door, tossing it to the side.

"Questions about why you're so suddenly friendly with the people who kidnapped you are being put aside for the issue of why you have super strength and I don't." I slowly stepped out of the car.

"It came with my cloak," Amanda said, defensively. "Dad says all of the cloaks have different powers."

"Just my luck to be stuck with the crappy one."

"*I heard that.*"

"I wanted you too!"

"Does he realize he sounds insane?" Cindy looked over at Diabloman.

"No," Diabloman replied. "He does not."

"As for why I'm being friendly with you. I don't think the Typewriter's zombie...survived for lack of a better term...crashing." Amanda's smile was big and satisfied—not at all the sort of look a superhero should be having at someone's death.

"Well, that's anticlimactic." Holding one hand over my wound, I burned it closed. I was relying more on movies and knowledge of basic First Aid than anything real. If not for my semi-useful invulnerability, I suspect I would have collapsed then and there.

Unbuckling my seat belt, I slowly slid out of the car and rolled onto the Falconcrest City Bridge. It was our equivalent to the Golden Gate Bridge, bisecting the cities' massive harbor and giving drivers a view of the hundred foot tall statue of Persephone holding a torch in the middle of the bay. Yeah, the city fathers hadn't had a single original bone in their body.

Dozens of cars were abandoned across the bridge as I saw the Typewriter's car burning nearby. Oddly, the other end of the bridge was cordoned off and there were signs a police barricade had been set up for some reason. There was no sign of the Typewriter, however, which made me nervous.

"I don't think he's dead," I said.

"What?" Amanda said, spinning around. She then looked at a spot where I suspect she'd seen his fallen frame. "He looked dead."

"That's because he's a zombie!" I shouted before scanning the area. "Fuck. Will someone check on Angel Eyes to see if the immortal demigod is, somehow, dead? I hope not. We need him. Kinda-sorta. Not that I like him or anything."

"*You're protesting far too much.*"

"Shuddap."

My inquiry was rewarded by having Angel Eyes' broken and battered frame tossed at my feet. Looking up, I saw his car had been totaled, its engine having been literally ripped out. Overlooking the destroyed car was the Typewriter.

Gone was the somewhat pathetic figure of before. Undeath agreed with the Typewriter, at least in terms of increasing his ability to inspire terror. Part of his prop mask was missing and it exposed the rotted corpse beneath with yellow broken teeth. Other holes in his costume exposed ribs and the gray twisted flesh that marked him as really most sincerely dead. It made up for the fact he no longer had his awesome energy-blast-shooting cane.

Obliterating any sense of intimidation was the fact that, also on the car, was a giant gorilla. A giant *zombie* gorilla. The Typewriter, it seemed, had come with backup to fight me. The thing was far larger than a normal gorilla, about Mighty Joe Young sized, and at least twice the size of a normal member of its species. Its jaw was distended and half of its face was missing. Oddly enough, the gorilla had a t-shirt with a GLG on it. I'd have wondered how he fit in the Typewriter's vehicle but I was starting to learn to just go with some things in this crazy mixed up world I lived in.

"Should I know this guy?" I asked.

"Ganglord Gorilla," Cloak said. *"The Simian Super-Crook."*

"Weird even by my standards."

The Typewriter hissed at me, pointing at me. "You have no idea what I've pondered doing to you. A month has gone by since you murdered—"

"Ahem." I coughed into my fist. "I'm sorry. I don't mean to interrupt your monologue. I appreciate them as much as anyone. However, what's with the zombie gorilla? I have to ask. It's like I expect him to start throwing barrels at me any time soon. Are you two like buddies?"

The Typewriter paused, stunned at my nonchalance. "If you must know, he's my brother-in-law! He has the strength of ten gorillas due to exposure to the Ultraforce."

"Your brot...you know forget I asked. Sorry, Amanda, I'm taking this one," I said, snapping my fingers.

Nothing happened.

"Mister Merciless?" Amanda asked, looking at me. "What are you doing?"

"Apparently nothing." I stared at my fingertips.

The Typewriter let out a nightmarish laugh, unnatural sounds exiting out a hole in his cheek. "If you're referring to your supernatural power to shoot fire and ice. I made a deal with the Brotherhood. They gave me an amulet capable of resisting your spells."

I grit my teeth. "I am getting sick of people having counters for my powers."

"*Blame my working in the city for eighty years,*" Cloak said.

"Kill these bastards!" I commanded.

Diabloman responded by lifting up the Nightcar and hurling it at the Typewriter, causing him and his gorilla to run away. Angel Eyes crawled out of his vehicle, still alive, and I saw his wounds healing over instantly. A third zombie-supervillain, a woman in a purple-sequin outfit with a domino mask with an open rib-cage I didn't recognize, started firing a magic wand at us. I dodged out of the way but this allowed Ganglord Gorilla and the Typewriter to regroup. This was going to be a fight.

The Typewriter tackled me, trying to strangle me with its rotting desiccated hands. "I was going to be rich, dammit! I was going to make millions selling her! Then you had to kill me! Now look at me!"

"Quit your whining! We all have problems!" I choked out, struggling to try and force his hands from my throat.

The monster's grip was tremendous, pressing against my trachea with force I didn't think possible. If I'd been a normal man, he would have snapped my neck then and there. Instead, I felt like the life was being choked out of me one second at a time. My attempts to press against his face and eyes did nothing. The Typewriter obviously no longer felt pain in his current undead state. Instead, it just salivated as it opened its mouth and moved to take a huge bite out of my face. Don't let zombie movies fool you, being eaten alive has no dignity.

Amanda Douglas, Nightwalker wannabe or not, then saved my life by striking the Typewriter in the head with a full-moon shaped shuriken. The monster fell over, hissing as the shuriken buried itself into the back of its skull. One of the benefits Amanda's Cloak granted was super-strength and those little throwing stars Sunlight used were now much-much more deadly.

The Typewriter was down, but not out, thrashing his arms wildly. I didn't know what was required to kill these zombies, precisely, but it seemed more extreme than the typical headshot you saw in movies. Destroying the brain did seem to work, somewhat, so I decided to go for that. I was just going to make sure I destroyed a lot of it.

"Do you mind if I do the honors?" I asked Amanda.

"Go ahead," Amanda gestured. "I'm going to enjoy watching this."

Okay, that wasn't creepy.

Noticing a piece of concrete had been knocked out of the bridge by the car crash, I reached over and grabbed it before using it to smash the

Typewriter's head in. It was a bloody, grizzly, gory process that ended only when I had thoroughly scattered the Typewriter's brain matter across the pavement.

"Nice," Amanda said, a giddy look on her face.

"You frighten me Amanda," I turned to Cindy who had just dispatched the purple-costumed supervillainness with her ray gun. "New plan, Cindy, I decapitate the corpses of everyone I kill."

"Good idea." Amanda coughed in her hand. "Mister Merciless... they're trying to distract us. I know how the cult operates. I've been studying them for weeks. They know we're a threat so they're arranging things so we're slowed down. We don't have time to let them—"

"The gorilla," Cindy said, interrupting her, "he's killing Mister Diablo!"

I looked up, only to see Diabloman thrown on the ground beside Angel Eyes' car. The vehicle's owner was still inside, having apparently decided to sit this one out. Either that or he was caught gazing at his reflection in the rearview mirror. That, or something like it, was supposedly his secret weakness.

Ganglord Gorilla beat its chest and reached up to pick up the Typewriter's punctuation-shaped car. Lifting it up effortlessly over its head, I tried to figure out a way to deal with it before it crushed us. Setting the super-strong super-durable zombie on fire seemed like it would only tick it off and I didn't know if the Brotherhood had given it a similar amulet as the kind the Typewriter claimed to possess. Before I could make any decision on what to do, the giant gorilla exploded into flaming pieces.

"That was unexpected," Amanda said.

Turning around, I saw Mandy had picked up the fusion cannon. She'd changed out the power pack with a replacement from the back of the Typewriter's vehicle. The cannon smoked and she looked sexy holding it. What could I say, I liked a girl with a big gun.

"Yeah, well, what can I say? My father taught me well." Mandy tossed the now-useless weapon aside. "I prefer the P-38, though."

"I love you," I said, smiling brightly.

"I know." Mandy grinned.

Angel Eyes climbed to his feet, taking time to dust off his outfit. He'd been utterly useless during our right. "This is not the most auspicious beginning to our business relationship."

"Kidnapping my wife wasn't the most auspicious beginning to our business relationship." I wanted to go over there and re-arrange his breathtakingly beautiful face. I couldn't, though. He was just so damned *pretty*.

"I wasn't kidnapped," Mandy corrected. "Try and remember that."

"Kidnapped like the helpless little princess you are." I adopted a playful mocking tone. "How could ever such a delicate flower survive the depredations of such a monstrous cretin as the one before me? Oh woe."

Mandy looked ready to kick my ass.

"Your sarcasm is duly noted." Angel Eyes glanced over at the Typewriter's corpse. "One less supervillain rival in the city, I suppose."

"He was a rival?"

"Not really."

Amanda pulled out another boomerang to threaten us. "By the way, I want you guys to know I'm only letting you go because I owe Mister Karkofsky and the city is in danger. After this, I'm coming after all you all."

Cindy aimed her ray gun at Amanda.

I shook my head and Cindy lowered it. I just gave a nod at our new partner. "Duly noted, Nightwalker."

Angel Eyes stared at her incredulously. "Where did you pick up this insolent little moppet?"

"You were there," I said, wondering if being immortal affected one's memory. I was about to shout before I found I couldn't. The words were difficult to speak and I suddenly felt woozy. "So, any objections to hot-wiring a car to continue our mission? We may have to loot some stores for Mandy to get some proper adventuring attire too plus any other equipment we need to case the place."

I felt like I needed to sit down.

Everything was blurry.

"*I'm sorry Gary,*" Cloak said, sounding heartbroken. "*I truly am.*"

"*For what?*" I thought back, confused.

"I'm all for stealing to save the city." Mandy took the initiative. "It's when you're doing it to satisfy your ego I object."

"Do you normally clear everything with your spouse?" Angel Eyes said, raising an eyebrow. In that moment, he showed me I'd never have to worry about him and Mandy. She'd never tolerate anyone talking down to her.

"Yes." I wondered if Angel Eyes had caught up with the 21st century regarding women's rights. "She wears the dress in the family and thus rules." I needed to find some place to sit down for a minute.

Angel Eyes looked at me like I'd grown a third head. "What *are* you talking about?"

I waved him away, looking down at Diabloman. I rocked back and forth on my feet, unable to properly balance myself for some reason. "D, you okay?"

"I am...alive," Diabloman said, sounding surprised. "You, on the other hand, are bleeding badly."

"What are you talking about?" I asked, surprised.

I noticed my cauterized wound had re-opened. A large amount of blood was pouring from it and sliding down the front of my torso. It was worse than before.

"Oh dear." I felt my legs buckle out from under me.

"*I appear to have led you to your death.*" Cloak's voice echoed in my head while my feet started to buckle under me.

I was dying.

I stumbled around, struggling for something to say before I passed out. "Yeah. Well, as my last words, I'd like Mandy to know I love her. That I like all of you but Angel Eyes. I love some other people. Also, I regret nothing. Nothing!"

I slumped over, face first, into the concrete.

Dead.

Bet you didn't see that coming.

Chapter Eleven

Death is the High Cost of Living

Then I died.

Well, maybe.

One thing I would learn is the difference between life and death isn't quite as clear cut as most people assume. Comas, unconsciousness, and even sleep are about halfway there. Halfway will get you a chance to wade in the Stygian darkness that is the Great Beyond.

Death, for me, felt a lot like getting drugged by the Ice Cream Man. This meant, perhaps, I wasn't dying.

Hopefully.

So what happened when I died? Where did I go? Well, I floated through the darkness of oblivion and past memories until I found myself once more solid and consciousness inside an elevator. The place had a faded stainless steel finish and the carpet was an ugly pattern stained with soot. There was only a down button on the right side of the wall and the place smelled vaguely of brimstone. *Paint it Black* by the Rolling Stones was playing in the background.

"Well this is odd." I looked around the elevator. "Not at all what I expected."

"*What did you expect?*"

"Fire and brimstone." I waved my hands around for emphasis. "Torture with hot pokers and rubber chickens. No possibility of seeing anyone I love ever again. The latter might still be true. Which is hell enough I suppose."

"*You have a very interesting view of the afterlife,*" Cloak observed, his usual annoyance absent. "*Quite possibly unique.*"

"Way to reassure me," I muttered.

"*I'm not here to reassure you.*"

"Obviously. We're going to Gehenna, aren't we?"

"*Yes. I'm afraid so.*"

"Bugger. I shouldn't have said I regretted nothing."

"*Probably not. That might have made all the difference in some religions.*"

"Not mine. If I'm dead, why are you still a cloak and not some hundred-year-old Hugh Hefner wannabe?" I asked, noticing I was still in the Reaper's Cloak.

"*I don't know.*" Cloak sounded genuinely perplexed. "*This isn't how I imagined my afterlife either. Why am I with you as opposed to being on the bridge seeking a new host. This isn't supposed to be how it goes.*"

"Well, only one way to find out." Reaching over, I tapped the elevator's lone button and lurched downward. "We can go ask the man himself. Samael, here we come."

"*You have no idea what you're doing.*"

"That's never stopped me before."

The elevator took an extremely long time to reach the bottom. "Carry on my Wayward Son" by Kansas played, "In the City" by the Eagles, and "Sympathy for the Devil" by the Rolling Stones. Say what you will about Death but she had good taste in music.

I was less afraid than I might have been because I knew the Reaper's Cloak tied me to Death. Be she angel, god, or anthropomorphic personification, Death was a literal being who powered my cloak. We'd only spoken a few words together since I'd gained my powers but all indications were she'd wanted to speak with me. I also knew she wanted something from me given she'd given me a dramatic power boost on the moon to save Gabrielle's life. I was hoping to talk my way out of being dead, even if bargaining with Death rarely worked out for most people.

"*You need to know a few things before you go to meet our master. This is a place formed by your impressions of what you expect the afterlife to be like. Hell is a mindset. You need to be in control of what you expect here.*"

"Our afterlives are formed by our perceptions?" I asked, surprised he decided to bring this up now of all times. "How very Discworld."

"*I have no idea who that is. I don't get half of your references.*"

"Half is generous."

Moments later, the elevator hit bottom and the doors opened up. I was rather disappointed to discover it was a typical fire and brimstone location with a long cavernous stone walkway leading up to a throne facing the opposite direction to the elevator doors so I couldn't see who sat inside it. Interestingly, the lava environment around wasn't hot but deathly cold. It seemed Gehenna was a place where fire burned low and without warmth. A fitting metaphor for evil I supposed.

"You should introduce yourself, formally," Cloak advised.

"Lucy, I'm home!" I shouted in my best Desi Arnaz impression, walking toward the throne.

Cloak was, for the first time, genuinely speechless.

"Welcome, Merciless," a voice spoke from the throne. It was pure sex, having roughly the same effect on me as my wife wearing a teddy. The figure stood up and walked around the throne. That was when I saw the form of the Great Beyond's ruler.

It was Mandy's.

She was dressed in a pair of tight leather pants and a black corset I remembered as Mandy's stage outfit. I barely remembered the Black Furies concerts I'd gone to but I remembered her wearing that. It still fit perfectly, despite her body type having changed a bit after our marriage. Curiously, her eyes were different. They were the eyes of my ex-fiancé Gabrielle's.

"Okay, that was unexpected."

"That's not your wife."

"No kidding," I said, sarcastically. Clearing my throat, I looked up at the woman who so clearly resembled my loved ones. "I don't believe we've had the pleasure of meeting. Would you believe you look like someone I once knew?"

"I'm Death," the woman resembling my wife said. Her lips were the shade of blood and just seeing them sent spasms of pleasure up and down my body. "I am known my many names. Hel, Persephone, Samael, Lilitu and her sisters, Azrael, and others. Everyone has a conception of Death but no one truly knows her. I am the Grim Reaper and the Loving Embrace."

Her voice was pure sex.

Even my toes felt aroused by her.

This was so wrong.

"There's a joke I could be making but I doubt Mandy would appreciate it," I was trying not to drool.

God damn, she was hot.

"Mind explaining why Death is appearing as my spouse, Lancel?"

"I am... at a loss for words. She appeared to me as a hooded skeleton with a scythe."

"Well, you're a traditionalist. Honestly, though, I prefer this look."

Death's look was a mixture of seductive and amused. "Lancel Warren summoned me with necromancy and bound me into the form he expected death to appear as. I decided, for our conversation, I'd adopt the form of your ideal mate. I'm surprised to see it's your wife's image. Most men dream about every woman in the world but their spouses." She paused. "Then again, perhaps you like this better?"

Her appearance altered to a mid-riff revealing black and white variation of Ultragoddess' costume. It looked like a cheerleader's outfit with a cape only with a strategically torn parts to give it a vaguely Goth look. Gabrielle's bronzed skin contrasted with Mandy's eyes and I couldn't help but feel both ashamed as well as tormented by the fact I loved both women. Mandy, though, was my *wife*.

"Choose whichever form you like." I looked down at the ground, unable to meet her gaze. "So, I take it I'm dead? Like, really dead? If so, I've got to register a complaint. I object to not only the manner of my death but that it happened period."

"You and everyone else," Death said, turning around her stone throne with a twirl of her hands. She sat back down in her, once more assuming the form of my wife. It was a head game I didn't appreciate.

"*Touché*," I replied, shrugging my shoulders. "You've got me there. In which case, I'd like to reserve six of the deadly sins to indulge in on a regular basis. I'll pass on Gluttony because I'm trying to lose weight."

Death sat down, crossing her legs and lying back languidly in a pose that turned me on in ways I hadn't been since, oh, last Halloween. Mandy had gone with a Guinevere costume and... well, anyway, that's none of your business.

"You're not dead," Death answered. "Not yet, at least."

"Thank God." I breathed a sigh of relief. "You know, if he had anything to do with it."

"He didn't." Death laughed, not at all reassuring me. "It is by my actions and my actions alone."

"Good to know." I looked for some place to sit down. Unfortunately, everything was burning or sizzling. Absent anything comfortable to sit on, I chose a large piece of rock jutting out of the lava river beside me. It was surprisingly comfortable. Apparently, the molten lava ran lukewarm in hell. Either that or this being the product of my imagination, nothing could hurt me. I was tempted to see if I could influence things like in *The Matrix* or *Inception*.

"Can I offer you any refreshment? Alcohol, food, or *dessert?*" Death enunciated the word dessert the way bad movie scripts did when they needed their two leads to have sex.

"Not interested in dessert." It took every ounce of my willpower to turn her down, calling into question my fidelity as a husband. I'd never been tempted by anyone the way I was by Death. Of course, she was tempting me by looking like my wife so maybe there was a loophole for my naughty thoughts. Nah. "I will take a Cherry Coke with rum in it. As for anything else, you may look like my wife but you're not her. I'm strictly a 'look at the menu but don't order anything' guy when it comes to attractive women who aren't my wife."

Death looked hurt, giving a cute little frown. "Your loss."

A human skeleton dressed in a butler's outfit walked up with a silver tray carrying a cherry coke with rum. A little stick of celery was sticking out of it as well as an M-shaped red straw. Taking a sip, I nodded. "My compliments to the bartender. This is the best I've had since grade school."

"This is not at all like my encounters with Death. He...she... it... threatened me with death and doom every other sentence."

"You don't have my people skills."

"That's a terrifying thought."

I sipped my drink. "By the way, do we have that time dilation thing where it's like twenty minutes here but only seconds passing in the real world? Because, honestly, I don't want to leave my friends up there. I know everyone can take care of themselves but I'd hate to miss helping them kick the Brotherhood's ass."

"Our meeting will only take a moment of your time. You have a lot of faith in your friends." Death sounded surprised. "Most would believe they would be killed by the Brotherhood given how the odds are stacked against them."

"I'm pretty sure I'm the least competent person in that group," I said, being more honest than I ever wanted to be. "I may have an edge on Amanda but that's only if she's listened to a single word uttered by Sunlight as to how to be a superhero. What do you want from me?"

"I want to offer you a job." Death rested her elbows on her knees and placed her chin in her palms.

"Could I have a chocolate chip cookie?" I asked the skeleton butler. "Fresh from the oven? Like my grandmother used to make?"

A moment later, another skeleton butler brought out a chocolate chip cookie on a black paper plate. It smelled absolutely delicious and I put down my drink long enough to tear into it. Hell was a lot nicer than I'd imagined it. Well, technically, it was exactly how I'd imagined it but that was neither here nor there. This is probably why I had a failing grade in philosophy. I aced Humanities, though.

"Merciless?" Death asked, looking somewhat annoyed. "Did you hear a word of what I said?"

Chewing my cookie, I took a few seconds to respond. Swallowing a mouthful, I answered, "Not interested."

"We're dead." Cloak sounded like he wished he could slap me in the face. *"Well, I'm dead anyway but we're deader than dead. Gary, you do not turn down an offer from the Grim Reaper. She... it... is one of the Primals, the cosmic constants that govern this universe. Only the Great Beasts are as powerful."*

As usual, Cloak's lessons probably would have had more impact if I had the slightest idea what he was talking about.

"I can, I will, I have," I said to Cloak before finishing my cookie and wiping off my mouth. "Listen Lady, I love the whole idea of Death as a hot chick. Neil Gaiman struck a chord with readers when he did it in *Sandman*."

"Greek and Norse mythology did it first," Death interjected, amused.

It was clear she either found my antics amusing or was doing an excellent job faking it. It was another way she was similar to my wife.

"Oh, right, Valkyries... Hel... Persephone... all that." I remembered my Bulfinch now. "Any-who, the simple fact is I didn't get into this whole supervillain business to work for someone else. I like being my own boss."

I expected Cloak to say something, anything, but he was silent. In retrospect, he was probably too stunned to say anything. It was probably a good thing. I didn't have the full picture of what Lancelot had done to make his pact with Death but it increasingly looked like he had gone and done something tremendously stupid. Of all the cosmic beings in the universe to screw over, the one responsible for your afterlife was probably not the one to do so.

Death wanted something from me. Which meant, unlike for every other poor schlub out there, I had some bargaining power. I couldn't be too eager in my willingness to agree to whatever she demanded because if she did, I'd probably end up her slave.

"You agreed to do anything she wanted on the moon in exchange for enough power to save Ultragoddess," Cloak gently reminded me of the biggest mistake of my life.

No, it hadn't been a mistake.

But it had been boneheaded.

I had to *try* and keep my freedom, though.

"I respect your decision." Death sat up straight and put her hands on the throne's arm rests. "But I believe you will change your mind if you learn of some extenuating circumstances."

"Like what?"

"Like the fact I can keep you here forever," Death said, her voice not changing in the slightest. "You're wearing my cloak after all and you made a pact with me on the moon. Likewise, you're not protected by any necromantic spells. I could just reach over and pluck your soul from your body."

Death reached over and made a grabbing gesture. I felt her fingertips reach into my chest as if they were tugging on something very essential to my being. I can't put it into words so I'll say it was like a cold chill running up your back taken to the extreme.

"Sorry. Threats don't work on me."

Death raised an eyebrow. "Oh?"

"Yep. I'm a sociopath. As a result, I have no fear of death or torture because I have no emotions."

"That's not how sociopathy works. Also, you're just suffering from a mild narcissism and trauma-based megalomania."

"She doesn't know that!" I said to Cloak.

"I'm pretty sure she does."

Death looked amused. "Yeah, sorry."

"How about I'm possessed of superhuman willpower? Thus, able to resist anything?"

"I don't believe that either. You're above average but that's not saying much."

"The cosmic beings are always so easily fooled in the comic books."

Death puckered her lips, looking like she had difficulty believing what she was seeing. "Indeed, I'm not sure if you're a genius or an imbecile."

"As my wife says, it depends mostly on the time of day. In any case, I'm serious about the not responding well to threats thing. Yeah you can kill me and torture me but I've seen way too many movies not to know making deals with vastly more powerful entities always ends up biting you in the ass. Name *one* instance in the *history* of fiction where it's worked out well for someone."

"The Devil went down to Georgia." Death showed a surprising knowledge of pop culture. "Johnny ended up with his soul and a golden fiddle."

I'd forgotten that one. "Okay, name two."

"Bill and Ted's Bogus Journey," Death said, a skeletal servant bringing her a Crown Royal on a dinner tray. It was Mandy's favorite alcoholic beverage. "They came back from the dead after beating Death at Twister."

"Really, you're going to use that one? Have some standards. The very least you could have done was cite the first movie. Would it applicable? No. However, I wouldn't be ashamed to admit I'd seen it."

"I can't help it if your mind is mostly filled with pop culture references," Death said. "I just picked the most suitable one."

I raised my hands up to draw an end to our present line of conversation. "I'm sorry but I'm not going to work for you. I'm sure you're a lovely person and I love the slutty shape-shifting Goth thing you've got going on but I became a supervillain to *be* somebody. Not become someone's pet monkey. I'm already starting to regret my deal with Cloak and he's a hell of a lot less scary than you."

"*Thank you. I think.*"

Death narrowed her eyes before they softened and she smiled. "Listen to my sales pitch and I'll give you an hour with your dead brother."

I didn't hesitate for a second. "I'm in."

Chapter Twelve

Where I Sell My Soul for Love (Again)

"So you agree to hear my offer?" Death fluttered her exquisite eyelashes. "I must confess, I'm a bit surprised at how quick you were to agree. Then again, you were eager to throw away your freedom on the moon."

"If you knew anything about me," I muttered, looking up to the seductive deity, "you wouldn't be *the least* bit surprised at what I'm willing to do for my loved ones."

"That's one of the qualities about you I love," Death said, surprising me. "It's why we're speaking rather than me seeking out a new vessel. Now, do I assume we have an agreement?"

"Yes."

Keith and I were as close as brothers could be. It didn't matter Keith was eleven-years-older than me, he always treated me as if I was his best friend in the world. In a way, I'd taken Keith's death harder than my parents. They'd had me to fall back on, at least.

The prospect of speaking with him again was almost too heady to think about.

Cloak interrupted my thoughts. *"Death will attempt to exploit your relationship to the deceased. You must be cautious and not reveal you're too interested in what she has to offer."*

"Is Keith in hell?" I asked, realizing he might be. "If he is, I'll take his place."

Cloak mentally sighed. *"You know, Gary, I'm going to stop trying to influence you into making sane decisions. Obviously, it's a lost cause."*

"Probably a wise idea." I tried to sort through my feelings.

Death laughed at me, seemingly amused at my breakdown. "I do admit I'm surprised at your having so obvious a weakness. Perhaps I should hold your brother's soul as collateral against the services I want from you."

I lowered my voice, glaring daggers. "What did you say?"

Death leaned back in her throne. "Merely that I might keep your brother's soul as a means of controlling you. It seems to be the one thing you respond to more than anything else. I could even make similar arrangements for your other loved ones."

Remembering this place was formed from my imagination, I conjured a spear in my hands. It was light weight and sharp with a long stone tip on the end. Without a second's hesitation, I hurled it at Death's head. The weapon struck against the back of her stone throne, missing her neck by inches.

Not bad for my first attempt to use one.

"You know that can't hurt me," Death said, her tone now reserved. At the very least, the spear had gotten her attention.

"Don't mess with my family," I growled, clenching my fists into balls. "I know you're probably all-powerful or damn near close to it. God knows you're probably above the typical near-omnipotent alien the Society of Superheroes fights on a regular basis. That doesn't mean I can't figure out something to do to you. I'm genre savvy. That means I know every conceivable weakness of an omnipotent super being that television writers could think of over the past forty years. Trust me, you do not want to mess with this."

Death narrowed her eyes, her voice becoming very cold. "You *dare* threaten me in my own domain?"

The lava around us started to bubble as the light in the room became an eerie shade of red.

"Damn straight I do. Also, you need to work on your dialogue. Who the hell says shit like that? This isn't the 1930s and you are not Ming the Merciless. Now answer the damn question: *is my brother in hell?*"

Death's shoulders tensed and for a moment I was sure she would strike me down. A second passed and another before she burst out laughing.

"Okay, not what I was going for but I'll take what I can get," I said, not sure what she found to be so funny.

Death giggled for a few moments before recovering her composure. "Your brother is not in hell, quite the opposite. Mercy is a quality of the Creator, even for supervillains who tried to take over Atlantis. Take note, Merciless, I could torture you until you were willing to do anything I wished. I alone decide when a man is given the release of death and I can stave that off for millennium. I am doing this the nice way."

"Yeah," I said, no longer remotely impressed with Death. "I saw how you were going to be nice to me. You tried to get me to cheat on my wife. Now we had a deal, give me an hour with my brother and I'll listen to your sales pitch. Just know there's no deal if you try and use my family against me. You might be able to torture me to insanity but I'm pretty sure whatever you need requires me sane."

"Don't be so sure." Death once more looking serious. Honestly, I liked her better when she was pissed off. It felt more authentic. I didn't like manipulators and Death was coming off as nothing but.

"Congratulations, Gary, you've managed to tick off the one cosmic being in the universe who was favorably disposed to you. Even for you, that's amazing."

"No one should love Death." I crossed my arms. "She's like every one of my ex-girlfriends rolled into one."

"Including Cindy?"

"Especially Cindy."

"I'm offended by that," Death said, gesturing to a wooden door free-standing in the middle of the room. It hadn't been there a second ago. "Your brother is inside."

"You'd better be telling the truth," I replied, heading to the door.

"I'm always honest. I'm one of the most straightforward beings in the universe," Death said, looking away. One of her skeletal man servants walked up with a margarita she took in hand, the glass decorated with a little skull on the side.

"Yeah, I suppose you are," I said, examining the door.

The door was a pleasant mahogany and was standing in the middle of the hellish landscape surrounding us with no room behind it. It had more than a vague resemblance to the door from the *Twilight Zone* series.

I felt a bead of sweat pour from the top of my brow. Rubbing it away, I stood there for a second. Strange, I felt more fear now than I did facing down the Extreme.

"It'll be alright, Gary. I'm sure he'll be glad to see you."

"I'm not so sure about that," I said, taking a deep breath and reaching the doorknob. It was weird, I had no idea where that sentence had come from. Why wouldn't my brother be happy to see me?

Chapter Thirteen

Meeting My Idol, My Brother, My Friend

Slowly opening the door to where Death had said my brother was located, I closed my eyes and stepped on in. When I opened them, I saw a surprising sight. In direct contrast to the cheesy pseudo-hell Death inhabited, I found myself in a tastefully appointed conference room. There was a large round table in the center of the room and a coffee table to the side.

If this was heaven, it was a tad underwhelming.

"It looks like my dad's office," I muttered, looking around.

In the back of the room, I saw a pair of extremely large black men wearing gray robes. Both of them sported feathery wings the color of midnight. They were heavily armed, though not with the traditional flaming sword but Uzis. I confess, they didn't fit my image of how angels would look but they certainly made an impression.

Keith was sitting on the other end of the conference table, looking so unobtrusive I almost missed him. He wasn't in his 'uniform' tonight— instead he was dressed in a plain pair of blue jeans and a Hawaiian shirt.

My brother was taller than me by half-a-foot, sporting sandy blond hair and a bleached blond goatee. His nose was crooked from where it had been broken a number of times. It was eerie seeing how Keith hadn't aged and still resembled the twenty-five-year-old he'd been when he died. I was older than my brother now, perhaps wiser than he'd been, which made the meeting all the more strange.

"*Wiser than?*" Cloak spoke incredulously.

"Oh hush," I snapped at him.

Still, looking at him, I couldn't help but smile. Sticking out my palm, I made a V sign with two pairs of fingers. "Live long and prosper, Bro."

Keith looked at me, smiling. "I still say *Star Wars* is the better of the two."

"I like them both. What can I say, I'm a rebel," I said, walking over to my brother. Keith stood up and the two of us embraced.

I'm not ashamed to say I cried.

"You okay, Gary?" Keith asked, patting me on the back.

I sniffed, wiping away the tears with my sleeve. "It's okay, I had onions for lunch. It's totally not seeing my dead brother again for the first time in a decade."

Keith smiled in understanding, a peaceful look on his face. He'd never had one before, at least which I could remember. My brother had always acted like he'd had something to prove, right up until the moment he died.

Looking over at the angels, I said, "So you went to the other place? They must have lowered the dress code for you."

"The Primals of Creation and Law decided to lend me out to Death for the evening. You know, Rabbi Sloan has it completely wrong. The universe works *nothing* like the Torah says it does."

"Depends on where you stand. The details may be different but I think the specifics are on the money."

I was proud of my status as both a Jewish man and a supervillain. There's actually a fairly long line of Jewish supervillains stretching back to Professor Bedlam and the Golem-Maker beforehand. By the way, yes, before anyone sends me a nasty letter there's also an even longer line of Jewish superheroes: Nazi Basher, Captain Victory, Professor Hellsinger, and Miss Liberty to name a few. Yeah, I was surprised by Miss Liberty too. She doesn't look Jewish.

Keith took me by my shoulders, staring directly in my eyes. "Gary, what the hell are you doing?"

"Is this a trick question?" I scrunched up my brow. "Because I thought I was catching up with my dead sibling."

Keith tugged on my cape before looking at me strangely. "I mean the fact you're dressed up like a Sith Lord and acting like a stand-up comedy version of Sauron."

"Thank you." I smiled, though weakly. "I think of myself as a sort of counter-culture Dark Lord."

"It's not a compliment," Keith said, shaking his head. "Dear God, Gary, why on Earth would you become a supervillain?"

This wasn't the reaction I was expecting. "I was trying to honor you. You were the best supervillain any kid could aspire to be."

"Seriously, Gary? *That's* your justification? You wanted to honor me?" Keith asked, his mouth hanging open. He lifted up his hands as if to strangle me.

"Yeah," I said, confused by his reaction. "You were my idol growing up."

"Gary, I became a supervillain because I was *poor*," Keith shouted, turning his back to me as he felt his head. "I had a daughter, a debt to several crime lords, and a wife with expensive tastes. I'd heard cops went easier on you if you wore a costume."

I bit my lip. My mother had told me this before. "That didn't mean you weren't impressive. The papers loved you. I mean, you fought the Silver Lightning—"

"The Silver Lightning was a *hero*, Gary. He *helped* people," Keith said, looking back at me in stunned disbelief. "I got caught on my first job and afterward, people broke me out of prison to join them in heists because they thought I'd be a useful distraction. I must have gone to prison at least fifteen times during my time as a crook. God, I can't imagine what sort of hell my daughter went through because of me."

I rolled my eyes, thinking my brother was being a drama queen. "Your wife wrote a book and she used the royalties to get your daughter acting lessons. Tina's already marked for a reality television series. The network needs a token super to show how diverse they are."

"That's not the point." Keith huffed. "You were out. You had a wife, a job…okay, that didn't work out, and a life that didn't involve people beating you up or threatening to kill you. I died at the age of twenty-five, two years after I started my 'career' as Stingray. This isn't the life mom and dad wanted for you. This isn't the life *I* wanted for you."

"Maybe it's the life I wanted for myself," I said, angry at my brother for not supporting me. I spent my entire life thinking the world of him and this was how he repaid me for it? It was a betrayal of the highest order.

Keith pulled back his hand to punch me in the face, I didn't move. If my brother wanted to hit me, I wasn't going to stop him. Despite everything, I still loved him and was glad to see him. Keith didn't punch me though. Instead, he looked at the ground and sighed. "I know what you did to the guy who shot me, Gary."

I didn't react for a minute. "He deserved to die."

"You were *fourteen*, Gary." Keith stared into my eyes, his face stricken. "Of all the things my actions cost our family that was the one I regret the most."

I still occasionally had nightmares about the night Theodore Whitman, a.k.a Shoot- Em-Up, came to our house. I'd been too stunned, too young, and too naive to react. He'd killed my brother in front of me and my father. Most people supported Shoot-Em-Up's decision to 'take the fight to crime directly.' I'd tracked him down, little more than a child, and shot him repeatedly.

Looking up, I met my brother's gaze and saw the guilt and self-loathing there. He blamed me for becoming a killer at an age when most kids were discovering girls. I had to wipe it away, somehow. "It's not your fault, Keith. It my first kill and I don't regret it or any of the ones that came after. You didn't take away my innocence, so absolve yourself of that. I'm an adult now and my path is my own."

Keith sighed and looked down at his shoes. They were Nike Reebok tennis shoes from the late Nineties. "I'm not going to be able to talk you out of this, am I?"

"Probably not." I felt sick to my stomach. I couldn't admit to my brother I'd been following his path in hopes of reconnecting with his memory. "I'm way too smart to ever let sense and rationality get in the way of me doing something stupid."

All this time, I'd been thinking my brother would approve. Instead, he was horrified by what I'd done. It made me want to tear off my cloak and burn it, impossible as that may be with it bonded to my body.

Keith gestured down to the conference table as he pulled out a chair and sat down. "I've occasionally gotten a chance to look in on you, Gary, here in the Great Beyond. I won't try to dissuade you further but know I'm looking out for you. You're not evil, Gary, I know that even if no one else does. Don't let anyone else tell you different."

"Well, I'm eager to prove you wrong," I said, pulling up a chair across from him and sitting down. "I'm looking forward to redefining evil for the Twenty-First Century. We're going to ditch atrocity and instead go with sexy-cool."

"Same old Gary." Keith smiled. "Always trying to make a square peg fit a round hole."

"Tell me about Heaven."

"It's incredible. I went on a date with Mary Ann from *Gilligan's Island*." Keith leaned back, putting his legs up on the table.

"Dawn Wells?" I asked, wondering if she was dead.

"No, the actual Mary Ann," Keith explained. "Fiction and reality tend to blur up there."

"Well don't let the Professor find out. Those two had a thing... "

I treasured every moment of the hour's remaining minutes.

Chapter Fourteen

Bargaining with Death isn't just a Stage of Grief

"The hour is up, Merciless," one of the angel's spoke to me, his voice sounding like a thunderclap put through a tuba.

"So soon?" I asked, looking up to him with a stricken look on my face.

The angel lowered his head, looking apologetic "I'm afraid so."

Keith had been telling me about how he'd finished the ninth *Lord of the Rings* novel. J.R.R Tolkien had apparently been writing up a storm in Heaven. He'd even done a collaboration with T.S. White. Damn, if I didn't want a collection of the whole set.

Keith reached over and took me by the hand. "We'll meet again."

"I'm not so sure about that." I slowly withdrew my hand. "I doubt we're destined for the same real estate."

"Heaven is a lot more forgiving than you'd think." Keith's eyes were filled with a peacefulness I couldn't put into words. "You should consider giving the good guys a shot. They're not a bad bunch."

I snorted, reluctantly standing up. "I would never belong to any club that would have me as a member."

Truth be told, I wasn't sure what I was going to do with my life now. I had enjoyed being a supervillain but Keith's approval meant everything to me. The only person whose opinion meant more was my wife's. I wasn't sure if I could handle both Mandy and he both disliking my career choice.

"If I can't persuade you, I'll see if I can get the big guys to send some aid your way. Time isn't the same in the Great Beyond as it is elsewhere. You're in for some serious shit." Keith smirked, reaching over to put his hand on my shoulder.

I looked over at the angels standing watch. "Should you be cursing in front of these guys?"

"Fuck no, he shouldn't," one of the angels replied, not changing his expression.

It was nice to know heaven's soldiers had a sense of humor. I shouldn't have been surprised. I'd always suspected God was a comedian.

That was the only way to explain my life. Well, that or the Devil had decided to make me his personal chew toy.

"Those two aren't mutually exclusive." Cloak had been quiet during my meeting with Keith—a fact I appreciated.

I rolled my eyes and stood up to give my brother one last hug. Stretching out my arms, I said, "Whatever happens, Keith, I want you to know I'll always remember you."

"Right back at you," Keith said, getting up and hugging me back.

The two of us broke apart and I turned around to leave. I had to focus on not looking back. I didn't want to watch my brother disappear from my life again, this time possibly forever. In a real way, I was losing him all over again.

"Are you alright?"

"Yeah," I said, gritting my teeth at the memory. "I remember both his death and Shoot-Em-Up's every time I close my eyes. There was more blood than I expected. Shooting someone isn't like it is in the movies. The movies don't show how disgusting the aftermath is."

There was no dignity in death, no matter how people romanticized it.

"No, they don't," Cloak answered, sounding disgusted. *"I'm sorry. What you endured is trauma no child should have to. It explains a lot about how you came to be what you are today."*

"Yeah, well, shit happens." I was uncomfortable with this topic. "I'm not the first kid to lose a brother to violence. I won't be the last either."

I turned the doorknob and the door opened to reveal a vast moon-lit cemetery. The faux hell from before had been replaced with a peaceful, albeit creepy, graveyard I recognized as Hightower Heights. It was Falconcrest City's largest place of internment and where we'd buried my grandfather.

Death was standing over one particular headstone, having changed out of her earlier stage attire into a robe more befitting the Grim Reaper. Even so, she subverted the look by having the robe surprisingly tight in certain places. Was it wrong to check out the Grim Reaper, especially given my surroundings? Maybe, but damn she looked good.

"Is this where you take me to my grave and reveal Tiny Tim will die if I don't change my ways?" I walked up beside Death. "Because, I never honestly understood that. Did the kid die because Bob Cratchit couldn't afford heating oil or what?"

"Don't ask me. I hate Dickens." Death shrugged her shoulders. "The only work of his I liked was *A Tale of Two Cities* and that's because there were decapitations."

"I'm starting to like you," I said, taking up position beside her. "You're funny."

"All gods are comedians," Death said. "Surely you've realized that by now?"

"Fair enough." I crossed my arms and stared forward, deliberately not looking at the headstone. "In any case, you lived up to your end of the bargain. I got to meet with Keith, talk to my brother one last time, and so on. I'm willing to hear your sales pitch."

"World domination," Death said, starting her offer off.

"Go on."

"Unlimited power. Mystical might enough to shake the foundations of the universe," Death continued, putting her arm around my shoulders. I could smell Mandy's perfume on her, causing my thoughts to become confused. It then reminded me of my childhood with Keith, my carefree days with Gabrielle, and the few moments in my life when I'd been free from darkness.

"Keep talking," I said, trying to keep my thoughts straight.

"The person beneath you will not die," Death whispered, her voice silky.

I didn't want to look down but I did. There, on the tombstone was the name: *Mandy Polly Karkofsky.*

"You spelled her name wrong," I said, staring at the tombstone. I wasn't happy about this, it was emotional manipulation of the worst sort.

"It's not your wife," Death explained, sticking out her hand. In an instant, a scythe appeared and she leaned in on it like a walking stick. "Your wife can take care of herself. Barring any overt godlike entities involving themselves, she'll manage to survive the Falconcrest City Zombie Outbreak just fine. Hell, I give her even money on surviving the rise of Zul-Barbas."

"What about Cindy and Diablo?"

"Dead. Also, the new Nightwalker, who isn't important to you yet but will eventually enter your social circle. Angel Eyes—"

"Yeah, I don't give a crap about him," I interrupted. "If it's not Mandy, who is this?"

I had a sinking feeling in my gut that I already knew. I'd shown Death my one weak point, the place where I was most vulnerable. My family.

"Your daughter," Death said, confirming my suspicions. "Of course, she won't have a tombstone like this in real life. She'll never be born. Poof, like that, she'll cease to exist. It's hypothetical it would even be a daughter. Genetic combinations are a bit like a box of chocolates. You never know what you're going to get."

"You get chocolates." My tone was very low and very gravelly. I had my villain voice now.

"Mandy and I aren't going to have children."

"Maybe she'll change her mind. It could be an accident. Maybe you'll have them with someone else. Either which way, I can assure you with one-hundred percent certainty you will be able to have a child to love and care for if you serve me. She'll also live to be born and enjoy the wonders of life if you serve me."

I looked down.

Death smirked. "I have you, don't I?"

"You know you do," I whispered to her. "How does it happen?"

"Without my help, you'll die," Death said, looking down at the headstone. "You're a clever man, Merciless, cleverer than the majority of supervillains by far I'd wager. Not the smartest or strongest, perhaps, but the most wily. Still, even that won't avail you against the forces you'll be facing. Without you, Little Mandy here will never have a father."

"I see." My voice was hollow.

"Do you need a minute?"

"Yeah. If you don't mind."

"We have all the time in the world," Death said, giving her scythe head a little spin, "or, at least, I do."

"*Cloak, am I being stupid?*" I mentally asked him. "*Am I letting myself being led by the nose here for a child who might never be born in the first place?*"

"*Yes. I wouldn't discount the fact she's lying either.*"

"Thanks, just checking."

"*You're still going to do it, aren't you?*"

"Yeah," I said, staring down at the headstone. "Yeah, I am."

"Are you ready?" Death's voice was almost sympathetic. Then again, she sounded like Mandy so maybe I was reading too much into it.

"Tell me what you need to do and I'm your man." I took a long deep breath.

"First of all, I need you to deal with the zombie outbreak in the city." Death gestured out to her realm. "Souls are being ripped from my realm and inserted back into dead bodies. I can fix your cloak so you no longer need to worry about accidentally creating more zombies but the other six cloaks are a problem. I need you to collect them from their owners."

"By which, you mean, kill their owners."

"Yes." Death didn't sugarcoat things. "Kill them and burn the cloaks thereafter. With my power, you'll be able to destroy their cloaks after they've been removed."

"I won't hurt Amanda. She doesn't deserve this."

"Not even to save your daughter?" Death said, tapping the tombstone. "You barely know the girl."

"No, and to be honest, I'd like to throw her under a bus since I hate rich people."

"*You're rich,*" Cloak said, sounding annoyed at my class warrior rhetoric. "*You have millions in stolen loot back at your basement.*"

"Shh! Don't interrupt my hypocrisy!" I snapped at my cape, looking back to Death. "But you said she eventually becomes my friend and I'm not going to turn on possible friends. That and my wife would probably object to my murdering a little girl."

Amanda, of course, was only ten years younger than me but I was feeling pretty damn old right now.

"Interesting how desperation so quickly turns to bargaining." Death looked at me intently. "Alright, Gary, take her on as your apprentice and I will offer the same deal I have offered to you. She can keep her cloak and help me gather up the wayward souls spread about Falconcrest City. The others must die, however. The entire Brotherhood of Infamy in fact."

"No problem. If the Society of Superheroes somehow ends up putting them away before I can get to them, I'll break into prison and kill them. The Brotherhood of Infamy, I mean. The shit they've done means they no longer deserve to be considered part of the human race."

Yeah, I was pro-death penalty and anti-superheroes killing people. Weird, huh?

"*Two,* I would like you to assist any souls you encounter in moving to the other side," Death said, looking mournful. "Lancel Warren spent the majority of his time hunting criminals and thus there's a substantial number of restless spirits moving about Falconcrest City. These ghosts are growing in number all the time."

"Maybe I'll start an exorcism business," I said, thinking of a certain movie starring Bill Murray and Dan Aykroyd. "I can't promise you I will prioritize it highly but if I have the time and nothing good is on TV, I'll deal with the city's spook problem."

"For a man that's supposed to be desperate, you're doing a lot of bargaining."

"Blame yourself for wanting to hire the wiliest supervillain in the world." I walked up to an angel statue before leaning up against it. "You should expect me to rebound quickly from life-changing traumatizing revelations."

"Well spoken," Death said, admitting I was right. "Finally, I want you to kill Zul-Barbas."

I nodded my head. "Sure."

"*Zul-Barbas is the size of a small city, capable of shattering planets with his mind, and a being even the gods fear,*" Cloak warned, sounding almost frightened. "*He's survived the destruction of several previous universes.*"

I vaguely recalled the Society of Superheroes fighting the monster several times during their long and illustrious career. Zul-Barbas had tried several times to destroy the world and almost succeeded. While the Society had managed to drive the monster back each time, Zul-Barbas only had to succeed once to win forever.

"I may need a couple of days to work on how to do that last one." I winced. "It's a bit of a tall order."

"The Brotherhood of Infamy exists for the purposes of destroying the world and Zul-Barbas's arrival is their endgame. They will have enough energy to bring him forth tonight." Death looked serious, her face as grave as you'd expect it to be. "Poof. No more Falconcrest City. No more Mandy. No more supervillainy."

"I see." I felt sick. We didn't have much time.

"Take this." Death lifted up her scythe before giving it a little shake. In an instant, the weapon transformed itself into a gold coin. Tossing the coin to me, I caught it in mid-air. "Give it a rub when you need help. Transform it back by thought."

"Okay," I said, looking it up. Running my finger on the ancient Greek king's face on the front, the coin transformed back itself into a seven-foot-long black-bladed scythe with two thick wooden handles. It was heavy, too, as if carrying the weight of the entire world. I ended up dropping it, which wasn't an auspicious start to my new job as Death's new hatchet-man or was that Reaperman?

"Your fire and ice powers should be capable of dealing with the majority of the zombies and cultists you face. You will face some opponents, however, who are not so easily dealt with. Hurl the Reaper's Scythe into Zul-Barbas, though, and my power will destroy the creature completely."

"Okay." I struggled to pick up the scythe but managed to succeed on my third try. It was big and ungainly, but not so heavy I couldn't swing it once I had a good grip on its handles. "Damn, I need to work out at the gym more."

"You must strike at him immediately, though. If you do not, he will destroy your planet and rewrite reality to his wishes."

Finally getting a good grip on the weapon, I gave it a few practice swings. "May I ask why you're so keen on stopping Zul-Barbas? You're Death. I'd think you'd be happy with the annihilation of reality."

Death sniffed the air. "Don't be ridiculous. I'd be out of a job."

"Fair enough," I said, holding onto my scythe. "What now?"

"Now, you wake up."

My eyes opened, I was once more on the Falconcrest City Bridge. Angel Eyes was giving me CPR.

Chapter Fifteen

Making Plans to Save the World Because We're the Only Ones Left (God Help Us)

I pushed Angel Eyes away from me, spitting up his saliva. "Gah!"

Angel Eyes sat up and wiped off his mouth. "He's fine."

Cindy had her cellphone out and had obviously taken a picture of me getting CPR. "I'm totally putting this up on Crimebook."

Getting up off the ground, I rubbed my mouth off with my sleeve. "Who the *hell* gives CPR for a shoulder wound?!"

"You're welcome," Angel Eyes said to me, looking annoyed. "As for your shoulder, I cast a healing spell."

"Oh," I muttered, reaching over to touch my shoulder wound. It was sore but had obviously sealed over. Apparently, Amanda had been correct about Angel Eyes' healing abilities. I owed the little moppet an apology. "Thanks, I guess."

We were still on the Falconcrest City Bridge with Ganglord Gorilla's, the Purple Woman's (who I finally recognized as a Silver Lightning villain), and the Typewriter's corpses next to the burning wreckage of our vehicles. Mandy, Diabloman, and Amanda were standing together with Cindy off to the side.

I could see fires were burning on the other side of the bridge. Whole buildings were ablaze without any sign that they were going to go out any time soon. Clearly the fire department was completely overwhelmed or, more likely, had completely failed.

Apparently, the zombie outbreak had gotten worse while I was unconscious. Falconcrest City was fighting to survive and it was up to us, well me really, to make sure it survived long enough to become capital of my future kingdom.

"You have a one-track mind, don't you?"

"Damn straight." I coughed before clearing my throat and addressing everyone. "I've returned from a meeting with Death. I'm not being figurative here, I mean I *literally* met with the Grim Reaper."

"Makes sense to me." Cindy nodded.

"I've encountered stranger beings," Diabloman said, going along with it.

"Cool!" Amanda exclaimed, accepting my explanation without question.

"Huh. I expected more resistance," I said, blinking.

"It's not like you're the first to meet a godlike entity during a near-death experience," Angel Eyes said, looking disdainful. His mask was missing and I wondered if he was aware he'd cast spells without it. I decided not to tell him because I didn't want to spoil the moment.

"I believe you, Gary." Mandy patted me on the hand.

"She has named ruler of the world and her chosen disciple. Furthermore, she has charged me with the most holy task of destroying the Brotherhood of Infamy!" I said, raising my hands in an almost spiritual manner.

Everyone stared at me blankly.

"Oh, come on! *That* breaks your suspension of disbelief?" I exclaimed, throwing my hands out.

"The irony is, for once, you're telling the truth."

"Right," Mandy said, rolling her eyes. "Listen, I'm glad you're okay. Things are bad, though. I've got a call from numerous refugee centers across town. A lot of them are under siege by the undead. The Brotherhood of Infamy is making their final push to take over the city."

That was bad. I still didn't have a full stock of what was happening with the city's zombie problem but if Mandy's militias couldn't hold them back then things were going to get worse before they got better.

There was also the little bitty tiny problem of the fact that all of these undead were apparently part of a larger plan to summon Zul-Barbas. When he arrived, it was in the words of a famous movie Marine, "Game over, man, game over."

"It gets worse," I said, sighing. "Death said the end of the world is happening tonight."

That turned out to be the wrong thing to say as all of the supervillains in my group shared a glance which told me they were no longer interested in hanging around.

Crap.

Angel Eyes spoke his objections first. "I suggest we abandon this place and head to some island in the Aegean. We can harvest a small population of humanity to breed as slaves and use magic to keep the rest of the world out. In a few centuries, after all of the zombies have rotted away, we can return to dominate the world's ruins. Simple and effective."

"I support this plan," Cindy said, raising her hand. "Especially the part about being on a sunny isolated island with Angel Eyes."

"Wow, guys. Way to show the team spirit," I said, shaking my head. I tried an alternative approach to convincing them it was in their best interests to save the world, though. I doubted appealing to their altruism would work. "That plan won't work, though. Seriously, do you know how much work rebuilding the Earth would be even with slaves? We might as well not take over the world if we have the responsibility of rebuilding it! Have you *seen* any post-apocalypse films? Everything's broken! I can't live without the internet or toilets."

"I hadn't considered that," Angel Eyes said, rubbing his chin.

"Are they good guys or bad guys?" Amanda looked to Mandy. "Because, I'm having difficulty telling."

"She's good, I'm bad." I gestured to myself then my wife then pointed my henchmen. "They're badder. The Brotherhood of Infamy? The worst."

Cindy lowered her head, faking hurt. "I'm more naughty than bad."

Diabloman made an annoyed grumbling noise. "I will help you save the world. I am going to, if you'll pardon the phrase, catch hell from my demonic masters for it, though."

"Thank you, D," I said, glad at least someone was on my side.

"Fine," Cindy said, sighing. "I'm in."

Adonis looked away. "I suppose I could barter this with my mistress and a few other gods to get favors. Besides, the worst that could happen is I'm banished to the Underworld for a few centuries. The benefit of immortality."

Amanda, though, was troubled. "What are we going to do? I should call Sunlight for instructions."

"Sunlight doesn't know which end his ass is on," I said to her. "Surely you've realized that by now."

I was being unfair to Sunlight and felt a little guilty for it. No, the guy shouldn't be fighting supervillains as an old man but he did a lot better than any non-superpowered person should. Besides, I had to admire anybody who had the balls to continue fighting crime when all the criminals were now cannibalistic undead.

"He's a hero but, no, you're right. Sunlight can't help," Amanda muttered, looking at her cellphone. "We need *The Book of Midnight*. If we stay on mission, we'll be able to salvage this. "Amanda put her hands on her hips, looking taller and more regal than her five foot two frame should allow. "Okay, I was willing to postpone my arresting of you on the grounds of the city about to be destroyed by an evil god and his zombie army. If you assist me in defusing the threat, I will even consider allowing you to go in hopes you'll reform and put your abilities to good use."

"I quake with terror at the possibility of your going after me," Angel Eyes said, his voice dull with sarcasm.

"You should," Mandy said, smirking. "She's taken down tougher villains than you."

"*Et tu,* Mandy?" Angel Eyes said.

For my part, I had to admire Amanda's brass. Spotting a golden light travelling through the air, I made a decision. "I don't think we should go straight after *The Book of Midnight,* though."

"Why's that?" Mandy asked.

The arrival of Ultragoddess was like a torch shining in the darkness of Falconcrest City's darkest hour. Gabrielle was wearing a white-and-gold form fitting alien polymer costume which had a long-flowing golden cape hovering behind her. She had ditched her short-skirt for a pair of shorts built into the top like a runner's outfit. Gabrielle wore her thigh-high boots over bare legs, more as a fashion statement than anything else since she was invulnerable to anything short of a nuclear bomb.

The Ultraforce appeared around her as a nimbus of light, a chain of glowing white energy extending behind her in a bubble which was wrapped about the Shadow Seven. There were actually six of them, Ultragoddess included, due to one of their number falling months earlier. I'd filled in for them on the moon and I supposed Mandy had been doing the same while they were visiting Falconcrest City.

There was General Venom the terrorist turned red, white, and blue power-armored knight in shining armor. Beside him the Red Schoolgirl, who was a cursed Goth samurai in a black and white sailor fuku. Bronze Medalist, an African American speedster who'd come out as the Silver Lightning's partner in two senses years back. The Black Witch, who was dressed in a tight black leather assemble and pointy witch's hat which made me very uncomfortable to look at given her relationship to my wife. Finally, there was the Human Tank, a transgendered woman in a bulky suit of metal armor which could level a city block.

The Shadow Seven were an oddball mixture of villains and heroes, each of them determined to do what was right even if they didn't get any credit for it or outright incurred the wrath of the wider world. They were champions I could respect, even if I still clung to my increasingly brittle justification that supervillainy was *cool*.

While it was more metaphorical than literal, the presence of Ultragoddess seemed to banish the dark energy gathered in the air around us. I felt less like giving up and more like doing some good, a strange feeling for me if you hadn't guessed.

I loved Gabrielle, always would, and while I wasn't going toss away five years of marriage to pursue something which would be toxic to both of us, I hoped I could renew our friendship. Keith had reminded me of a time when I wasn't so angry at the world and it was probably a good idea I start to work on recovering that period.

"*So does this mean you're abandoning supervillainy?*" Cloak asked.

"Ask me again when the world isn't ending," I said, shaking my head. Looking up to Gabrielle, I said, "Hey."

"It's good to see you're back, Gary," Gabrielle said, smiling at me. "Though, perhaps not at the best of times."

"Eh, the world is always ending," I said, shrugging. "Either Entropicus is attacking us with his Cross-Time Empire, Pyronnus is trying to destroy the galaxy, a Great Beast is coming into this universe, Mister Hoppy is rewriting reality, or one of the interstellar powers is trying to bomb Earth into submission."

"*You forgot Atlantis invading or the Ultraterrestials,*" Cloak said. "*There's also a few Dimension Lords you wouldn't know about I used to tangle with.*"

"I'm not mentioning P.H.A.N.T.O.M, Unity, the Emerald Sign, or various world-ending supervillain plots either," I told my Cloak. "We've survived all of those, we'll survive this."

"Your optimism is encouraging," Gabrielle said.

"Except the bad guys only have to win once," Cindy said, frowning.

Diabloman said, "Not necessarily true. Good cheats. One time I destroyed the world only for them to reverse time."

"No shit, they can do that!?" Cindy said, staring.

Diabloman nodded.

"Those bastards!" Cindy said, shocked.

Gabrielle looked at Mandy. "Hello, Munin."

"Hugin," Mandy said, back.

"Pardon?" I asked.

"They're the codenames we use to communicate via radio," Gabrielle said, looking back at me. "Mandy and I have been coordinating our defense of the city since the dome went up. You've married a very formidable woman, Gary."

"Thank you," I said.

The Black Witch waved to Mandy.

Mandy waved back, embarrassed.

I frowned, trying not to let my jealousy get the better of me. He who lives in glass houses, shouldn't carry a rocket-launcher and all that. "We were just discussing our next move. We're hoping to get *The Book of Midnight* to prevent Zul-Barbas from getting summoned."

I looked over at Amanda, seeing her positively bouncing up and down at the presence of Ultragoddess.

Apparently, she was a fan.

"It's an honor to meet you!" Amanda said, grinning from ear-to-ear.

"Uh, thanks," Gabrielle said, not really looking too comfortable with the adoration. She'd started her covert ops team precisely because she'd gotten sick and tired of the limelight. "Getting the Book is a good plan. It may work."

"May?" Amanda said, stopping in mid-squee.

"We don't know where the Brotherhood is operating their ritual from but it's very likely they've already gotten everything they need to know from the book," Gabrielle said, frowning. "I've identified the leader of the cult as a woman named Lucretia Despayre. She's going by the moniker of the Nightmaster and possesses powers easily equal to anything we've faced before. The Nightmaster has a cloak like yours, Gary, but with much-much greater powers."

"Who names their child Lucretia Despayre?" I asked, missing the point of what she was saying.

"Someone who wants to raise their child to end the world?" Cindy asked.

"Point taken."

"What's the situation?" Mandy asked, still checking on her radio feed. "I know the attacks are getting bad but I don't know how bad."

"Very bad," Gabrielle said, looking at me. "We've come here for reinforcements."

Gabrielle was one of the most powerful superheroes in the world.

That was not good.

Amanda surprised me with her next statement. "Gary, we don't have time to waste on saving people here."

"Saving people is never a waste," Gabrielle said, looking down at Amanda.

"It is when it kills other people," Amanda said, looking back and meeting her gaze head-on.

"What's the biggest target right now?" I asked, wheels starting to turn in my head.

"The Falconcrest Football Stadium," Gabrielle answered, looking up at the invisible dome above our heads. "When the dome came, we tried to move as many of the unevacuated there as possible except for those we needed to run essential services. There are a few minor supers we've drafted for the defense as well as military personnel but nothing which will hold out against the Brotherhood's necromancers, Amazons, and dinosaurs."

"Hold up," Cindy spoke. "What were those last two?"

"Amazons and dinosaurs," I said, shrugging. "Get with the program, Cindy."

Cindy shot me a glare. "Excuse me, Mr. I've gone to the moon now I'm too cool to hang with my henchwoman. Some of us are still adjusting to the high-grade stuff. We're going to fighting dinosaurs and feminist separatists now?"

"Amazons aren't separatists," I said, surprising everyone. "Speaking as a feminist myself, they're also not particularly devoted to the cause of female social justice either—at least beyond believing they're the equal to any man. The Daughters of Ares are a multi-racial tribe of warriors who just happen to restrict their military traditions to women."

Everyone looked at me.

I paused. "I dated a couple in college."

Simultaneously.

Fun bunch.

Scary, but fun.

Diabloman looked at me then Ultragoddess, Mandy, and Cindy. "I am confused on every conceivable level."

"You and me both pal," the Black Witch said.

"The Amazons are not invincible," Angel Eyes said, speaking as if he knew their tactics from personal experience. Which, now that I thought about it, he probably did. "They are very well-trained warriors with access to P.H.A.N.T.O.M weaponry, magic granted by their father, and super-tech provided by their alien contacts. They can be killed if the protection spells on their armor can be overwhelmed, though."

"Why would they be helping the Brotherhood destroy the world?" Amanda asked.

"Most likely money," Angel Eyes said, shrugging. "The Daughters of Ares will never break a contract even if it is not in their best interest. They have no fear of death, either, since loyalty to the gods guarantees them a place in Elysium—even the God of War and Cowards."

"Do you think any of the Reaper's Cloak wearers will be joining in the attack?" I asked.

"A good third of the Brotherhood's forces are presence. The rest are spread through the city," Gabrielle said, frowning. "Why?"

"It's a long-shot but with only a few hours to midnight, we need to hit the cult hard in such a way as to weaken them. I say we go there, wipe out the bastards, and save a bunch of lives. It might weaken their plans to raise Zul-Barbas. If it doesn't work, we'll still have retrieving the book to fall back on."

"That's an awfully risky plan if they're summoning their god now," Amanda said, showing, again, she was probably the most ruthless of us.

I didn't want to admit my plan was because I didn't want to leave however many refugees they'd saved to die. I was a bastard but not that much of a bastard. "Every which way we go is risky. I'm asking you to follow m...Gabrielle's lead. Mandy?"

"I agree, we should help," Mandy said, making me breathe a sigh of relief. With her support, I had everyone.

"Good," Gabrielle said. "Let's go make some dinosaur steaks."

Chapter Sixteen

Where We have a Big Splash Page Fight

Ultragoddess looked at Mandy's torn and battered evening dress. "We should probably get you something a little more functional before we head off. Selena?"

The Black Witch nodded and raised her stage-wand at Mandy before saying, "Abracadabra!"

The Black Witch was the avatar of Hecate or her chosen one, I wasn't sure which or whether it made a difference. Created by Professor Thule in much the same manner as myself, she wielded magic by force of will rather than spells or focus objects. As such, she was prone to using cheap costume shop props and generic wizardry words than things used by more "serious" mages.

I'd, I kid you not, seen her kill a man with an *Avada Kedavra* spell.

The Black Witch's magic whirled around Mandy's tattered attire and then did a swirl of white pixie dust which resembled the effects from the animated Cinderella movie. It was Selena's idea of a joke, I think.

Mandy's attire melted away and she was briefly naked before her outfit was replaced with a black leather costume, long overcoat, and a silver N amulet at the base of her neck. If not for her Eurasian features and the amulet, I'd have said she was a pretty close ringer for Kate Beckinsale in *Underworld*.

"That's your costume?" I asked, blinking.

"Do you like it?" Mandy asked, smiling.

"Yes and no."

"No?"

"You look outrageously hot. However, now I'm afraid I'll be utterly distracted during battle."

Mandy rolled her eyes.

Cindy interrupted our moment. "Cool costume, but can you do anything?"

"I kick a lot of ass," Mandy said, staring. "That's enough."

Cindy looked at her, blinked, and then shrugged. "Works for me."

"I'm not comfortable teaming up with these guys," Bronze Medalist said, surprising me. "Gary is okay, he's not like most supervillains. However, Diabloman is a murderer and a madman. I knew the Guitarist and Spellbinder. They were good people and he took their lives or as much did."

"We don't have a choice," Gabrielle said, staring down. "We need all hands on deck. Besides, I made this team to redeem the wicked as well as fight evil."

"There is no redemption in Hell," Diabloman said, his voice cold but certain. "That does not mean I will not help."

Bronze Medalist didn't look happy but I doubted anyone would given the situation. It wasn't like the friends and family of the Black Witch or General Venom's victims would feel any different than he did. He would let it go, though, because he was a professional. Both he and the Silver Lightning had worked with worse than Diabloman in New Angeles to protect the innocent.

"Hell is for other people," I said, making light of his statement. "Also, Heaven. Let's get going."

Gabrielle nodded and extended the Ultraforce around our group, raising us all up in a bubble behind her which carried us in much the same way as the Shadow Seven. Much to my surprise, Mandy took my hand and stepped forward through the bubble's exterior.

It sloshed around us and I briefly thought we were going to fall before finding myself floating through the air at speeds identical to what we were travelling at. An aura of Ultraforce was clinging to us and Mandy took us down into a swimming like pose before speeding us up fast enough to come just behind Gabrielle's flying form.

"I thought you'd like a chance to be up front," Mandy said, smiling. "Gabrielle taught me how to manipulate her aura through thought."

"Wow," I said, staring forward, blinking. "I'm flying for real. This is...wow." I then blinked, doing a double take. "Wait, are you two friends now?"

Cause that wasn't awkward.

At all.

"Oh yes," Ultragoddess said, hovering directly in front of me. I briefly wondered if this was why she'd switched from a skirt to shorts. "Your wife is a fascinating woman. I've completely forgiven her for trying to kill me with the Black Witch."

"What's that?"

"You knew I was in love with her," Mandy said, looking away.

"There's a difference between being in love with a supervillain and aiding and abetting a murder," I said, with a great deal of hypocritical moral outrage.

Mandy looked at me.

"Yeah, I've not got a lot a leg to stand on, I know," I said, still troubled by it. "I'm just not a very forgiving sort. I don't know how you can work with so many people who have tried to kill you, Gabrielle."

"Of course not," my wife grumbled. "You're Merciless."

"Forgiveness is the path to healing. It's also the path from turning an enemy to a friend, which is the sweetest victory," Gabrielle said. "It's not just a song by Survivor."

Silent, I looked down and saw the beating my hometown had taken. It looked arguably worse from above than it did on the ground. With only a few superheroes to guard against the hordes of supervillains, zombies, and zombie supervillains—plenty of them had chosen to go to town. The WFCR Radio Station was covered in a glacier, for example, and I could see places where fires were still burning unattended.

The one saving grace was it didn't look like they were anywhere near the city's population in undead shambling down below. As bad as the deaths had gotten, it seemed the vast majority of the population had been evacuated. There were thousands of shamblers below, tens of thousands even, but a good number of them were raised from the existing dead. I wanted to believe not that many had been killed.

"*Eighteen thousand, seven-hundred and fifty-two,*" Cloak said, his voice low. "*That's how many the Brotherhood of Infamy and their monsters have murdered in the past month. That's not counting those who have died from starvation, exposure, thirst, accident, disease, lack of medical attention, or suicide. I can feel their spirits calling thanks to your pact with Death.*"

Sometimes there were no words.

Then there were.

"We're going to kill these bastards," I said, my voice low and cold. "Every last one of them."

"Yes, we are," Gabrielle said, her voice surprisingly calm and cool.

"Isn't that against the superhero's code?" Mandy asked.

"Not during war," Gabrielle said, her voice cold.

Mandy gave my hand a squeeze.

She'd killed her first person to save my life.

Now I was going to ask her to kill more.

This whole superhero and villain thing wasn't working out nearly the way I'd wanted it to.

"*It just took the end of the world to make you realize that,*" Cloak muttered.

"Oh like that doesn't happen every Thursday," I muttered.

"We're here," Ultragoddess said, slowing us down.

The sight which greeted me was less like a superhero battle and more like a war zone. The Falcons Stadium had been barricaded up by a gigantic wall of cars, presumably moved by Ultragoddess and Black Witch's powers, with lots of towers manned by courageous mundanes fighting with weapons taken from the National Guard Armory.

Laser bolts sailed through the air against the thousands of zombies formed into a horde by the black robed-necromancers interspersed with them. They weren't wearing the Reapers' Cloaks, I would have felt it if they were, but their clothing was clearly inspired by the Nightwalker's attire. Hundreds of them were present, many using scavenged weapons in place of spells or staves. They had managed to roll over a number of ground based defenders and were either eating them, hacking them to pieces, or just celebrating their kills even as the horde was shot at from above.

They weren't the real threat, though, but merely the support for the mounted dinosaurs which were breathing fire and shooting laser-beams from their eyes. They weren't just dinosaurs, you see, but cybernetic dinosaurs which meant the Brotherhood of Infamy either had looted the stash of or had the help of Doctor Dinosaur.

Which was a shame because I liked that guy.

The Amazons on top of brachiosaurs, triceratops, and a pair of Tyrannosaurus Rexes were tearing through the stadium's meager defenses. They were tough-looking women, some beautiful, others not, but all wearing modernized Grecian armor and helmets with specialized lenses which allowed them to see in the dark. They were working methodically, murdering the defenders one by one, showing no sign of the crazy slaughter their associates were engaged in. They were professionals doing a job, which made them so much worse than the insane cultists they'd been bought by.

There were even some supervillains in the air, both living and dead, like long-time Ultragoddess annoyances Nega-Goddess, Xerox, Blood Eagle, and the Smog the Elemental Spirit of Corruption. There were also the dead and zombiefied forms of Canadian heroes Avro Arrow and Ms. Mountie, presumably having come across the lake to help the city with the Backwoodsman. I felt for the guy and hoped he was still alive out there somewhere. Either way, all of this was a massive amount of overkill for

---

butchering a stadium full of helpless people. If this was supervillainy, I wanted no part of it.

"How many people are in that stadium?"

"Twenty-one-thousand," Gabrielle said.

"Drop me down."

Like that, Mandy dropped my hand and the battle was joined. I levitated down onto the head of the closest Tyrannosaurus Rex, landing right behind one of the Amazons who was using a weird saddle with levers and buttons to manipulate the creature's brain. I felt guilty placing my hand on her shoulder, filling her lungs up with ice, and then causally dumping her over the side of the creature's body.

The controls weren't terribly complex, a little more difficult to manage than your average video game and I'd played a lot of video games. Moving the central lever to one side, my T-Rex buddy moved in a similar direction and a pulling of the trigger on its side resulted in glowing red death shooting from its eyes.

It was a testament to how thoroughly pissed off I was that *riding a frigging cyborg Tyrannosaurus Rex with DEATH RAY EYES* was not something I could take the time to enjoy. Instead, I turned the monster against the necromancer's down below.

Deliberately targeting them rather than the zombies around them. As they screamed, going up in burning flame, much of the zombie horde below became a disorganized mass of mindless hate-filled monsters which turned on the non-necromancer cultists around them. Dozens of them died, then perhaps as many as a hundred while the rest of my time went to town on the enemy army.

As Ultragoddess said, it was war and no effort was spared to keep alive the Brotherhood forces. Well, let me correct that, no exceptional effort was spared. Bronze Medalist did his best to knock out living cultists then tie them up against the side of the fortifications outside of the zombies reach with his kinetic energy bands.

He could afford to do that since he could reach speeds of several thousand miles per hour. Ultragoddess, likewise, did her best to knock out the living rather than kill them. None of us hesitated against the dead, though, and no one objected when the Human Tank fired rocket launchers into the gun-wielding black-robed sadists who'd unleashed this horror on the city or their Amazon allies.

Really, I couldn't help but be proud of my henchmen as they showed off their own fighting skill. Angel Eyes floated in the air, blasting zombies with glowing beams of arcane might. Cindy plopped herself down on one of the towers and pulled a Foundation for World Harmony laser rifle from her basket and shot Amazons off their mounts into the zombie hordes below.

Amanda threw big objects around, even grabbing a stegosaurus by the tail and hurling it into the air at Nega-Goddess. I was particularly impressed by my wife. She moved like a ninja, using a pair of eskrima sticks charged with magic that seemed to cause the undead to explode when touched while having a taser-like effect on humans. I'd have to, very reluctantly, thank the Black Witch for providing those.

The one who did the most damage of our group, though? That was Diabloman. He went to town with his summoned tattoo monsters and enhanced strength. A man who had struggled against a super-enhanced gorilla was going to town in a way not seen since his heyday in the Eighties.

I suspected he planned to die here.

"He has a family, he wouldn't do that," Cloak said, conspicuously silent as I launched a pair of rockets on the sides of my mount into the other T-Rex. I ducked underneath the eye beams it shot wildly as it died, collapsing into the ground.

"Unless he thinks he isn't worthy of them," I said, watching an Amazon run up and jump on the side of my mount. She was climbing up the side of the creature like it was an obstacle in basic training.

She was a rough and tumble dirty-blonde haired woman with an eyepatch, a bloody knife in her mouth (which couldn't be sanitary), and a host of scars across her face. Her armor looked like had been scarred by Ultragoddess' energy blasts and I was surprised at the vehemence in her eyes. Reaching the top of the T-Rex's head, she stood across from me and pulled the knife from her mouth before holding it threateningly at me.

"You killed my sister," she hissed.

I supposed she meant the one I'd seized the T-Rex from. I'd like to say being confronted with this display of my attack's humanity affected me. That it reminded me every single person I killed, living or dead, had relatives who loved them. I'd like to say it did, but I'd be lying. I just hit her in the face with a fireball, knocking her off the side of my T-Rex, and then I brought the cyborg-dinosaur around to stomp her. I even sang *Walk the Dinosaur* by Was (Not Was) during it. Because there was no way in the world I was going to ride a T-Rex and not sing it, inability to enjoy my situation or not. Perhaps I'd have to wean myself off supervillainy a little bit at a time.

"You're enjoying this too much," Cloak muttered.

"I'm not enjoying it at all," I said, growling. "They're the ones who brought this fight to the people inside. Not me."

It was a good lie to tell myself. The truth was I was getting angry again. Seeing all this slaughter, mayhem, and bloodshed on both sides was reminding me I'd become what I hated. My brother had been killed by a fanatic who thought he was making the world a better place by murdering people. These assheads were doing the same thing, though I wasn't sure how they thought summoning a giant god of chaos would help. Cultists were funny that way. The fact was, I was killing them because I thought it would make the world a better place.

Talk about irony.

"*That's more apropos,*" Cloak said. "*Murder is in the details, Gary. You are killing to save lives.*"

"Am I? Or am I just doing it because it feels good to let all that rage out?"

Cloak had no answer.

Nor did I when one of the Amazons on the ground fired a rocket launcher which blew up the T-Rex's head underneath me.

I flew through the air, on fire, and hit the ground amongst a horde of hungry dead.

Blacking out.

This was getting to be a habit.

Chapter Seventeen

Where We Discover Our Princess is in Another Castle

I didn't stay blacked out very long, only a few seconds. Long enough for a pair of zombies to grab my leg and start biting down hard on it.

That woke me up real quick.

"Argghhhh!" I screamed, incinerating every one of the damned monsters around me.

I lashed out in a rage thereafter, bleeding from my leg wound as I destroyed every single monster I could throw fire at. I didn't stop burning, slashing, and killing until the better part of ten minutes had passed.

And that was because everyone was dead. Everyone on their side at least. Spread out around me was the burning remains of a lot of cultists, zombies, and more than a few of Ares' daughters.

If this was Greek mythology, I would have really offended said deity by my actions and now be under some kind of curse. As such, I was under a curse. I couldn't help but look at what was around me and feel like throwing up.

Guilt.

Sickness.

Horror.

It had to hit me sometime.

Falling down to my knees, I felt my face and tried to figure out whether I'd gone insane. No, that was obvious. Sane people didn't put on costumes to become supervillains when they had happy lives. Hey, they didn't do that when they had unhappy ones. No, I was afraid I was becoming sane. Which was so much worse.

I just sat there, collapsed, for a long time. I tried to muster my strength to move but I couldn't bring myself to do it. I wasn't cut out for this life and now was realizing it. It was a hard realization, like you just woke up one day and discovered everything you'd worked to for your entire life was pointless.

Time lost all meaning as I focused on this one thought, Cloak leaving me to it.

I appreciated that.

"Gary?" I heard a feminine voice behind me. It woke me from the self-pity was throwing myself.

I thought it was Mandy, before I looked over my shoulder and saw it was Gabrielle instead. She'd descended down behind me and was hovering a few inches over the ground. Mandy was interrogating one of the captured cultists alongside the Black Witch. The Shadow Seven and my gang were off to the side, not interacting and doing their best to avoid one another.

"How long have I been sitting here?" I said, looking up.

"About twenty-minutes."

"I don't think I'm cut out for supervillainy," I said, taking a deep breath and getting up. It felt like confessing to murder.

"Gary, can I tell you a secret?" Gabrielle said, walking up toward me and putting her hand on my shoulder.

I looked over to her. "What's that?"

"Whether you're the good guy or the bad guy depends greatly on your perspective," Gabrielle said, helping me stand up. A glowing bandage appeared around my leg, remaining there even when she broke away.

"Should you really be telling me that?" I asked, surprised to hear it coming from a hero.

"Let me show you," Gabrielle said, extending her Ultra-senses to me.

For the briefest moment, I felt the world the way she did. I heard Mandy, Diabloman, Angel Eyes, the spirits hovering over the bodies, and the presence of the twenty-one thousand people in the stadium. The latter were discussing the battle which had just taken place. They were a mixture of scared, elated, relieved, and hopeful. Most of them focused their gratitude on Ultragoddess and Nighthuntress. Others were grateful *I* was there, which stunned me.

I heard one old woman say: "Did you hear? That Merciless guy who killed the Extreme is outside. He's fighting the zombies."

"Isn't he a bad guy?" A man said back to her.

"Yeah, but the Extreme blew up a bridge. He's *our* bad guy!" An eleven-year-old child said.

A middle-aged woman replied, "Maybe need some bad guys to get things done."

"I'll follow anyone-good or bad as long as they get us out of here." That came from a seventy-year-old man.

They were already making up contrived stories as to why Ultragoddess and I would be allied together even as they had similar tales of

Nighthuntress and the Black Witch. It was flattering. I hadn't realized I'd made quite such an impression.

"*For better or worse, superheroes and supervillains are a part of this world's ongoing mythology,*" Cloak said, sighing. "*You are one. Both hero and villain. Don't ever believe otherwise.*"

Gabrielle held my hands in hers. They weren't smooth but covered in tiny healed scars from countless battles. I had forgotten how warm and reassuring they were. "I grew up amongst the Cape and Cowl crowd, Gary. I know every conceivable type of hero, villain, anti-villain, anti-hero, fallen hero, risen villain, and everything in-between. I don't see the archetypes anymore but the people under the mask. You're the same person you've always been to me, whether you have superpowers and a codename or not."

I wasn't ready for this sort of pep-talk. "You can't tell me you can look at all these bodies around me and say I'm the same person I was in college."

Gabrielle blinked. "No, you're not. If you were like this, I might have believed you could survive my enemies. We might still be together."

Wow.

That...was awkward.

Stumbling for something to say, I said, "Careful, you might ruin your clean-cut image."

Gabrielle snorted. "I'm not in this for my image, Gary. I'm in this to help people."

I stared at my hands. "I got to talk with Keith's ghost, recently. He's not proud of who I've become."

"Don't be ashamed of who you are," Gabrielle said, looking at me. "Be who you are for you."

"*That is appalling advice, Ms. Anders,*" Cloak said in my head.

Gabrielle could hear Cloak's voice, just like her father. "Eh, I call 'em like I see."

I thought about what Gabrielle was saying and tried to parse it in my mind. I couldn't be a superhero. I was too selfish, too stubborn, too mean, and too ruthless. I would never *not* be these things. I also couldn't turn a blind eye to all that was going on around me either. The Nightmaster and her insanely stupid flunkies were turning my city into a cemetery.

My city.

For years, decades even, I'd been trying to use Keith as an excuse for doing what I wanted to do from the very beginning. I'd made supervillainy into a code rather than a label people slapped on people they feared.

I'd made it a game.

Well when I played games, I played to win.

"Then let me be a villain," I said, looking down at his hands. "A villain who does what he wants, when he wants, and how he wants. I'm going to follow my own code, screw society's, and I'm going to fix what I hate about this planet. I'm also going to get rid of the people who I hate about it. I'm not going to do it for Keith, I'm not going to do it for America, I'm not going to do it for Death, or even God. I'm going to do it for me."

I conjured a ball of flame and a handful of ice in my hands.

Then made them disappear.

Gary Karkofsky was dead.

Now there was just Merciless.

And I was okay with that.

"It's a hard road putting on a mask," Gabrielle said, staring at me. "The mask compels you to become more than who you are under your birth name. It demands an immense toll and enacts an immeasurable price. It also grants strength greater than you could ever imagine if you believe in what it represents. That's why your mask should also be of someone you want to be."

I understood that. "Are you happy with who you are, Gabby?"

Gabrielle gave a half-smile. "Sometimes. It would be easier to be Ultragoddess if there were more people she could not be her around."

I took her hands and looked at her. "You should come visit more often."

"Thank you," Gabrielle said, blinking away mist from her eyes. "I'd like that. I need to take a vacation after this. The world can take care of itself for a few months."

I nodded. "I think we all will need one. Know any nice beach planets?"

"A few," Gabrielle said, smiling fully. "I'll recommend Mandy some sexy swimsuits."

I thought about mentioning she preferred to swim in the nude but this conversation was already awkward enough as is. "You'll always be part of my family, Gabby."

"I..." Gabrielle started to say something.

"Gary, we need you over here!" Mandy called to me.

I stepped away from Gabrielle, gave her a smile, then levitated over toward Mandy. My leg felt much better now and it seemed whatever healing effect was spreading to other wounds over my body. It didn't help with the guilt I felt over the slaughter I'd just enacted but maybe that was how I was supposed to feel. I'd been bottled up for decades after killing Shoot-Em-Up and felt nothing after killing the Ice Cream Man or Typewriter. Maybe confronting Keith had allowed those emotions to finally pour forth.

"There's also a difference between killing two people and killing a hundred," Cloak said.

"Yeah, whoever said the million is a statistic thing was a dumbass," I said, stepping over a couple of bodies to get to Mandy.

"It's falsely attributed to Joseph Stalin—not the best source of wisdom."

I walked over to the Black Witch and Mandy, the former looking like I'd interrupted a moment they were having. I'd never liked Selena, even when we were classmates, and that feeling hadn't changed now that I'd married her girlfriend. The pair of them were standing over the body of a black-robed cultist who was now drooling out of the sides of his mouth.

"We've found out some vital information," Mandy said, looking at me. "Are you okay?"

"Yeah, I killed a bunch of people but I'm fine," I said, giving the peace-sign.

"Excellent," Mandy said. "We've managed to take down a third of the cult here but the strongest of their necromancers as well as the Reaper's Cloak wielders are elsewhere."

"Your Princess is in another castle," I said, giving a tired smile.

Gabrielle snorted behind me, laughing.

Mandy looked confused. "Okay, sure. Whatever the case, I need you at your fighting best, can you do that."

"Aye-aye, Skipper." I saluted. "So what did you learn?"

"The final ritual to summon Zul-Barbas is at midnight," Mandy said, coldly. "Which, along with the black robes is just one of the many clichés they're following."

"There's nothing wrong with black robes," I said, frowning. "Well, aside from a few of those guys on the stadium fortifications shooting at me."

"We've located another of their bases and Ultragoddess' group is going to try to stop them but the actual location of the Nightmaster and her inner circle of spellcasters is unknown. This entire city is one gigantic summoning circle and they only need to do the ritual from anywhere in the city to do it. It'll have to be a place of great violence or significance to the citizen's residents, though."

Great.

It was like finding a needle in a pile of other needles. "It seems like a good idea to split up then. Gabrielle's team should go deal with this other base while carry on with our original plan to retrieve *The Book of Midnight*."

Angel Eyes seemed thoughtful before giving a short nod. "A wise plan. I will follow your lead on this."

Diabloman, on the other hand, looked troubled. The older supervillain was sitting nearby, looking exhausted with several wounds regenerating as his tattoos moved across his body. He seemed almost disappointed at his survival "You should go on without me. You have surpassed anything I ever accomplished as a supervillain and have no further need for my counsel. I am an old man and would only slow you down."

The last thing I needed right now was my second in command quitting.

"You're my wingman," I said, looking at him with an even look on my face. "I still need you for many important tasks that only you can do."

"Oh?" Diabloman questioned.

Pointing at Diabloman then myself, "You're part of a proud and illustrious tradition, you two. It is an Every Big Bad needs his top enforcer. The Emperor had Darth Vader, Sauron had the Witch King, and I've got you. I'm awesome but, honestly, not that scary. I need you to stand around looking menacing so people don't think I'm too nice to punish them. That's why I pay you the big bucks."

Diabloman, I suspect, smiled under his mask. "You are too good to me."

"I really am." I looked at Cindy. "What about you?"

"If we're going to save the city, I want to be famous because of this. Like talk-shows, television appearances, book deals, and Shirley Manson playing me on television."

"Will do," I said. "I want Wentworth Miller."

Cindy snorted. "You wish."

"I'm going with you. You will do what I say and not try to stop me." Mandy's gaze brooked no interference.

The Black Witch seemed disappointed, then nodded. "Good luck."

"Our prayers will be with you," Gabrielle said, looking between her fellows before wrapping them all in Ultraforce bubbles and taking to the sky.

"Thanks, you two," I said, knowing only Gabrielle could hear me. "Okay, Amanda, whatever you can tell us about your father's defenses would be great."

I was expecting state of the art security systems because of the man's billionaire status. It was also likely he had some magical defenses due to his membership in the Brotherhood of Infamy. With my group's combined strength, I was pretty sure we could tear through that like wet tissue paper.

"Well, I don't know how much has changed. I had to flee the mansion when the cult killed my father." Amanda looked bitter. "They slaughtered the cleaning staff and their families too. Some of them were friends of mine."

"End of the world, Amanda. Try to keep your brooding to a minimum here." I immediately regretted saying it.

Amanda shot a withering glare to me before Mandy put a helpful hand on her shoulder.

"Please, just try and remember." Mandy said, her voice calm, even soothing. "We're on your side. Mostly."

Amanda took a deep breath. "Well, if I had to narrow it down to one single thing you have to worry about I'd probably tell you to look out for the giant robot."

"The giant robot," I repeated, looking over to the cyborg dinosaurs. "Right, okay, sounds about right."

Amanda nodded. "My Dad is... was... a collector of a lot of weird superhuman stuff. One of them is the German *Automatisch Ubersoldatten*, a twenty-foot-tall machine from WW2 powered by the souls of the damned. My Dad never used it but I'm sure the cultists have reactivated it."

"A magical *Nazi* robot." Mandy blinked rapidly. It was as if she couldn't quite digest what she just said.

"You've had a very interesting childhood," I said.

"Tell me about it," Amanda said, wiping her face off with her sleeve. "It kind of put a crimp on inviting anyone over to play."

"I call cultural dibs on smashing this thing to pieces." I raised my hand. I needed to apologize to God for my blasphemous boast earlier.

"Ditto," Cindy added, grinning from ear-to-ear.

"You'll have to wait in line," Amanda replied, smirking. "I've lived my entire life with that stupid thing in our living room. Nothing on Earth is going to keep me from smashing to pieces."

"How are we going to get there, though?" Cindy asked, gesturing to the wreckage spread across the bridge. "Our cars are trashed."

No time to deal with that now, though. "When you're a supervillain, there's a never-ending supply of cars to steal. To the Merciless Mobile!"

"There is no Merciless Mobile," Cindy pointed out. "You trashed the Nightcar."

"I know that," I said, having gotten caught up in the moment. "We'll improvise."

We, instead, hijacked a minivan abandoned on the side of the road.

Chapter Eighteen

Where We Go Visit a Creepy Castle (Yes, Really)

The journey to the Douglas family mansion wasn't long. They lived just outside of the city limits, still under the dome erected by the Brotherhood of Infamy. Their home was in a picturesque region of Falconcrest City filled with golf courses and houses worth more than some countries' national debt. Amanda's childhood home wasn't hard to pick out from the row after row of forty -room-plus villas.

Hers was the only castle.

The place was either a genuine Medieval castle transplanted to the United States stone-by-stone or a damn fine reproduction of one. It was complete with creepy towers and overgrown grass. A wrought iron fence surrounded the place with a large metal 'D' hanging over the gate. I expected bats to fly out of the tower belfries any minute. Storm clouds were gathering behind the castle, the edge of the bubble-like dome over the city shimmering behind it like the Aurora Borealis.

"We're in a van heading to a creepy castle. All we need is a talking dog and this is officially an episode of *Scooby Doo*," Mandy muttered, sitting beside me in the passenger's seat.

"If so, I'm Daphne," Cindy called from the very back of the van. Diabloman and Angel Eyes were sitting in front of her with Amanda between them.

"I am not Velma," Mandy's voice brooked no disagreement.

"Well I'm obviously Shaggy," I said. "Angel Eyes is Fred. I suppose that makes Diabloman Scooby."

"This conversation has gone a direction I find insulting to a man who has overthrown governments," Diabloman grumbled. "Besides, I like Velma."

Angel Eyes just ignored us, doing his nails.

I shrugged and switched topics. "How did you end up living in a place like this anyway, Amanda? Most teenage girls only wish they lived in fairy tale castles. Albeit, in your case, the original dark and disturbing Brother's Grimm version."

"It's not as bad as you might think," Amanda said, smiling. "My dad bought it from Vincent Weird, the sorcerer. It came with a lot of cool stuff like secret passages, giant spiders, and other cool things I got to play with as a child."

"You're like the debutante version of Wednesday Addams," I said before turning around and reaching towards Cindy. "Henchperson, hand me my Merciless Binoculars."

"You mean your regular binoculars? The ones we stole from an Omegamart on the way here?" Cindy said, handing them over.

"Yes, *my Merciless Binoculars.*" I shook my hand for emphasis.

Cindy sighed and gave me a pair.

Taking my binoculars, I surveyed the area before the mansion's entrance. I saw the place was surrounded by a group of about a hundred skin head punks. They were armed with a mixture of automatic weapons, bats, chains, and machetes.

I did my best Harrison Ford impression. "Nazis, I hate these guys."

"You and me both, pal," Cindy said.

There was also a giant Nazi robot coming around the back, waving its arms in front of it like it was a monster from an old black and white science fiction movie. The *Automatisch Ubersoldattan*, as Amanda called it, was a classic art deco design. It was mostly blocky with a square head and body with rectangular arms as well as legs. A number of blinking lights dotted its crude face. Instead of hands, the robot had claw grips and there was a long spinning radar dish on the top of its head. The thing honestly looked like an oversized child's toy with the exception of the steel swastika on its front chest.

"I have never wanted to destroy something so much in my life," I muttered, narrowing my eyes. "Why the hell is the Brotherhood using a Nazi robot, though? I mean, at the very least, they could have scraped off the insignia. I mean, aren't supervillains today enlightened enough to avoid the sheer *tackiness* of it?"

"*The Brotherhood of Infamy has often made use of Nazi remnants and their imitators across the decades,*" Cloak explained. "*The Brotherhood claims they will be rewarded with a purely Aryan world upon the destruction of civilization by Zul-Barbas. This is, of course, nonsense.*"

"So, they make use of Neo-Nazis and a Nazi robot because they're idiots?"

"*Yes.*"

"*That,* I understand."

"Don't you hate the way he talks to himself?" Cindy asked Amanda.

"Let me ask my Dad," Amanda said, staring at her cloak. A second later, she said, "No."

"Spoilsport," Cindy said, pouting.

Mandy took the binoculars and took a look through them herself. "The robot seems to be patrolling around the castle grounds rather slowly. We should probably wait until it's moved to the back of the castle grounds to move in."

"Yes, and all we have to do is kill a hundred or more Neo-Nazis," I said, smiling at the prospect.

"It would not be difficult to kill them all," Angel Eyes said, rubbing his facial scar. "Apparently, Aphrodite has not abandoned me completely. Between my magic and your fire powers, we could kill them all in under a minute."

"Simple but effective, I like it. Who's up for an old fashioned Nazi bash?"

Cindy's hand shot up, oddly so did Angel Eyes'.

"May I use lethal force?" Diabloman asked.

"As much as you want. In fact, if you *don't* kill every one of them, I'll be disappointed."

"We're not killing a hundred people," Amanda said, taking charge. "Even Nazis."

"Really?" I looked back at her, raising an eyebrow. "*National Socialists* are where you're going to draw your 'no killing' line?"

"Well..." Amanda trailed off, looking guilty. "It's not that I like them—"

"Even Ultragod killed Nazis both before and after taking down the Fuhrer," I said, raising my forefinger for emphasis. "Superheroes can kill three types of people: Robots, Ugly Aliens, and Goose-Stepping Morons."

"Don't forget zombies," Mandy said, seemingly amused by our discussion. "That's important."

"Yeah, the undead don't count either. They're soulless abominations," I said, throwing my hands up in mock surrender. "Besides, Amanda, you're not going to be killing them. *I'll* be killing them. Angel Eyes too."

"I have no objection to killing fascists," Angel Eyes said. "I killed more than my fair share during the Second Great War. I confess, though, I mostly ended up killing Italian fascists. They were not kind to Greece."

Diabloman simply said, "I am at your service."

"My family would never forgive me if I *didn't* kill Nazis," Cindy said. "Even poseurs."

"Could you at least *try* and cut down on the mass murder in my presence?" Amanda sighed, exasperated.

"After what happened at the stadium?" I asked.

"Because of what happened at the stadium." Amanda corrected.

I sighed, realizing she was probably still traumatized by the slaughter there. "Fine, though this goes against my every instinct."

I crossed my arms and leaned back in my chair before rubbing my chin. "How powerful is this 1940s robot, anyway, Amanda? Do you know?"

"It was designed by Doctor Terror," Amanda said. "So it's got all sorts of bells and whistles like super strength, near invulnerability, and—"

"Wait, *Tom Terror* worked for the Nazis?" I interrupted, shocked. "Uh, duh," Amanda said. "Didn't you know that?"

"I'm more a Silver Age fan than the Golden Age." I felt sick to my stomach. "That son of a bitch. I can't believe I didn't kill him when I had the chance."

"That was probably a mistake," Angel Eyes said. "For both the world and humanity."

"Bastard." I cursed myself.

Mandy patted me on the shoulder. "It's okay, I'm sure you'll be able to kill the global-trotting terrorist the next time you meet."

Mandy always knew the right thing to cheer me up.

"Thank you," I said, looking back over at her "In any case, please finish up what you were saying, Amanda."

"The robot has death rays—"

"There's a classic," I interrupted, smiling. "I've always admired Ming the Merciless for having one of those."

"Don't be racist, Boss," Diabloman said. "It's getting annoying."

"I'm not racist!" I snapped. "Just... okay, yeah, Ming the Merciless was a pretty racist. Sorry."

"The robot also has motion sensors and radar. It's limited by its human pilot, however," Amanda ignored us, rapidly developing one of the qualities necessary for survival in my group.

"A human pilot, huh? Interesting," I said. Facts started coming together in interesting and peculiar ways. Okay, I have a plan."

Everyone was curiously silent.

"Nobody is going to complain?" I asked.

"Your plans have an oddball way of working," Diabloman replied. "Against all the laws of physics and good sense."

"I think you're insane, Gary," Mandy said. "I don't think you're stupid."

"Yet, you married him," Cindy pointed out.

"I love lunatics," Mandy said. "What can I say?"

"That explains why you're here," Amanda deadpanned, showing there may be hope for her yet.

"*Anyway*," I said, "here's what we're going to do..."

Twenty minutes later, when the robot was safely on the other side of the house, the majority of the Douglas family mansion front yard exploded. A colossal wall of fire rose from the ground, illuminating the place for miles.

My distraction had begun.

Chapter Nineteen

Where We Fight a Giant Robot and Try Not to Die

Seconds after the explosion tore through the front gate and most of the Douglas family estate front lawn, a towering column of flame arose from the ground at least twenty-feet-high. Above it I hovered, back-lit by the fire, as I shouted with an exaggerated voice, "Doom is upon you! Beware!"

At the end of the day, all a supervillain has is his capacity for *showmanship*. Well, in my case, at the end of the day all I have is my capacity showmanship, a magic cape, and a team of extremely talented henchmen. Whatever the case, it would be theatricality that carried the day.

"Holy shit!" One of the skinheads shouted. "It's the Nightwalker!"

"It can't be him! He's dead!" Another exclaimed.

"Tell him that!" A third screamed.

A few of them started firing at my levitating form. Given I was insubstantial, their weapons were utterly useless. I made sure I was visible enough that they were able to see it. Nothing inspires fear like seeing your opponent shrug off your strongest attack.

"Your souls are mine, so speaks the Dark Lord!" I shouted, conjuring a bunch of hailstones to fall down upon them with my ice powers.

Oddly, it was the ice that did it. The skinheads, to the man, panicked and started running in every conceivable direction. The robot was still on the other side of the castle and thus we had plenty of time to rush on in before it arrived.

Levitating downward, I settled down a few feet away from the heat less fires and surveyed the empty area with no small degree of satisfaction. The ground was covered in abandoned guns, melee weapons, and even a rocket launcher.

"I must confess, Angel Eyes, I'm impressed with your skill at illusions. I never would have been able to make a conflagration like that myself." I looked up at the massive inferno. The fire was still burning brightly, almost like a work of art. I would have been exhausted making something a quarter of its size.

Angel Eyes walked through the wall of flames behind me, treating it as it were no more than a wall of mist. He took a moment to survey the landscape and gave a proud smile. "I still believe we should have killed them all. Still, I admire your theatricality. Aristophanes would be proud."

Amanda Douglas, having pulled her mask on again, followed Angel Eyes through the harmless flame. "Please, you stole all of that from *The Princess Bride.*"

"I always steal from the best."

Cindy, Diabloman, and Mandy passed through the illusionary wall of fire one by one. We'd left the minivan parked outside the estate in case the giant robot decided to smash it to pieces while we were inside.

From its halting, jerky, movements I figured we had at least six or seven minutes until the *Automatisch Ubersoldattan* finished its rounds about the estate. I'd waited for it to start on its journey away from the mansion and was counting on its sensors not picking up the illusionary fire we created. That gave us time to be cautious in our investigation of the mansion interior.

"Okay," I said. "Here's my plan. We move to the front door, Amanda and I turn insubstantial, and then we scout ahead. You guys stay on the outside until the robot comes or we give the all-clear. We'll then proceed to—"

"Duck," Angel Eyes said.

I immediately threw myself on the ground. A glowing blast of red energy sailed over my head and struck the ground behind me. A three-foot-deep crater appeared in the resulting explosion, showering me with charred dirt and burning grass. My face and back stung like hell as my ears rung from the noise.

"*Sieg Heil! Das ist ein Überfall!*" a deep robotic voice shouted as the *Automatisch Ubersoldattan* started tromping around from the back of the castle, moving at a far faster speed than I would have thought its blocky legs capable.

Its palm was sticking out and I saw a hole in the center of it, smoking from the blast it shot out at us. Obviously, I'd severely miscalculated the robot's self-awareness and speed.

"God damn World War 2 super-science!" I grit my teeth and looked to the Heavens. "Is there no end to the evils you bring!?"

Mandy tackled me out of the way as a pair of twin rockets fired from the machine's back and landed where I was standing, causing another explosion of dirt and flaming debris.

Mandy slapped me across the face. "This is no time for jokes!"

Her words stung. "Sorry, I don't know how to react to danger unless I'm joking."

"Running and screaming is good!"

"But that's a joke by itself!"

"Shut up and fight!"

"*Eliminieren! Eliminieren!*" the robot shouted, waving its arms around wildly.

Angel Eyes began casting something, only to have the robot bat him away like a toddler knocking away a toy. It wouldn't be lethal to the Greek demigod but I suspected it would hurt like hell. Cindy, being the sensible soul that she was, ran like hell for cover and never looked back. Diabloman, brave but foolishly went for the rocket launcher dropped by one of the skinheads. I suspected it wouldn't even put a dent in the machine's reinforced steel hide but admired his courage.

"*Gary, this is a pointless distraction,*" Cloak said to me.

"Oh really? Cause, I thought it was us trying to stay alive!" I shouted, running alongside Mandy as the robot fired a number of energy blasts at us. I got to repay Mandy back for saving my life seconds later, pushing her out of the way as another energy blast exploded beside us.

"*There's no reason this place would be as heavily guarded as it is unless one or more of the Brotherhood's Inner Circle was present here,*" Cloak said. "*This might even be the location they're summoning Zul-Barbas from. You should dispense with fighting this mindless creature and focus on getting into the mansion.*"

The *Automatisch Ubersoldattan* picked up Amanda Douglas in one of its claw grips, the young woman trying to keep it from crushing her. Diabloman fired his rocket launcher, striking the machine in its shoulder. While it didn't do much damage, the resulting explosion caused smokes and sparks to pour from the spot.

The giant robot turned its head to the damage. "You little shit!"

"That's not a stock German phrase," I said, wrinkling my brow. "Mandy, are you pondering what I'm pondering?"

"Why you keep joking despite imminent danger of death?" Mandy said, ironically going with my joke.

"No," I said, trying to think of a response before shouting at Amanda, "Shoot the radar dish!"

Amanda, still held in the robot's claw grip, nodded and threw back her hand like she was pitching a baseball. A second later, a huge bolt of blue lightning shot forth and struck the machine's radar dish.

Electricity moved up and down the front of the creature before it lifted its claw grips up and started fumbling backwards, flailing its arms. To my amusement, the *Automatisch Ubersoldattan* did a semi-decent rendition of 'The Robot Dance' before it fell over.

Amanda, having leaped out of its grip as soon as she'd thrown her lightning bolt, cheered and gave a fist pump in the air. "Ten points! My first giant robot! Woo!"

"Yeah, it's a super-heroic milestone." I walked up beside her. "Hold on, *you have lightning powers?*"

"Yeah?" Amanda inquired, looking at me. "What's wrong with that?"

"Lightning and super strength is *way cooler* than fire and ice powers," I muttered. "Why couldn't I have had all four?"

"Don't be greedy, Gary," Mandy chastised, taking up position beside me. "So, what do we do now?"

"Wait to talk to someone who might actually know something. It's likely one of the Brotherhood's inner circle if they're trusted enough to have a giant robot and smart enough to know two different languages," I observed, staring at the ruined robot. "You know, if Amanda's lightning bolt didn't fry him." It was also possible it was another Amazon and I hoped she was alright. For some reason, I felt sicker having killed them than the myriad cultists back at the stadium.

Amanda winced, the look visible through her mask. "Alight. Let's crank her open."

Diabloman and Angel Eyes took up position behind me as Cindy reluctantly crawled from behind an uprooted willow tree. Moments later, the front panel of the *Automatisch Ubersoldattan* popped open, smoke pouring out of the front. An elderly man stumbled out, well into his sixties, and obviously wearing one of the seven Reaper's Cloaks.

"You... imbeciles!" The Brotherhood of Infamy cultist screamed. "Do you have any idea what you're interfering with?"

His voice sounded familiar and the closer he got, the more I could make out his features. I was gobsmacked when I realized who it was. "No way. *Chief Watkins?*"

The Chief of Police, Bill Watkins, was a member of the Brotherhood of Infamy? The man supposedly in charge of keeping the city safe from supervillains? It explained a lot, not the least bit including why our city sucked so bad. He'd been willing to let me go after killing the Typewriter, despite the fact I'd been involved in an earlier bank robbery. Watkins probably thought I'd eventually get myself killed fighting the other supervillains in town and that would allow him to recover the Reaper's Cloak I was wearing.

Damn.

"He would have gotten away with it too if not for you meddling kids!" Cindy piped in from the back.

I waved behind me. "Not now, Cindy."

"*I don't believe it.*" Cloak was horrified. "*I was friends with that man for thirty years. I was friends with his father for almost as long. How could I have been so blind?*"

"Save the self-pity for another time." I stared daggers at the crooked cop. "Does he have any oogie-boogie powers I should worry about?"

"*He's wearing the Cloak of the Oracle,*" Cloak said, still sounding upset. "*It grants the ability to tell the future. You don't have to worry about him turning insubstantial or throwing fireballs like you and Amanda are capable of doing.*"

"Good to know," I replied, gesturing to the man. "Diablo, beat this guy up."

"As you wish," Diabloman answered, advancing towards the Chief of Police, his hands extended as if to crush the cultist.

"Wait!" Chief Watkins shouted, raising his hands in surrender. "We can make a deal."

"Why did I know he would say that?" I sighed, rubbing the bridge of my nose.

"Because criminals tend to be a superstitious cowardly lot?" Amanda said.

"Yeah." I nodded, before doing a double take. "Hey! Wait a damn minute, we are not!"

Amanda giggled while Mandy grinned.

Chief Watkins took a deep breath. "It's not like I'm insane for joining the Brotherhood. I had very good reasons."

"I'm pretty sure summoning an eldritch abomination to destroy the world is the very definition of insane."

"The world is doomed," Chief Watkins replied, staring at me. His eyes blazed, filled with a hate I couldn't even begin to describe. "Hundreds of people die every year in this city due to supervillains. Men, women, children... especially children. My father waited until I'd seen how people ignore the horrible things supervillains, people like you, do before inducting me into the Brotherhood. My God, have you ever stopped to look at how *insane* this world is?"

"You mean how supervillains can kill a hundred guys or blow up a city in Florida only to get out on good behavior in a month? How superheroes can never kill people despite facing people objectively worse they'd fight in wartime?" I asked, my voice getting higher with each example. "How the masses are entertained by superhero and supervillain fights despite the fact they're risking hundreds of lives every time they brawl in the middle of downtown?"

"Yes!" the Chief shouted.

"No," I said. "Not really."

Chief Watkins looked frustrated but undeterred. "Zul-Barbas will destroy the world by reducing it to chaos, yes, but the ambient magical energy left behind will be greater than anything our world has ever seen. The Nightmaster, our leader, will use *The Book of Midnight* to harness that energy. We can remake the world overnight! Think about it! No more superheroes, no more supervillains, and the entire world running on the principles of science alone!"

"So, let me get this straight," Mandy said, staring at him. "You intend to destroy the world with magic... so you can rebuild it with science?"

"Yes!" Chief Watkins hands shook as he spoke. "Not insane science either but the solid earthy kind. We'll have cars that don't fly and space that's an empty void we need gigantic rockets to visit. That's the kind of world we want to build!"

"You, Sir," I said, pointing at his chest, "are a disgrace to Einstein and Tesla."

It occurred to me the world he was describing wasn't too different from the one where Tom Terror stored his stuff. It made me wonder if the Brotherhood of Infamy's doppelgangers had succeeded on that world. It was a depressing thought. A world without aliens, magic, or phlebotinum-based technology scarcely bore thinking about.

"So, technically, we could let the world be destroyed and use the book to remake it as something we like?" Cindy interjected, leaning up between Mandy and me. "Like Mercilessland with the city of Cindyopolis?"

"No," Mandy replied, her voice like steel.

"Mandyopolis?" Cindy suggested.

"No," I snapped, just as forcibly. "We don't kill kids. Wiping out the entirety of humanity and remaking it with a bunch of new humans is the very opposite of not killing kids. I don't have enough scruples to start violating the few I do."

"I agree with Merciless... and I never thought I'd be saying that," Angel Eyes said, even more haughty than usual. "Here, I am a living god.

Who knows what sort of reality might be created with such magics or whether it would even work? It's much too risky."

Cindy gave me a sour look before staring daggers at Mandy. "Fine. I don't even know why I bother anymore."

"Me either." I was annoyed. "Weren't you supposed to be a doctor?"

"Yeah, but this pays better," Cindy answered. "That's what's important."

"*Ms. Wakowski's character in two sentences.*"

"Tell me about it. Okay, you've got one chance of making this out alive. Is *The Book of Midnight* still in there? Is the house guarded by anything else? Where is the ritual going to take place? Three questions and you live."

Chief Watkins took a deep breath. "It's not too late to make a deal, Merciless. Even if you thwart the ritual, this town still needs a Mayor. Both he and Douglas were too stupid to realize the far reaching power of our cult. We could be very good to one another."

I set Chief Watkins' foot on fire with a wave of my mind.

"Ahh!" the Chief screamed.

"I'm sorry, did I break your concentration?" I said, my low and threatening. The number of people the cult had murdered was fresh in my mind. I was a villain, willingly so, but he was a monster. "Answers, now."

Torture was an imprecise and, frankly, useless means of getting information but I suspected Chief Watkins would try to make a deal with us if he was scared. Intimidation tactics and coercion were viable means to get knowledge.

"Shouldn't you be arguing against that?" Cindy said to Amanda. "Being a superhero and all?"

"He killed my father, so... no." Amanda looked down.

"I like you," Cindy said, playing with one of her bunches.

The Chief finally stamped out his foot before saying. "*The Book of Midnight* is still there. Dick Gleeson and I weren't able to get past Douglas' wards so we set up perimeter around the place rather than relocate the tome. The Nightmaster is doing the ritual from notes the cult made in the past at the top of the Falconcrest City Clock Tower. Dick is a sorcerer and can do all sorts of seriously weird stuff so I don't know what you'll encounter in the mansion. Fine, are you satisfied?"

"Yeah. I am."

Chief Watkins burst into flame, burning to ashes before my eyes as I concentrated more flame into him than I had anyone else prior. He didn't have time to scream before his body started collapsing onto itself as his bones melted before our eyes, his entire frame becoming nothing more than a fine powder.

With his death, Chief Watkins cloak floated up above his body, apparently seeking out a new wearer. I briefly considered giving the cloak to Mandy, violating my deal with Death but she'd played straight with me and I owed it to do the same. Supervillains may not have ruled, but we had standards.

Or I did, at least.

Grabbing it in mid-air, I focused my will through it and the cloak burst into flame. This flame, however, was a pure white and I felt the cloak disappear into it. Death had claimed one of her seven cloaks back and my deal with her was partially filled. All I had to do now was kill five other people with magical cloaks and a physical god.

Super.

Mandy looked down at the man's ashes, all that remained of the former Chief of Police. "That was murder."

"Pretty much, yeah." I stared at the flames as they died down. "I'm sorry I didn't clear it with you ahead of time."

"I don't mind you killing people plotting global genocide," Mandy said, putting her hands on her hips. "That's about the limit of what I'm comfortable with, however. Don't take it as a blanket permission to start killing people."

"I'll bear that in mind," I said, making a mental note not to tell her about all the other people I'd killed.

"I can't believe famed radio commentator Dick Gleeson is evil," Amanda said, her voice chipper and full of naivety. "I mean, he's a radio commentator. If you can't trust the Fourth Estate, who can you trust?"

It took me a second to realize she was being sarcastic. "Ah. There may be hope for you yet, young padawan. Being a smart-ass is the first thing you have to learn as a supervillain."

"I'm a super*hero*," Amanda corrected me.

"Sure you are," I said, turning around to head to the mansion. "I dub you Merci-Lass."

Chapter Twenty

Where I Explore the Castle from Hell

"I am *not* Merci-Lass." Amanda wasn't amused by her new appellation.

I smirked, walking towards the Douglas family mansion front door. "Well, we can also go with Merciless Girl, Lieutenant Merciless, Mandy Merciless, or Kid Merciless. I'm flexible."

Mandy reached down to the ground where the skinheads abandoned their weapons and picked up a pair of Colt .45 automatic pistols. Lifting the two weapons up, all trace of her pain vanished. Somehow, Mandy had managed to suppress it under a sea of determination. "If we're going to fight more zombies, I should get some upgrades. How do I look?"

"Amazing," I said, worried my wife was embracing the hard-edged path of superheroism a little too quickly.

For years, I'd taken it for granted that superheroes didn't kill and supervillains did. A lot of the public tried to shame them for this, saying the world would be a much better place if Tom Terror was executed by Ultragod or Mister Chaos was stabbed in the head by Guinevere. They never quite made the connection that if they wanted these individuals dead, they could do it themselves through the courtroom or themselves. Superheroes tried to hold themselves to a higher standard and got called to task for not lowering themselves to the depths of everyone else.

The thing was, the world was getting darker again. Most of the Nineties had been filled with superheroes willing to kill, inspired by Shoot-Em-Up and the Extreme's example. Those days had never truly left us. It was estimated more than half of the Society of Superheroes had killed under some set of circumstances or another, even if their official policy was to not. I couldn't condemn them for it but it seemed more and more, the world was trying to put the Anti in front of every hero out there.

I bore some responsibility myself.

I needed to figure out a way to encourage my wife, Douglas, and any other heroes I met to stay away from this path. If that required sparing Nazis and crazy doomsday cultists, ugh, so be it.

Cloak was silent then said, "*I am proud of you, Gary.*"

"*Thank you.*"

"Your wife is tenacious," Angel Eyes observed, watching her as she strode past Diabloman. "She didn't even look at me when I was speaking to her."

I took a moment to look at Angel Eyes, reevaluating him. Honestly, he looked like hell. His suit, the one which probably cost more than the Greek national debt, was in tatters. His gorgeous hair was caked with mud, no longer possessed its overwhelming beauty. Even his posture had changed, losing its superhuman grace. Angel Eyes looked tired. Worse, he looked beaten.

It occurred to me that Angel Eyes was an immensely lonely man. He was immortal, which meant he didn't have much in the way of prospects for long-term commitment. The Greek Gods weren't exactly paragons of fidelity. Angel Eyes was also the sort of man that men and women would instantly fall under the sway of, meaning he didn't have many peers. I doubted the man had any more than a handful of friends. I'd feel sorry for him if he wasn't an immensely rich and powerful douchebag.

"Yeah," I said. "My wife is awesome that way. I don't know why she loves me but she does."

"If I could kill you to take what you have, I would do it. I hope you realize that," Angel Eyes said to me, his voice threatening.

"Yeah," I said. "Also realize that I have the Reaper's Scythe now and I'm pretty sure that will kill immortals."

Angel Eyes looked like he was debating testing that theory then shrugged. "Perhaps you might be a worthy opponent for Mandy's affections, after all."

I smiled, realizing Angel Eyes didn't get it. Even if I got jealous and sometimes had doubts, love wasn't a competition. I hoped Angel Eyes would learn that. Otherwise, well, I'd have to kill him and that would require whole *hours* to get Mandy to forgive me. "May the better man win."

"How generous of you," Angel Eyes said. "I accept your concession."

"Yeah, I'm totally killing you after this," I said.

"We shall see," Angel Eyes said.

Heading up to the door, I took in the front of the mansion. The exterior was illuminated by Angel Eyes' illusionary flame, allowing me to see all of the castle's details. The door was an impressive double-door wooden edifice with gargoyle-shaped knockers and no doorknobs. A large stone family crest was built into the wall above the doorway, incorporating a pair of crossed swords and a skull. It made me wonder if the previous owners of the mansion had been pirates.

"Seriously, I want to know if all of the architects in this city went to the same school or belong to the same agency. If so, the first thing I'm doing after all of this is burning down their place of business," Cindy muttered, pulling on the door knob. "It's locked. You want us to knock it down?"

"I'll handle it." Turning insubstantial, I walked through the door. With that, I entered into the main hallway and immediately found myself surrounded by hundreds of ghosts.

Literally, hundreds of ghosts.

The main hallway was a two story chamber with two spiraling staircases on either side of the chamber, heading up to the second floor. The place was dark but had a soft illumination from the dozens of spirits standing on them and on the marble tile floor. They glowed like little fluorescent light bulbs, most of them translucent with only a small number as physical looking as the little girl had been.

They were dressed in a mixture of outfits, ranging from the 1930s to the Modern Era. To my disgust and horror, at least half of them were adolescents or teenagers. There were kids holding bloody newspapers as if they were killed hocking them on the street, a girl in a poodle skirt with her throat slashed, and a boy holding a 1980s-era Nintendo game controller with a bullet hole in his head.

I surveyed the scene. "Well dammit."

Now, by this point, I had become somewhat jaded to ghosts. I'd encountered only a few but I had the basic principle down—restless spirits hanging on despite the fact that they had a better afterlife waiting for them on the other side. At least, you know, if they were good. I had no idea they could exist in such vast numbers.

"*This is going to hurt. Brace yourself.*"

"What do yo...gurk!" I said, before being immediately being washed over by agony beyond measure.

Encountering the little girl had nearly killed me, my 'spook senses' feeling like a heart attack encountering one eighty-year-old ghost. Here, it was like being shot in the chest, repeatedly. I didn't know why I didn't sense them through the door but I fell to the ground, grabbing my throat as if I was being strangled. The pain was excruciating, like nothing I'd ever experienced. It was the Reaper's Sense, a horrible gut-wrenching feeling which occurred when I was surrounded by ghosts.

"Mandy..." I choked out, falling over and feeling my head as the world's most severe migraine began.

"Gary, you have to hold on. You're feeling the pain of these restless spirits pouring onto you. It's all in your mind. If you absorb too much of it, they'll drag you into the Place Between with them."

"No," I said, reaching into my cloak and pulling out the coin Death had been giving me. "I'm not going to die like this."

Rubbing the coin, it transformed into a scythe and I braced myself against it. Climbing up the wooden shaft, I leaned on it for dear life as the pain continued. It was agonizing, beyond words, as if a lifetime of horrible deaths were crammed into every single moment I drew breath.

"I am Merciless! The supervillain without mercy!" I shouted, slamming the end of the scythe into the ground, cracking a marble flagstone. In the distance, I swear, I heard a crack of thunder. Instantly, the pain vanished.

"That was probably not a good idea."

"Why?" I said, gasping for breath.

"The Reaper's Scythe is recognized by all ghosts instinctively," Cloak explained. *"You've drawn everyone's attention."*

"What?"

I noticed there were over a hundred pairs of ghostly eyes staring at me. All of the spirits, which had been standing there motionless before, were now turned to me. All of them had regained the light of comprehension, more than a few of them growling at me as if I was dinner.

"Dammit," I grunted. "Why does this shit keep happening to me?"

"Because you're a terrible person."

"In a way, that's comforting." I leaned on my scythe for support. "It makes the world make a kind of perverse sense."

A ghost dressed like John Travolta in *Grease*, all slicked back hair and leather, pulled out a switchblade and advanced on me. "Kill you, kill you, kill you."

"Back off, John, I loved you in *Pulp Fiction* but I am *not* in the mood.

I considered using the scythe on him but I could already see several dozen other ghosts advancing towards me. In a few minutes, it would become open season on supervillains. I wasn't about to dump that problem on my henchmen.

So, I decided to improvise.

Sticking my fingers in my mouth, I blew on them. The whistle was loud and shrill. "Alright, you damn dirty spooks, it's time for your annual evaluation!"

"Oh this, I've got to hear."

"As a duly appointed necromancer and psychopomp of Her Majesty, the One True Death, also known as the Hot Chick Who Looks Like My Wife, it is my duty to reap your souls. You have been derailed from the Circle of Life, which is not just a song from *The Lion King*. It now falls upon me to correct this grave, no pun intended, imbalance. Please note that if you have any objections to this, you can file a complaint at your local divinity's gateway to the underworld. The gateway to hell is under Omegamart. Seriously, I've seen it." I spoke so fast *I* didn't know what I was saying.

Which happens a lot to me.

The ghost dressed like John Travolta paused, along with a large portion of the other spirits. "What?"

"I'm here to help you move on," I said. "Free you from your eternal imprisonment in a painful half-life. You know, all the stuff that makes being a ghost awesome. Heaven is great and if you're a bad person, well hell has its perks too. I hear they've traded in the fire and brimstone thing for nonstop television and sex. They get more recruits that way."

"You're the Grim Reaper's agent?" A female ghost dressed like a hippie asked, having a hole where her heart should be.

"Obey the Merciless Scythe!" I shouted, slamming it down on the flagstones again. That got everyone's attention. Even the ghosts advancing on me were stopped, looking more confused than anything else. "Now, I need a quick summary of what is keeping you tethered to the mortal plane."

"Pardon?" A bald ghost a mustache and horned rimmed glasses asked. He had no visible wounds but was the most problematic to look at, mostly because he was naked. Damn, that was a cruddy way to die.

"Dude, imagine some clothes." I looked away. "Tell me why you're here."

The bald ghost looked down at his naked form and squinted, a pair of suspenders, striped shirt, and suspenders appearing. He looked like an accountant now. "Wow, it worked!"

"Of course it did," I said. "I have the Merciless Scythe. *Anyone* want to answer my question?"

The hippie, thankfully, answered. "We were all sacrifices for the Brotherhood of Infamy's rituals. They invited us here, tortured us, sacrificed us, and bound our spirits to the castle's walls. Professor Weird tried to help us but he was forced to sell the mansion due to lawsuits from the Falcon Corporation."

I squinted at her. "That just begs for further explanation but I'll leave it alone. Okay, I'm your answer. With this scythe, I'm going to send you all on your way."

"You're going to kill us?" the hippie said. "Again?"

I had to wonder what everyone was thinking outside. Did they think I was having trouble with the lock or did they think I'd been eaten by whatever was lying on the other side of the door? It was hard to tell. I had to reassure the horde of spooks that I was on the level, though. You know, before they ate me.

"No," I said. "I'm going to use my scythe to sever your ties to the Earth and allow you to move on."

"*That's not going to work,*" Cloak said. "*In fact, I find this whole thing you're doing despicable.*"

"Any volunteers?" I hefted up the Reaper's Scythe.

None of the ghosts volunteered immediately, most looking at me like I was a crazy person. I can't imagine why.

Finally, the one who looked like John Travolta threw aside his switchblade. "Do me first."

"Okay, close your eyes and think 'ascension.' It's as easy as dying. You know, unless you had a horrible and violent death. In which case, it's quite a bit easier."

The ghost closed his eyes and I swung the scythe beside him, striking the ground. The ghost opened his eyes and stared down at his body as he faded away. "It's working!"

"Oh yeah!" I said, watching him disappear. "Who ya gonna call!"

"*I have no words,*" Cloak said. "*At all.*"

"Dumbo's magic feather," I thought at Cloak. "If these guys think I can make them ascend, I can."

"*That's... brilliant,*" Cloak replied, seemingly unable to believe it. "*I'm disturbed you came up with it.*"

"Who's next?" I called out.

Dozens of ghostly hands shot up and I went to work, sending one spirit after another to the Great Beyond.

About six or seven ghosts in, a head popped in through the back of the door. It was Amanda Douglas, my unknowing sidekick. "Gary, are you okay?"

"Sorry, ran into a little spook trouble. I should have it dealt with in about five minutes."

"Uh, okay," Amanda said, surprised at the scene before her.

Amanda's head turned to a ghost in a nightgown, a long trail of blood flowing down her front. She stopped cold, her gaze focused with a haunting intensity I couldn't put into words.

"Mom?" Amanda said. "They killed you too?"

Her father had murdered her mother.

Oh God.

Chapter Twenty-One

Where I Therapist for a Bunch of Ghosts

I looked between the two. "Oh crap. This is going to be one of those awkward family moments, isn't it?"

Amanda shot me a look which could have melted steel. You'd think a twenty-something girl who was five-foot-two at best would be less intimidating. It didn't help the ghost she identified as her mother gave me the *exact same look*.

"Sorry," I said, raising my palms as I let my scythe rest on my shoulder. "Really."

"It's... alright." Amanda stepped through the front door. Her insubstantial frame moved with a dancer's grace.

"It is? My, you're forgiving."

"Mister Karkofsky, could you leave us alone for a minute?" Amanda's mother asked, giving me a sidelong glance.

"Alright." I couldn't begin to imagine what Amanda was going through. It was bad enough losing your family. To discover your mother had been sacrificed on an altar somewhere to the Brotherhood of Infamy's evil god? Possibly by your father?

It was unforgivable and he was bound to her cloak. That would make for some rather dreadful conversations.

"Sure." I gestured to a spot across the ghost-filled front hall. "I'll be over there, harvesting souls."

"Thank you," Amanda said, showing a remarkable maturity for her age. "You're a good man, Gary Karkofsky."

"No, I'm not," I corrected, looking at my costume. "Right, Cloak?"

"*I've looked into his soul. He's at least sixty-two percent evil.*"

"You're quipping to someone who can't hear you."

"*I know. I think being linked with you has finally driven me insane,*" Cloak grumbled. "*Do you think Ms. Douglas will be alright?*"

"Not at all," I said, turning to the ghosts and walking to the other side of the room. "*Finding out your family has been murdered is pretty damning. I should know.*"

"So do I."

Turning to the rest of the ghosts, I noticed they were all looking at me with expecting gazes. I guess when all of them were waiting for rescue from a permanent state of hellish limbo, it was important to keep your attention focused on them.

"You might want to help them move on. You know, if your plan works beyond the testing stage."

Clearing my throat, I addressed the assembled spooks. "Okay, I want everyone to form two single-file lines. There's to be no shoving, no punching, no complaining, and if you're a kid don't worry I'm going to kick the ass of whoever did this to you."

That brought a smile or two from some of the ghosts around me. Once the ghosts formed into lines, I started swinging around my scythe to send them on their way. I didn't know what I'd do if it ever stopped working but, at least for the first six or seven, it seemed to be continuing on like before.

Swinging a scythe was a lot harder than it looked, however, and I was exhausted by the time I'd claimed my twelfth soul. Even singing, "Don't Fear the Reaper" didn't make the experience any less tiresome.

"I have a new found respect for field hands in the Middle Ages," I said, huffing and puffing.

"Perhaps you should take a breather," Cloak said. *"After the world is saved, provided you don't bungle it, I also suggest you exercise more."*

"Yeah, yeah," I said. "You and my mother." Making a time-out gesture, I started walking past the ghosts in line toward the front door. "Five minute break time, people. Better let in everyone before they think I've been eaten alive by ghouls."

"Ghouls don't eat live meat," Cloak said. *"They first have to kill you."*

"What an interesting fact." I was surprised to realize there were over eighteen locks built into the side of the door. There was also a wooden board barricading the entrance. I hadn't noticed any of this earlier, which told me I was probably the single most unobservant human alive.

"I would agree with that. What with you taking a break from trying to save the world to deal with a bunch of restless spirits."

"Yeah," I said, wrinkling my nose. "I'm sorry. It's too easy to get distracted by dead children and all. I'll try and avoid it in the future."

"Was that sarcasm?"

"You better hope it was." I started turning the locks one by one. "How could you found a group like this? They've killed kids, kids. Plus, the whole end of the world thing. You were a lot cooler before I learned about this whole idiotic cult connection you have."

"*Founding the Brotherhood of Infamy made sense at the time,*" Cloak said. "*World War 2, the Depression, and the rise of communism—*"

"That's crap and you know it," I said, finding a combination lock. Freezing it off, I moved on. "Tell me about the real reason."

"*You know the reason,*" Cloak said, its voice losing its usual echoing quality. "*Loss.*"

It was common knowledge Lancel Warren had lost his family in a gangland shooting. The event had inspired his brother to become the city's Santa Claus for close to a century due to the tragedy. I knew you didn't turn to selflessness and compassion after events like that. There was a period of anger and hatred as a result, a questioning of 'why me?' For some, namely myself, it never ended.

"Yeah, but tell me anyway," I replied, reaching the halfway mark with the locks. "I need something to pass the time and Amanda looks preoccupied."

I stuck my thumb over my shoulder towards Amanda and her mother. They were talking to the left of the hall, engrossed in a conversation I couldn't hear. A part of me envied her, the opportunity to talk with lost loved ones was one I'd come to appreciate and wish I could do again and again.

I think we all would like that.

"*Alright,*" Cloak, no Lancel Warren, said. "*I'll tell you.*"

"Thank you," I said. "I mean that."

I needed to know what was motivating these psychos. If I did, I had a chance of getting into their head. With that knowledge, I might be able to manipulate them into doing something stupid so I could kill them easier.

Being an evil mastermind was easier than it looked.

"*Everything lost its meaning after my wife and child died. I lost my faith in God, the goodness of man, and myself. I sought some way to contact my wife and child beyond the grave. I ended up finding something more,*" Lancel Warren whispered, his voice quivering a bit. "*From there, it seemed logical to try and recreate the world into something better.*"

"Yeah, replace logical with batshit insane," I finished unlocking the door. "I can't say I blame you, though. If Mandy died, I'd want to burn the world to the ground too."

"*We're not having a bonding moment are we?*" Lancel Warren asked, sounding upset.

"No, we're not," I snapped.

"*As you wish,*" Cloak said. "*Eventually, I realized how insane the cult's plans were after I met my brother's children. He talked me out of my madness and we worked together for years thereafter. I vowed I would prevent the Reaper's Cloaks from every being misused. It's the reason why I support your endeavors, even if they are insane.*"

"We're going to fix this, Lance," I said, finishing unlocking the door.

Opening it up, I saw my group standing outside looking more than a little annoyed. Diabloman was standing straight up, breathing audibly as he flexed and un-flexed his fingers. Mandy, on the other hand, looked forward as if she'd been waiting for me to open the door. Cindy was trying to chat up Angel Eyes and he was looking off into the distance, obviously bored out of his mind.

"—I also play racquetball," Cindy chattered on, smiling. "So, Angel Eyes, do you believe in the whole dating thing or are you into casual sex?"

"Oh thank the gods," Angel Eyes said, seeing me open the door.

"Gary, what the hell were you doing in there?" Mandy asked, staring at me. "The city is being massacred out there."

I frowned and leaned in on my scythe. "A hundred or so ghosts need their souls sent onward. It's tiring work. Oh and Amanda found her dead mother's ghost. I'm guessing they have some issues to work out."

"Gary!" Amanda shouted from behind me.

"You never said it was a secret!" I shouted back, not bothering to turn back to look at her. "I haven't seen hide nor hair of Dick Gleeson, so he's either deeper in the house or he fled when we defeated his buddy's robot. I'm going to be a bit longer so I suggest we split up and go after *The Book of Midnight* separately."

Cindy, stared at me in horror. "Split up? Gary, are you crazy? That's against all horror movie logic! I'm an attractive single woman who has lots of sex, I'm bound to die!"

"This isn't a horror movie." Then I looked over to the horde of ghosts behind me and my surroundings. Looking over at a nearby grandfather clock, I noticed we only had about forty minutes left until midnight. "We're running out of time."

Diabloman replied, looking inside the house. "Can your spirit friends wait until we are done saving the city before you send them on their way?"

"I think they've waited long enough," I said, thinking of all the childish faces eying me. "Besides, they might know something."

They weren't happy but I was in charge.

For the time being at least.

"Do you need any help with the scything?" Mandy asked, crossing her arms. "It's best if we take care of that first."

"Can you see ghosts now too?"

"No, but I figure that you look ready to pass out." Mandy pulled the Reaper's Scythe from me. I tried to hold onto it but she got it away from me rather easily. "I figure that between you and Amanda, I can do some of the heavy lifting for you. Just tap where I need to hit and I'll do it."

I took my scythe back, albeit with some difficulty. "I'll handle it. Could you please watch out for anything which looks like a Ring-wraith, though? I wouldn't put it past Dick to attack me while I'm depleting the spectral population of this place."

"Ahem," Mandy coughed, looked down at my outfit then at Amanda's own. "Anything that *doesn't* look like you two?"

"Point taken," I said, feeling embarrassed. "Anyone *else* who looks like a Death Eater, the Grim Reaper, or Sith Lord."

"Understood," Mandy said.

"I'm uncomfortable with the prospect of a woman being our primary protector," Angel Eyes said. "It was appropriate when we were fighting amazons but now we'll be fighting male opponents."

"You can have him, Cindy," Mandy said, rolling her eyes. "I don't even want him mooning over me anymore."

Cindy wrinkled her nose in distaste before turning away from Angel Eyes. "Nah, it's okay. I'm sure there's someone out there with stunning good looks, a godlike body, and an aura of power. Wait, what was I saying?"

"I feel I am being mocked," Angel Eyes observed.

"You're a real Aristotle, aren't you?"

"I prefer Plato, myself," Angel Eyes said, wrinkling his nose. "Fine, I'll go along with this perversion of the natural order. For now."

God, I hated Angel Eyes. I hated every part of him, including his big beautiful blue eyes and flowing blond hair.

Ignore that.

"Alright, we're going to have rush this along my spooky friends. So, everyone close your eyes and I'm going to send you off on your merry way at once." I shouted, turning around to face the ghosts. Jabbing my scythe down in the ground, another thunderclap resounded. Combined with the organ music, I felt like I'd stepped into an old Hammer Horror movie.

"That's ridiculous," a ghost missing half his head shouted. "We demand to be treated separately!"

A chorus of shouts came up from the many spirits behind me, voicing their agreements.

"Okay, now you're starting to piss me off. If you guys don't close your eyes and go along with this, I'm going to soul-kill you with my scythe. It can do that, I've read the manual. If you're lucky, it'll just *send you to hell*," I said, accenting the last words. "Do I make myself clear?"

"Even the children?" the ghost missing half his face said, sounding afraid.

"No, contrary to what Pat Benetar said, hell is not for children. They get into heaven regardless. On the count of three, people."

"Is Gary really talking to a hundred ghosts?" Cindy whispered behind me.

"Yes," Diabloman said. "I was trained to sense their presence by the monks of my order. This house is a great mystical convergence, much like the rest of the city, but more so."

"God, I hate this town," Cindy grumbled, following me. "First thing I do after I make my first billion is buy one of the Hawaiian Islands. One of the ones without an active volcano."

"You may want to go for a smaller island," Diabloman said. "A billion doesn't go as far as it used to."

"You're right," Cindy said, nodding. "I'll have Gary ransom it from the government. I figure by then he'll control at least the lower forty-eight states."

"I'm debating getting Canada first."

"Why Canada?"

"Why *not* Canada?"

Amanda coughed and pointed to the horde of spirits around us. "The ghosts, Gary."

"Oh, right."

Reluctantly, but uniformly, the ghosts all closed their eyes. The only exception was Amanda's mother, who was still talking with her. It was somewhat gratifying to see I'd managed to shake them all out of their post-death lethargy through the simple power of my presence. Well that and the huge otherworldly artifact I was wielding.

"Shouldn't we be saying something to these souls as we send them off?"

"If you see Marilyn Monroe, tell her I'm sorry the press hounded her so much in life," I said, addressing the ghosts. "Oh and tell my third grade teacher to rot in hell. I'm sure she's there."

"I don't even know why I bother."

"Neither do I," I said. "One... two... three!"

Slamming down my scythe into the ground, the entire mansion shook. One by one, the ghosts around me disappeared, until whole groups started to fade away. A few of them screamed as if being consumed by fire while the majority reacted as if they were waking up from a long nap. That told me more about the afterlife than my visiting it had.

Only a single ghost remained, a man in a tuxedo with a pencil thin mustache and slicked black hair. "Ha! I knew you were a fraud!"

Mandy put her hand on my shoulder. "Are they gone?"

"Most of them," I said. "There's always one jackass in a crowd."

"What are you going to do about him?" Mandy asked.

"Not a damn thing," I said. "He can have the cold satisfaction of sticking around this joint. Besides, the house is infinitely cooler being at least a little haunted."

"Now all we need is to find *The Book of Midnight*, cast whatever who-zit spell is needed to undo the hex, and save the world. Oh and kill Dick Gleeson." Mandy put her hands on her hips.

"You got it," I said. "Let's hope we can find it in this place."

Amanda left her mother's side and walked over. Her face was grim, lacking all of the joy I'd had at meeting my brother. "My mother will show us the way to my father's resting place for *The Book of Midnight*."

"That's good news," I said, having a distinctly feeling about this. "Right?"

Amanda looked up. "Not quite. Apparently, Dick Gleeson got through the wards about an hour ago. He's trying to destroy *The Book of Midnight* so we can't use it."

Chapter Twenty-Two

Finding the Douglas Family Vault

"Sweet Mother of Solomon!" I spit, clenching my fists. "He has the book already?"

"Probably," Amanda said, looking pedantic. "I'm sorry."

We'd come all this way to try and get *The Book of Midnight*, only to find the damn thing might have been snatched up while I was reaping souls.

"I'd say the person responsible was an idiot," I said, "but since that's me. Someone else must be. Angel Eyes, I blame you."

"What?" Angel Eyes looked up.

"*George Orwell wrote a book on the way you think,*" Cloak said. "*He called it doublethink.*"

"Nah," I said. "I would have been in the Inner Party. Julia and I would have been chilling while the world burned."

"*Wait, you got that reference?*"

"I went to college, Lancel. I just didn't get a degree in anything useful," I replied, trying to think of what to do next. "We are screwed every which way from Saturday."

"And not in a good way," Cindy piped in. "So, Dick and the Brotherhood have *The Book of Midnight*. What's the worst that could happen?"

"Well, the end of the world is already happening." Mandy was holding her pistols downwards so they weren't aimed at anyone. Good gun safety. "So I can only assume it's going to happen faster if he brings the book to his boss, this Nightmaster character."

"Which would be bad," I added.

"I think we got that," Mandy said.

"Just making sure," I said, holding my palms up. "We should get moving as soon as we've got our plan for dealing with him laid out."

"Are we sure the Society of Superheroes can't take care of this?" Cindy said. "Hey, Amanda, did you make any super-secret teen hero friends during your training?"

"No." Amanda said, "And teen heroes? I'm five years younger than you and Gary."

Cindy blinked. "Really?"

"Oh yes." I said, "The sex tape proved it."

Amanda looked like she was going to throw a shuriken at my head then just blushed, which was surprising.

"I think we can safely assume we're alone here," Mandy said, holding tightly to her pistols as expecting monsters to show up at any point. "Gary, Amanda, I need you to ask your cloaks what sort of powers the others have."

"Ten-four, Sexy Boss Lady," I said. "Cloak?"

"*The other cloaks*—"Cloak started to say before he was interrupted.

"Dick Gleeson has the Cloak of the Dragon," Amanda interrupted, looking between us.

"It allows him to become a dragon. The literal fire-breathing kind."

Try as she might, she couldn't look intimidating in her outfit. It looked adorable on her.

"Well, that's a bit on the nose isn't it?" I asked, chewing on my one of my thumbnails. "Anyone have any experience in dragon slaying?"

"Does *Lances and Labyrinths Online* count?" Cindy inquired.

"No," I said.

"Then no," Cindy said. "Which is a pity because I had a 40th level Chaos-aligned Orcish thief who would have been perfect for this situation."

I lost a lot of respect for Cindy in that moment. After all, I had a 60th level Chaos Elf Warlock. Obviously, she didn't have sufficient devotion to playing our mutual computer obsession. I really needed to buy the latest expansion pack. Supposedly, they were bringing back the King Below by promoting one of his Wraith Knights.

"The others?" Mandy asked.

Cloak said, "*The Nightmaster's Cloak grants all the abilities of the other cloaks combined as well as vast knowledge of sorcery. The price of said cloak is the subject goes steadily insane, however. The other cloaks are eso-morphic, transferring abilities as based on the personality of the wielder but one can expect they're at least going to grant the ability to become insubstantial as well as powers related to the elements.*"

Great. I got stuck with one of the crappy cloaks.

Cloak, somehow, glared at me.

I could feel it.

Explaining, Mandy and Amanda listened before discussing their battle plans. Mandy proved to be a good leader, taking in everyone's opinions and formulating a strategy based on consensus.

Mandy pointed to each of us as she spoke. "Angel Eyes, if you have any protective magic or things you can cast on us, I need you to do that now. Diabloman, protect Gary, it's your job and I'll be very cross with you if my husband dies. Cindy, you quip and be useless."

"Righto," Cindy said, saluting her. "I'll even throw in a cowardly back-stab before running away. I'm good at those."

"Good to know," Mandy replied, not bothering to look at her. "We're going to hunt down Dick Gleeson and take the book back from him. If he turns into a dragon, we'll hit the wings first and then the underbelly. It worked in Tolkien and it worked in folklore. Any objections?"

Cindy raised her hand, standing on her tippy-toes. "Ooo! I've got one."

"Except from Cindy," Mandy said, looking between the rest of us. In that moment, she looked like the world's sexiest drill sergeant.

"I do." Angel Eyes coughed into his fist before raising a hand. "I can work my magic on you, Fair Lady, but there will be a risk. Aphrodite can bolster your strength, give you limited invulnerability, and perhaps even enhance your firearms but she is a jealous deity. The fact I am asking her to help a woman I care for will likely result in something ill befalling you."

"You can tell that Hellenistic ocean-born bitch nobody threatens my wife," I snapped, fully willing to scale Mount Olympus and kill her if it came to that.

Another thunderclap was heard outside, this time accompanied by a lightning bolt hitting a tree visible through one of the hallway windows.

"Gary, please don't threaten my goddess, I'm in enough trouble as it is." Angel Eyes said, wincing, before glancing back over at Mandy. "Are you still willing to take that risk knowing the potential price you might be asked to play?"

"Yes," Mandy said without hesitation. "I am."

A pained expression passed across Angel Eyes' visage. For a brief second, I actually thought he cared about my wife. Then I remembered he'd only known her for the space of a few days and rolled my eyes. What a drama queen.

"Very well. I will work the magic," Angel Eyes said, stepping behind Mandy and muttering something in Ancient Greek. I could feel a surge of power in the air that wasn't easy to put into words, like someone was rapidly changing the room's temperature up and down.

"Does anyone else have any objections?" Mandy asked, completely ignoring Angel Eyes' spell-work.

None of us raised our hand. We didn't have any further time to dawdle. Mostly because I'd taken compassion on a bunch of spooks. I wasn't going to make that mistake again. No good deed goes unpunished, it's an immutable law of the universe.

"Okay, then, good. Time to move on," Mandy said, waiting only a few seconds for Angel Eyes to finish chanting before starting to walk off. Amanda's Mother, probably realizing she was supposed to be leading us, floated over in front of her and started heading down one of the mansion halls. Amanda quickly followed her.

"Mandy, such a Type-A personality, she could even order around the dead," I muttered, hoisting up my scythe over one shoulder.

"I still don't know why we're risking our lives for the brain-dead masses." Cindy sounded better. "They'd hang the lot of us if they could. I mean, you leave a pair of scissors in someone's torso during surgery and you're out for life. What sort of world is that?"

Well, that explained what had happened to her medical career.

"Try and think of it less as us saving the world than us saving ourselves, which coincidentally saves everybody else." I started walking after my wife, Diabloman and Angel Eyes following me.

"Well *that* makes sense," Cindy said, running to catch up.

The interior of Amanda's house got no less creepy the further we got in. It was pretty much the ultimate embodiment of spooky interior design. There were cobwebs, dusty bookshelves, oil paintings with moving eyes, and even the occasional suit of armor.

Amanda herself was pretty silent, mostly just telling where her mother was moving so we knew where to go. It would be easy to get lost in her home and I wasn't about to waste any more time doubling back to find our way.

I wanted to ask what she and her mother talked about, none of my business or not. Amanda was too old to be called a little girl, especially after blowing the head off that robot, but I still felt pretty protective of her. Maybe it was because she did remind me of Mandy as a younger woman, the kind of person I'd imagine our daughter being like.

Daughter.

Yeah, that was a conversation I was looking forward to. We'd agreed not to have children. Yet, Death had shown me one. A daughter who was a little piece of Mandy and me, carrying our legacy into the future. You might think it's stupid I was thinking of my relationship with my wife when the world was ending but it was the primary thing on my mind. I didn't want to reopen a painful wound and the last time we'd discussed children, it had ended badly.

Really badly.

My staying in a hotel for a week, badly.

I wanted a child and Mandy didn't.

It was that simple.

"You have hidden depths, Gary."

"Forget everything you heard or I swear I will destroy you, even if it kills me." I mean it too. I did not like Cloak listening in on what I'd been thinking. There were few things I considered private and my relationship with Mandy was one.

"As you wish."

I considered grabbing the edges of my costume to try and strangle them. Instead, I just shook with rage.

"Gary, are you okay?" Amanda asked, looking over her shoulder at me.

"No, but don't worry about me. I'm tough like the noble turtle. The turtle is the most underappreciated of the animal kingdom, you know. They can become mutants and ninjas but do you see them topping anyone's favorite animal's list? No."

Amanda looked bewildered. Kids today, no education.

"You realize he distracts people from questioning his actions by acting like a lunatic, right?" Angel Eyes said, behind me. "It's obvious."

"Who's acting?"

The ghost of Amanda's mother paused in mid-air, floating in front of a pair of wooden double doors. The doors had a bloody giant inverted pentagram drawn on them. Stretching forth her arm, she gestured to the doors and gave a silent nod.

"Yeah, in no way could we have found this on our own," I said, looking between them. "*Clearly*, Amanda, your father knew how to cover up where his valuables were hidden."

"Gary, I like you like a weird sociopathic big-brother but please don't ever mention my dad again." Amanda looked between me and the pentagram. "He's dead to me. Deader than he already was."

I wondered how that was going to work with his soul bonded to the cloak she was wearing. Given my relationship to Lancel, probably not well.

"Alright," I said, deciding not to push it. "Your call."

Amanda sighed, looking to the ghostly apparition of her mother. "My mother, says that the door is impenetrable to any physical force and all magic. Not even the Brotherhood of Infamy can get through it. Somehow, Dick Gleeson figured a way to get past the barrier after about month of trying various spells and explosives. He's been in there for about an hour. Mom doesn't know how he did it."

Diabloman ran his hands over the door, a glowing aura wavering wherever he touched it. "Powerful magic. I can feel it from here."

Angel Eyes rubbed his chin, taking in the strange phenomenon. "As long as the pentagram is unbroken, I don't think we're going to be able to penetrate it. Given a few hours, I might be able to break it."

"We don't have a few hours," Mandy said, hoisting up her guns as if in battle posture. "Especially if there's a window in there he can get out of."

I hefted back my scythe. "Okay, guys, let the master go to work here. Let's see how this magic door

"Wait," Mandy interjected. "Is it possible he found the room key?"

I paused in mid-swing, holding the scythe over my head with both hands ready to slash into the door. "Would that work?"

Amanda reached over and turned the door knob, there was a resounding click as the pentagram broke. "Huh."

"Occam's razor," Mandy said, gesturing with her automatics. "Let's go pay Mister Gleeson a visit."

"Allow me," I said, kicking open the door. "I love making a dramatic entrance."

"No wait!" Mandy shouted, trying to stop me. "Don't!"

Unfortunately, it was too late. Kicking open the door, I got a glimpse of the room inside. It was a ballroom-sized chamber filled with more antiquities than I could count. There were statues, paintings, piles of jewelry, books, swords, armor, and chests overflowing with gold. The looked like cross between a warehouse for the Louvre's castoffs and a pirate den. In the center of it, though, was the single most ugly thing I'd ever seen in my life.

The creature almost completely filled the room, dwarfing the objects around it like Godzilla dwarfed the little cardboard buildings he regularly knocked down in his original 70s monster movies. To call the creature a dragon would probably be *technically* accurate, but the thing utterly lacked the elegant majesty found in fantasy art and miniatures worldwide.

Instead, it was a disgusting legless monster which seemed half-shadow and half-molted serpent. It had only two appendages, tiny arms sticking out in front of it like a Tyrannosaurus Rex with leathery bat-like wing sticking out from its back.

The creature's face was the most horrible part of it. It was a terrible, almost-human-like visage, with squashed nostrils and giant yellow eyes that seemed to bore into your soul. It was completely black, blacker than my cloak, and seemed made of a substance not of this Earth.

The creature let forth a roar that was so loud, I stopped being able to hear it after a few seconds, temporarily deafened. The beast pulled back its neck and breathed forth a column of flame so brilliant that it was like pure white washing over me and my friends.

A word to the wise: dramatic entrances are stupid.

Chapter Twenty-Three

Where We do Battle with a Dragon No I'm not Kidding

Killed by a dragon.

I confess that wouldn't be in the top ten ways I'd expected to die. Maybe not even top forty. Those included being shot by the cops, eaten by a shoggoth, killed by ghosts, and chopped to pieces by a boat propeller. Strangely, my first worry was for Mandy and the others.

I would gladly die for my wife over and over again, but I was surprised at my concern for my henchmen. Cindy, Amanda, Diabloman, and even Angel Eyes occupied my final thoughts. The last one honestly disturbed me. I mean, I didn't even like the guy.

Surprisingly, though, all of us lived.

A glowing shield in the shape of a discus appeared in front of us at the last second. The glowing circle crackled like a bug-zapper, diverting the flame at the last second. The heat was still intense, raising the temperature to painful levels, like having a sunburn over my entire body, but it was better than the alternative. Even looking at it was painful, like staring into a floodlight.

"*Aegis*! *Aegis*! *Aegis*!" Angel Eyes shouted, repeating the word over and over again. Looking over my shoulder, I saw he'd crossed his pinkies and was gesturing at the flame with them. His eyes were closed and his face was locked into a mask of intense concentration.

"Okay, I admit that was impressive," I said, not taking my eyes off the fireball being blown in our faces but speaking to Angel Eyes. "I'm going avoid making any more jokes about you for.... at least ten minutes. Maybe twenty if I'm in a good mood."

"Gary!" Mandy shouted.

"Mister Karkofsky!" Amanda added.

"Brad!" Cindy threw in.

"Rocky!" I added. "I know, I know. I'm a horrible person who doesn't understand the gravity of the situation. Don't worry, I've got a plan. Plan X."

"Plan X?" Cindy said.

"Plan X!" I proclaimed, lifting up my hands.

Tapping my scythe, it transformed back into a coin and I put it away. Clapping my hands, I focused on my ice powers. I was more a fire-boy than an ice-man and I'd neglected my cold abilities for the majority of my short career as a supervillain.

It was time to change that.

At first, it was like dropping water droplets on the surface of the sun but I tried harder. Thinking about the Arctic, freeze-rays, penguins, snowmen, ice cream, and all the cold things in the world. Surprisingly, the flame was forced back as a giant cloud of steam was created, spilling over the shield and into the hallway around us.

The dragon, surprised by my actions, ceased its assault. Pulling back, it looked at our group curiously. "What treachery is this?"

"Did he seriously say, *what treachery is this?*" I asked, staring at it.

"Yeah," Cindy said, crossing her arms and nodding. "What a loser. What does he think this is, the *Lord of the Rings?*"

"The fiend is powerful," Angel Eyes said, falling to one knee before me. Never had he looked more regal. "I have never faced such raw intensity in a fiery attack before. I suggest you pull forth every reserve of energy you have to smote this beast."

Cindy immediately changed her tune. "Gary, I think the way they talk adds dignity and posh to our confrontation with the dragon! You should stop talking like you're straight out of high school."

"*Et tu*, Cindy?" I said, raising an eyebrow before asking in mock astonishment, "How could you betray me for a pretty face?"

"He's a *very* pretty face," Cindy pointed out.

"Let's kill Puff here and get the book," Mandy said, lifting up her guns and firing, walking forward as she unleashed a horde of enchanted bullets onto the dragon. The creature reared back, trying to cover its face with its wings.

Bullets, even enchanted bullets, seemed to be little more than pinpricks to Dick Gleeson's dragon form but there were a lot of them being fired at him right now. Mandy moved methodically, targeting his wings first and then his eyes, forcing the dragon to cover its eyes with its tiny hands while retreating.

"When did my wife go insane?" I muttered, rushing after her.

"This is what happens when women enter combat," Angel Eyes said. "It always goes to their heads."

"Gee, and you wonder why you're alone," Cindy said, following me.

"If you'll excuse me, I have to go save her from being killed." I ran after my wife at top speed.

Grabbing Mandy by the arm, I managed to turn us both insubstantial just in time for the dragon's tail not to take our heads clean off. Ironically, the tail hit Amanda who grabbed it and pulled. The titanically strong debutante pulled the dragon down from where it was raising its neck to blow flame again, only to be punched in the face.

"Gary, get the book!" Mandy shouted, pulling away from me.

"Are you going to get yourself killed if I leave you alone?" I called back, horrified by how crazy she was acting. I mean, seriously, assaulting a dragon? By herself? This wasn't like her. My wife was normally one of the most settled individuals in the world. Yet, here she was, acting like she was the Terminatrix.

"Let me worry about that!" Mandy screamed, causing me to back away. Lifting up her guns again, she once more began assaulting the dragon. Angel Eyes' spell apparently gave her infinite ammo since she had shot well over a hundred rounds into him with nary a microsecond between pulling the trigger.

"Fine, I will," I said, realizing talking to her was useless. "Everybody, double time! We've got a dragon to slay, as a team."

Diabloman, grabbed a marble statue of Pallas Athena and hurled it at the dragon. The massive stone thing probably weighed more than my car, but Diabloman somehow managed to throw it like a baseball, smashing it across the dragon's head. Angel Eyes conjured a Spartan spear, helmet, and loincloth which somehow replaced his ruined business suit before charging. As for Cindy? Well, Cindy hid behind a pile of coins, but she was reaching into her picnic basket, so maybe she wasn't going to be completely useless here.

The dragon once more breathed out fire at us, but it was weaker this time. Apparently, he'd spent the majority of his load. Reaching out with my hands, I once more managed to drive it back with a current of ice from my hands. Either I was getting better at using my powers or I was seriously overdoing it, I wasn't sure which.

Still, it prevented the dragon from killing us at once.

"*I believe your wife is lost in the euphoria of being a superheroine.*"

"No kidding," I said, wondering if I was as bad.

"*She's not wrong, though. If you get The Book of Midnight then we can end this disaster here and now. The book has power of its own, enough for you to destroy every zombie in the city at once. Hell, enough power for you to summon and bind the Grim Reaper herself.*"

"Not worth it if she gets herself killed."

"*To be a superhero is to risk your life to help others. To sacrifice yourself, if need be, for the greater good. She is no less in danger than if she held back. Attack is the wisest strategy for beating it.*"

I still didn't like it and suspected that was how she felt when I was out there fighting and almost getting myself killed.

Karma was a cruel mistress.

Surveying the piles of treasure gathered from all parts of the world, I spied a plain black metal book stand off to one side. On top of the book stand was a brown leather volume which looked decayed and wrinkly, as if its leather cover had putrefied over the years. It probably smelled worse than my sock drawer had during my college days.

Underneath the book stand, inscribed on the ground, was a red pentagram similar to the one which bound the door. I wasn't sure but I suspected it was keeping Dick from the book. Dudley impressed me with his foresight. Even if Dick had managed to figure out a common sense solution to getting into his treasure room, there was no guarantee he could find one to this problem.

Running at the circle, I stopped within inches of its edge. Pushing my fingers against the air around it, it felt like I was touching an invisible wall of stone. The surface was entirely smooth but completely solid, preventing me from being able to enter.

"*It's a Circle of Thanatos. It prevents any living being, good or evil, from passing through the barrier. Even touching with a staff or object will utterly obliterate the owner. It's one of the most powerful defenses any necromancer can erect against intrusion.*"

"Any living beings huh?" I asked, thinking on that.

"*Yes, the ancient necromancers of Acheron would send zombies and other creatures of the undead to fetch the book. It is my suggestion we attempt to defuse the ritual by warping the runes one at a time. We must be extra careful less we accidentally detonate one of them, releasing the magic within.*"

I picked up a piece of rock from one of the shattered statues and used it to knock the book off the pedestal, sending it onto the ground nearby. The book slid across the floor enough to move it slightly out of the protective circle. Reaching over, I picked the volume up into my arms. It was heavier than it looked.

"*That shouldn't have worked,*" Cloak said. "*The late Mister Douglas must have altered the spell. Made it so that a common sense solution would work where magic wouldn't. The ancient Atlanteans couldn't have been so stupid as to leave a weakness that a ten-year-old boy could exploit.*"

"When I'm Evil Overlord of the world, I'm going to have ten-year-old children proof all of my plans," I said, proud of my solution. "It would have saved the Emperor's life in *Return of the Jedi* to have those big bottomless pits covered. Hell, how much trouble would Sauron have saved himself if he'd had Mount Doom fenced off?"

"The worst part of that is I can't disagree. Ugh, how far I've fallen."

The Book of Midnight was a hideous black tome made of human skin, a fact that revolted me to no end. The front of the book had a face carved into it, two eye holes and a mouth with nostrils. I tried reaching for the clasp, hoping to see whatever secrets it might contain. Instead, the book proceeded to bite me on the wrist, causing me to drop it on the ground.

"God dammit!" I said, kicking the thing across the floor. "What the hell!?"

"Yip! Yip!" *The Book of Midnight* yelped, opening its pages and bouncing across the floor. It then bounced up, growling at me.

"I should probably have mentioned The Book of Midnight contains a portion of Zul-Barbas's power, manifested as a hell hound."

"Damn," I said, staring at the book yipping at me like a Chihuahua. "I kicked a dog-book... thing. I am the scum of scum."

"Oh you were the scum of scum well before now."

"Thank you," I said, trying to think about how to calm it down. Extending out my hands I tried to say the magic words.

That was when the dragon's tail hit me in the back, sending me flying through the air before I landed in a bunch of clay pots. The pots, probably priceless cultural artifacts of unparalleled historical value, shattered to pieces beneath me.

"Perhaps we should have a conversation about awareness of your surroundings. I suggest you deal with the dragon first then worry about finding a spell to save the world."

"You just said the opposite dammit!" I shouted, climbing up out of the shattered pottery. A shadow passed over me as I looked up to see the form of the dragon falling backwards on top of me. "Meep."

Once more, I turned insubstantial, levitating up through the creature's remains as they collapsed on me. It felt like passing through a big black inky ocean, old and filled with an unnamable evil. One which came from either the fell forces he'd made a bargain with or the fact he was a conservative radio host.

Hovering up, I came through his belly and turned substantial on top of him. It was like standing on a mound of gelatin. To my pleasant surprise, I saw my henchmen had brutalized the dragon within an inch of its life. Dozens of tiny bullet holes were spread across its underbelly, leaking out blackish blood as if it had been stabbed with a needle repeatedly. Its malformed face was missing many of its shark-like teeth and one of its eyes had been knocked out.

The dragon growled at me, lifting its mouth back as if to breathe fire once more. You'd think he'd have learned by now.

"I hate one-trick ponies." I held my palms together as in prayer. I concentrated on my powers and iced over its mouth and nostrils. I drew on every ounce of my power to super-compact the ice.

The creature thrashed and struggled, trying to shatter the miniature glacier I'd created around its face but it was wounded and not fighting at its full strength. The ice cracked after a few seconds but I merely reinforced the icy prison, causing him to thrash more.

The creature batted its wings at me, trying to knock me away with the wind it created but the holes Mandy had punched in it prevented the monster from generating anything more than a light breeze. I took a grim satisfaction when its head fell backwards, smashing against the floor of the ballroom beneath us.

"This is where the victory theme kicks in," I said, doing a little dance on the monster's belly.

Just like with Chief of Police Watkins, a black cloak flew from its dead body. This one was the size of a small house. Despite its massive girth, I grabbed it and set alight with my powers. The shadowy substance burned in the air, vanishing in a puff of flame and shadow. Two Reaper's Cloaks were down, three to go.

"Gary!" Cindy called from behind me.

"What? I'm having a moment here." I threw up my hands in frustration.

"Idiot! Turn around!" Angel Eyes screamed.

All of my jubilation left me when I saw the source of his distress. There, between the rest of the group, was Mandy. She was laid prostrate on the ground, Amanda holding her head as Diabloman checked her pulse.

"Oh shit," I said, running off the belly of the dragon and rushing over to her side.

Mandy looked like she'd been struck in the chest, blood visible from where her ribs had been smashed to pieces. She'd been hit by yet another tail strike from the dragon, easily equivalent to getting struck by a Mack truck. This time, I hadn't been there to turns us both insubstantial. This time, I hadn't been there to protect her.

I'd ignored my wife's safety and let her go off half-cocked into the middle of the beast's mouth. The fact she'd managed to almost single-handedly slay the dragon herself meant nothing to me. The only thing I cared about right now was making sure she lived.

"Can you do something?" I questioned Angel Eyes, looking at my wife. Mandy wasn't breathing and was still as a corpse.

"No," Angel Eyes whispered. "I can't."

"I'm sorry," Diabloman said, letting go of her wrist. "She's dead."

Chapter Twenty-Four

Where Things Get Necro-mantic (Get it?)

In an instant, my world ended. There's no other way to describe the pain that losing your spouse gives. People suffer losses like this in movies all the time, trivializing the destruction of one half of a person's soul. I don't think you ever fully recover from something like that. I don't believe any of those lovey-dovey romantic comedies where beautiful widowers and widows end up falling for some plucky romantic hero or heroine.

"Gary...." Cindy reached up to touch me on the shoulder. "Mandy died protecting me from Mister Gleeson's tail. She shoved me out of the way as it was coming down on me. She was a hero." It was spoken without irony or subtext. I didn't think Cindy had it in her.

"I have not met a woman like her since Medea. I am sorry to have dishonored your marriage with my actions. Mandy was a worthy woman. She will never be equaled in this generation." Angel Eyes placed his right hand on my shoulder.

"I'm sorry." Cindy had the audacity to speak. "I liked her a lot. She was a great musician in college. We even got to talk a bit while you were gone. It turns out we're both huge fans of Sigourney Weaver. I'm sorry she died."

Diabloman started to say something as well, "Gary—"

"*Perhaps I can offer my own condolences—*" Cloak started to speak.

"Guys," I lifted my hand, wanting to kill them all. "Shut up."

I made a zip-it gesture with my fingertips. "Seriously, everybody, be quiet. I need to think about how I'm going to bring her back from the dead."

"Excuse me?" Amanda asked, the first one to speak. Her mouth hanging open fully as she cocked her head to one side. "Could...could you repeat that?"

Diabloman turned to me, nodding his head. "He said he is going to bring her back from the dead. Perfectly rational."

"In the span of one night I've fought a demigod, zombie supervillains, a Nazi robot, cyborg dinos, Amazons, and a dragon. You're not going to tell me that it's exceptionally difficult to resurrect someone from the dead." I was surprisingly calm about this. I would bring Mandy back from the dead, no harm, no foul. It was the only thought keeping me sane.

Angel Eyes coughed into his fist, his eyes not meeting mine. "Gary, resurrection is not something to be done lightly. I point out that my friend Orpheus tried it and it didn't work out so well."

"Cool idea," Cindy said, pulling out some chewing gum from her Red Riding Hood basket. "Gum?"

"Thank you." Taking the gum and stuffing it in my mouth, I started chewing before blowing a bubble and letting it pop. "Okay, where is *The Book of Midnight*? Hopefully, there's something to get me started on reanimating my wife."

"The words reanimating and wife shouldn't be used in the same sentence." Amanda got up, wringing his hands as she looked around the room, unable to meet my eyes. "Has television taught you nothing? How many times has this exact same plot played out with the mad scientist or wizard ending up dying bemoaning tampering with fate? It never turns out right! They always come back wrong or undead or evil!"

"Stop that," I said, stepping away from both her and Angel Eyes. "I'm set on this. If the Society of Superheroes can keep their loved ones from dying no matter what supervillains do to them then I can bring mine back from the dead. There's nothing you can do to dissuade me."

Angel Eyes approached me, extending out his hands. "Gary—"

"Don't call me that. You call me Merciless or Lord or Boss or Master. Let's get one thing straight, you're all great."

"Gary—" Amanda tried to speak.

"Don't interrupt," I snapped, my voice sharp as my eyes flared. Clenching my fists, I tried to keep my voice level. "Any of you."

My head felt like it was going to explode. My hands shook as I looked away from my wife's corpse. I couldn't look at it, it was too painful. A sign that reality was threatening to destroy the fantasy I'd built up around me. It was a reality I couldn't live with. I needed to retreat fully into the world I'd created where I was a supervillain who could do anything, make any dream possible. They needed to understand that. If they didn't, I had nothing to live for. Falconcrest City could burn. Hell, the entire world could die for all I cared.

They had to know what I was.

"Amanda, you're the kind of girl that makes me wish I had a younger brother to hook you up with. Diabloman, you're like the evil Mexican Wrestler Uncle I never had. Cindy, you're the best henchwench a guy could have. Angel Eyes, I still pretty much hate you but you have your uses. However, if I need to kill you all to resurrect Mandy, I'll do it in a heartbeat"

I meant it too. I might never forgive myself for killing an innocent like Amanda. I sure as hell wouldn't forgive myself for killing my old school girlfriend. I wouldn't even forgive myself for killing an old super criminal like Diabloman. Yet, everyone one of them was expendable compared to my wife. Mandy might leave me for it but she'd be alive.

I could live with that.

"Do you understand that?" I wanted to hurt someone. Anyone. Even my so-called friends. "Do you *understand*?"

"Yes, we understand." Amanda stared at me. "We all do."

Angel Eyes, Diabloman, Cindy, and Amanda all stood together. They, thankfully, blocked my view of Mandy's corpse. Cindy looked the most hurt out of the group, unable to look at me. I think that was because Mandy and she had somehow managed to build a friendship in the past month. Even more so than the fact I was threatening to kill her, she was hurt by the loss of her friend. I would pay her back for that sympathy, I didn't know how, but I privately vowed I would.

Right after I raised Mandy from the dead, whatever the cost.

"*I once believed as you did,*" Cloak said. "*There is a spell that can raise her from the dead in The Book of Midnight.*"

"Spill," I said, searching the room for *The Book of Midnight*. The cursed book had bounced away, hiding itself under one of the piles of treasure surrounding us. "Now."

"*It will cost you your immortal soul.*"

"Bargain." Not that I hadn't sold it twice already to Death.

"*On page sixty-six of The Book of Midnight, it is possible to summon a representation of Zul-Barbas. He will grant the wish of whoever summons him and then proceed to consume their soul.*"

"Sounds good." I checked for *The Book of Midnight* under a table covered with Ming dynasty vases. "Why didn't you sacrifice yours?"

It was a horrible question but given everything Lancel had done in the name of his dead wife and child, I felt it was a valid one.

"*I couldn't decide whether to bring back my wife or my son. I have only one soul to give, after all. So, I ended up wanting to destroy the entire world.*"

"Logical," I said, nodding my head. Conjuring a little icy bone, I started shaking it. "Here boy. Come on. Come get your bone."

Truth be told, I sympathized with Lancel's plight. I was going to miss sympathizing with people. When I lost my soul that was probably the first thing that would go.

"You do realize that it's a book and a hellhound, not a dog, Hell, even if it was a dog, your bone is made of ice."

"Lancel, remember the context of what's just happened," I said, shaking the icy bone in midair. It was a desperate, ridiculous action meant to deal with a situation I had no context for. "If I'm coming up with some seriously stupid plans right now, there's a reason for it."

"Sorry."

"Good." I checked under some antique Victorian cabinets. "Otherwise, my soulless form is going to very pissed at you."

"Yeah," Lancel's voice cracked, lacking its earlier echo. "I suppose so."

"So, will you be bonded with soulless Gary or will you move on to some other schmuck? I don't know much about what happens to a man with no soul." I wasn't even sure I'd even exist afterward. Zul-Barbas might instead drag me down into whatever hell it hailed from.

"I think my soul will be sacrificed with yours."

"Oh," I said, stopping my wagging of the icy bone. "I didn't know that."

"We're linked, now and forever." There was a wistfulness to it, utterly lacking the fear such a statement should engender.

"I can find another way." I wasn't ready to sacrifice Lancel. I'd kill for Mandy but I wasn't sure I could sentence the old man to eternal damnation. I would, perhaps, do it. But I would look for a way around it first.

Maybe for an hour.

"It's alright, Gary. I've been trying to make up for what I did for the better part of a century. Maybe this is Death's way of illustrating to me that I could never escape the consequences of my action. Your wife is a hero. Perhaps by saving her, we'll find our redemption."

"In our damnation."

"Err... well, yes."

That's moronic. Also, put back up the creepy echo. If you continue talking like a human being, I'll confuse you for one." I looked back at my group. They were all standing together, watching me as if I was a creature from another world. I couldn't blame them, I'd just threatened to kill them after all.

"That would be dreadful."

A moment later, *The Book of Midnight* peeked itself around a statue of Hades. The book moving into pouncing position with the two sides of its binding making it stand up. It yipped at me like a dog, acting adorable despite being made from human skin and black magic.

"Seriously. You were incredibly messed up when you made this thing."

"*Blame Abdul Alhazred's brother Abu for this, not me,*" Cloak said, sounding apologetic. "*I found this particular copy of it in an old antique store. It was more than a year later I started wondering why the store owner was selling accursed books of magic written on human skin.*"

"Funny. You'd think that would be the first thing you questioned."

"*Actually, I was more curious about why it was written in English and how human skin kept legible writing for the better part of a thousand years. Have you ever tried writing on human skin? It's not easy.*"

"I can't say I've had the pleasure." I struggled to stay calm. It was good to joke around; it helped distract me from the horror of my situation.

Waving my ice bone at *The Book of Midnight*, I tossed the frosty treat on the ground. The book bounced up at it, scooping it up in its covers and crunching it to pieces. This allowed me to grab the book, prying it open as it struggled to get free.

"Oh quiet!" I said, holding the book open with my elbows as I flipped through the pages. "This is for your own good."

Finally, I reached page sixty-six. There, I saw a short poem-like spell across from an illustration of a witch summoning an image of a gigantic multi-tentacled dragon-god with wings. It reminded me of some of the more lurid images I'd found on the cover of fantasy-horror novels.

"Is that Zul-Barbas?" I asked, grimacing at the image.

"*Yes,*" Cloak said. "*The Great Beasts are the ultimate evils in the Multiverse, powerful monsters existing beyond any conventional ideas of time and space. They have no comprehensible motivation and exist only to rewrite reality to their dread design. We can summon an image of him but it'll be equivalent to talking with a computer simulation. A magical construct meant to imitate its power. We're beneath the real Zul-Barbas's notice.*"

"All I care about is whether or not he can bring Mandy back," I said. "Can he do that?"

"*Yes.*"

"Then let's do this thing." I took a deep breath. "If you're okay with it, I mean."

I couldn't proceed without his blessing, don't ask me why.

"Let us dance with the Beast. Read the spell."
I did.

Chapter Twenty-Five

Where I Meet Zul-Barbas (He's Overrated)

"I invoke thee, Zul-Barbas, in the name of the eight Primals. By Death, Life, Chaos, Law, Destruction, Creation, Fate, and Choice I bring you forth." The words for the spell tumbled out of my mouth, the book becoming hot in my hands.

The chandeliers in the ballroom fell from the ceiling, one by one, shattering to pieces across the floor. I could feel a power rising in the room, a power which seemed to flow in and out of me as I recited the words within the living tome.

"I invoke thee, Zul-Barbas, Lord of the Dread City Which Lies Beneath the Waves. I invoke thee, Zul-Barbas, One Who is Neither Dead Nor Alive. I invoke thee, Zul-Barbas, whose return shall bring the end of the world!"

The shelves and art around me began to rumble and shake, as if my words were disturbing the very fabric of the universe. Antique books flew against me, slamming against the side of my head and back while I read. Paintings began to float off the ground and I felt my own body slightly levitate, a familiar feeling made disturbing by the fact it was not by my power that I rose.

That didn't stop me from reading, though. "I offer unto you my entire being in exchange for my fondest wish come true. Bring your most unhallowed attention onto me, this unworthy mortal. I compel thee, amen!"

A crack of thunder echoed outside as I slowly floated downwards.

I shook my head, disbelieving the cheesiness of what just happened. "Seriously, Lancel, is this what passes for magic nowadays? I mean, it's not even in Latin. Pyrotechnics aside, there's no way this is going to work."

"Gary, don't mock the evil ritual you don't understand."

"Why? Will Zul-Barbas show up and kill me?"

"Yes."

"Oh. Never mind then."

Much to my surprise, I saw that the ballroom had vanished around me. Where once I was standing next to a dead dragon's corpse in the middle of a vast treasure room, I was now surrounded by nothing.

Lots and lots of nothing.

It wasn't even a black and empty void like Outer Space, since that would be something. It was surrounded by nothing. Nothing at all. You'd be surprised at how genuinely unsettling that is.

"Okay, I admit that's impressive," I said, allowing the book in my arms to snap closed. "Magic is a lot cooler than I expected. I wonder if this is the place I'm going to get to see alien geometries and nameless cities where sleeping elder god-thingies dwell."

"*No. There is nothing here,*" Cloak said. "*We're in the Nothing Beyond, which lies beyond the Great Beyond.*"

"What's beyond the *Nothing* Beyond?" I asked, genuinely curious.

"*Nothing.*"

"That was terrible, Cloak." I rolled my eyes, impressed by the sheer awfulness of his joke.

"*Ask a stupid question, get a stupid answer,*" Cloak said. "*You should know that by now.*"

"I should indeed."

As much as I wisecracked, I felt empty. Completely empty. I didn't feel love, hate, pity, mercy, forgiveness, or warmth. Mandy's death was like someone had killed me too and I was only going through the motions of life. I was, in a word, going on autopilot. It was a good thing I could do this, too, because otherwise I'd crawl into a hole and start crying.

Which wouldn't do Mandy a damned bit of good.

The Book of Midnight managed to pull itself free from my grip, bouncing on the ground before starting to bark at me once more. It was clearly unsettled by its surrounding, jumping up and down as it circled around me.

"It's okay, girl," I said, waving my hand at her gently. "We're just in a crazy place. After we finish this, I'll take you for a walk to the park and we'll play fetch while people scream at you. Does that sound good?"

"Yip-Yip!" *The Book of Midnight* called, plopping itself over as if it had rolled over on its stomach.

"Stay," I pointed at the book.

It came to a halt and sat itself upright.

"Good girl." I looked around the endless nothingness. "Okay, where is Zul-Barbas? I'm expecting some tentacle-y goodness here. I hope he's at least a hundred-feet-tall with a squid head and batwings."

"Ahem." Something cleared their throat behind me.

"Gah!" I said, jumping up and spinning around.

Behind me, dressed in my dark black cloak and turban-like mask, was me. The outfit hid most of my features but my build was still visible. My eyes were also visible, the only difference being they were utterly without emotion. Say what you will about me, but I've never been cold and unfeeling.

"You, sir, are a very handsome man," I said, pointing at my doppelganger. It was amazing how much humor I could do without finding anything funny at all. "Zul-Barbas, I presume?"

"In the flesh," the figure spoke, his voice a dry shadow of my own. "So to speak."

"Yip! Yip!" *The Book of Midnight* shouted, hiding behind my legs. Apparently, there was no love lost between the book and its master.

"I confess a little disappointment," I said, cocking my head from side to side, trying to see if there were any differences between us. "I was expecting someone a bit taller."

"The spell conjures me as the single most terrifying thing you can think of. You have either a very high opinion of yourself or a very low one," Zul-Barbas said, his voice completely lacking in any mirth.

"Thank you," I said, knowing I was the person who'd gotten his wife killed. That made me the worst monster in the world. "I was hoping for something a little more Lovecraftian, though."

"Everyone is," Zul-Barbas said, not having blinked since his arrival. "Would you like to see my true form? With all of its multiple dimensions and angles no human mind can comprehend? The form which can drive a man utterly mad?"

"Yeah, kinda."

"*Wait, Gary, no!*"

What followed was my doppelganger becoming a thing involving hundreds of mouths, tentacles, eyes, and orifices. I really didn't like looking at the orifices. I'll spare you the 'things no words can describe' and instead go with 'butt ugly.' It was also ridiculously large, easily the size of a skyscraper.

"Now that's more like it!" I said, giving two thumbs up. "Now let's get with the wife raising."

In an instant, Zul-Barbas was once more in my form. It continued talking in its dull accountant-like tone. "I'm surprised by your reaction. In the 1930s, this sent people running of screaming to mental institutions."

"I guess people are a bit more jaded nowadays," I said, shrugging. "You know why I'm here."

"You want to sell your soul," Zul-Barbas replied, pressing its palms together and gazing at me intently. I was a bit creeped out, especially since my doppelganger had no concept of personal space. "I confess, I'm a little surprised. Death is going to be pissed beyond measure. She chose you out of all the beings in the world to be her champion and you're going to throw it all away for your mate."

"Pretty much."

"How peculiar," Zul-Barbas responded, smiling. It was a complete parody of a smile, lacking anything resembling emotion. "I'm willing to make a deal. Your wife will be... restored."

"You made a suspicious pause there," I said, closing one eye and looking at him intently.

"What?" Zul-Barbas replied, sounding surprised.

"A suspicious pause, like you're going to be fulfilling the letter of the agreement rather than the spirit."

Zul-Barbas' right eye twitched. "I don't catch your meaning."

"Like, I'll sell my soul to you in order to get Mandy resurrected only you bring her back as a zombie or something." I didn't like where this conversation was going. "It happens all the time in movies. The genie or whatever twists the intent and we're all supposed to think the human is foolish for making the wish in the first place when the real lesson is the wish-granter is a douchebag."

"I see," Zul-Barbas said. "She won't be... a zombie."

"See, there, you did it again!" I shouted, appalled.

"No I didn't," Zul-Barbas said, wrinkling his brow.

"God dammit!" I kicked the endless blackness around me. "You're going to screw me!"

Zul-Barbas assumed its true form and made threatening gestures more terrifying than anything I'd ever seen. They were the sort of thing which could drive a man to rip out his eye sockets. There were a few things involving a suggestive wiggling of tentacles which aren't fit for publication.

"Do not mock the God Who Lies Between!" A chorus of voices filled my mind, each sounding like a screaming banshee. My entire body was shaking, my hands most of all. I wanted to find a corner to hide in but there was nowhere to go in this place.

"That would have worked if not for the fact it's my wife on the line," I said, taking a deep breath and struggling to calm myself. "Now are you going to make a deal or not?"

The Book of Midnight popped back out from behind me and began yipping wildly, growling at the skyscraper-sized thing threatening me. I had to admire the little books tenacity. It was a brave little tome of evil.

"Good girl," I said, leaning down to stroke the back of her spine. "I'm going to totally get you a treat when this is all over."

"Yip-Yip!"

The gigantic monstrous horror was silent, its withering tentacles slithering back and forth as if deep in thought. Slowly, but surely, the monstrous thing began to shrink. After several seconds it was once more my size and twisted itself until it was humanoid in shape. From there, it covered itself in a fleshy-mask which once more resembled me.

"God, that's gross," I said, repulsed. "You couldn't have come up with something a little less hideous?"

"No." Zul-Barbas' voice was as dry as dust. "There will be consequences for your wife's resurrection. I can breathe life back into her but those who pass through the veil of true death are not brought back untouched. I will not be the one who inflicts the consequences upon her, however. Of that, you can be assured."

"I confess, I would have preferred something a little more concrete," I said, creeped out by the Great Beast's behavior. "You're not reassuring me I'm getting my money's worth here."

"Soon, your planet and all of its peoples will be destroyed. Everyone you've ever known will die in a flood of chaos, reducing them to nothingness as I devour their souls," Zul-Barbas said without a trace of pride or malice. "I am not sure you will be capable of getting your 'money's worth' in this deal."

"You should work on your sales pitch, Zul." I wrinkled my nose. "That was terrible."

"I desire souls," Zul-Barbas said, not even breathing I realized. "They are the one currency of the Great Beyond that has value. Therefore, it is in my best interest to provide what a subject desires in order to avoid accusations of cheating them. I was not attempting to do so earlier. I was merely confused."

"Sure you were." I was annoyed the Great Beast was backpedaling. "I've heard that before."

"I've looked into your soul, Gary Karkofsky. You are a person who only cares about a very small circle of friends and loved ones. What happened to you in your childhood burned your ability to empathize with any but a small group of trusted souls. Your wife, by contrast, is the one who would sacrifice herself for the world. Indeed, she was willing to sacrifice herself for a person who might as well have been a complete stranger," Zul-Barbas explained. He wasn't being insulting, merely factual.

"Yeah," I said, remembering Cindy's description of how she'd died. "She's crazy like that."

Wonderful too.

"You realize she will attempt to stop me after your soul is taken. You will have wasted your eternal existence, cost you your only chance of destroying me, and ruined the pitiful few remaining minutes of your resurrected wife's life by costing her husband—all for nothing. She will die with the rest of humanity. That's even assuming I can bind her soul to her resurrected form, which is a big if."

"Again, your sales pitch sucks. You would do terrible in politics." I'd thought about all of his statements and didn't care. I couldn't leave Mandy dead, not for a moment longer than I absolutely had to.

I wanted her to live forever.

"If I may offer an alternative suggestion," Zul-Barbas said, still talking as if he was teaching math class. "You should not sell your soul to me. Instead, I suggest you assist the Brotherhood of Infamy in completing my summoning. The world will be destroyed, yes, but you will be able to shape it to your wishes. You can recreate your wife and all of your lost loved ones. It will be as though she never died."

"I don't get why you're destroying the world if the Brotherhood of Infamy can just remake it. It seems counter-intuitive for an ancient godlike evil out to eradicate everything."

"I devour souls," Zul-Barbas explained, as if I was saying something terribly stupid. It was the first real emotion I'd heard in his voice. "If I destroy all of creation, I won't have any place to eat in the future."

I mentally processed that. "So, whatever I recreated wouldn't be Mandy? It would walk like her, talk like her, and look like her but it wouldn't be her."

"Only by some definitions," Zul-Barbas said, his voice once again dry as dirt. "Many humans don't even believe in the soul."

"Yeah, but I do." I was horrified by what he was suggesting. Zul-Barbas devouring the world's souls was infinitely worse than him just killing everybody.

"So you will not agree to this?"

"I don't want a clone of Mandy to live. I want *her*."

"Even if she will die again in a few hours and have her soul devoured for all eternity?" Zul-Barbas asked, gazing at me with crossed eyes.

"Yeah," I said, sighing. "I've got faith in the Society of Superheroes. They'll stop you, Mandy will live, she'll go on to marry some other guy or girl and everything will be roses and cupcakes. You know, except for me. I'll be in your stomach or wherever you store the souls you eat."

"*Zul-Barbas keeps the souls he devours in a dimension of darkness and terror,*" Cloak said. "*A place of horror and nightmare where your worst fears live on forever.*"

"Wisconsin?"

"*That doesn't even make any sense.*"

"Clearly, you've never been to Wisconsin. My cousin's farm? Horror beyond imagination."

"The Society will cease to exist when I enter this world," Zul-Barbas laughed. "They will be actors, has-beens, and comic book artists. Nothing more than dreams in the imagination of children and fools."

I wasn't sure what bothered me more. That there was a half-way decent plan for destroying the world or that there were enough morons in the world to carry it out. If I'd had any faith in mankind left to lose, I would have lost it then and there.

"Mandy will stop you," I said. "She and Gabrielle have more good in her than all of the world's heroes combined. *Before* you rewrite reality."

I was surprised to realize I believed that.

Zul-Barbas chuckled. "They'll have to work quickly. The world will end in forty-five minutes and fifty-three seconds."

I took that in. "Shit."

"Fifty-two seconds."

Chapter Twenty-Six

Where I Scam Zul-Barbas

"You can't destroy the world," I said, biting my lip. "For reasons I have yet to figure out."

Zul-Barbas gave me a sidelong glance.

"For example, I'm using it. I intend to rule it and it's not your place to destroy my property. Seriously, though, people will stop you. Heroes. Heroes who are willing to sacrifice their lives. People who aren't me."

"It will work because those who sacrifice themselves are fools," Zul-Barbas said, stretching out a hand and clenching his fist as if to crush something. "I feel compelled to tell you all this because I am assuming your form. Which means, of course, you believe those who sacrifice themselves are foolish. Ironic."

"It's not so much ironic as sad. Like the Alanis Moirsette song. Most of those things weren't really ironic and—"

"Are you quite finished?" Zul-Barbas interrupted, raising an eyebrow.

"Yeah, I think so," I muttered, looking away. I was more embarrassed than anything else.

Zul-Barbas stretched up its right hand and snapped its fingers. "There. It is done."

A part of me worried that, in the midst of our conversation, everything had been destroyed. "You... killed everyone? Killed everyone and ate their souls?"

"No," Zul-Barbas said, its expression remaining utterly lacking in emotion. "That is for later. I have restored your wife to life, or what passes for it. She will rise from her slumber within moments. Now, it is time for you to sacrifice your soul unto me. To become a meal for the one true master of the—"

I pulled out my scythe coin, rubbed it, and swung the resulting blade. The end of the scythe through sliced through the representation of Zul-Barbas. The scythe went through its side like a hot knife through butter, leaving a free-standing hole where his abdomen used to be. Strangely, his upper torso didn't fall over, it hung in the air where I'd slashed through him.

"You betrayed me," my doppelganger cried out, shocked. He looked unable to comprehend what just happened.

"Nothing gets by you, does it?" I said.

Zul-Barbas's body exploded into a thousand pieces of free floating black shadow. The shadows caught fire in midair, burning into tiny little cinders before vanishing into nothingness. I was now alone, free from the curse of Zul-Barbas, in the vastness of the Nothing Beyond.

"Yip! Yip!" *The Book of Midnight* happily jumped around my feet, eventually nuzzling against the side of my leg.

"Gary, what have you done?!"

"Saving our ass," I said. "I figured anyone who calls themselves a Great Beast, has magical books written in human skin, and takes the appearance of whatever terrifies a summoner is a royal douchebag. I figured I could manipulate him into trusting me and double-cross him at the last second."

"You realize you haven't actually killed Zul-Barbas. You just killed your image of Zul-Barbas using his power."

"Yeah," I said, hoisting my scythe over one shoulder. "I don't get why it seemed to know a lot about what the actual Zul-Barbas is doing but I figure that's just one of the oddball facts of magic."

"Wait, you killed your image of Zul-Barbas, which you were only able to kill because you thought you were smart enough to outsmart. But you were only able to outsmart him because you thought you were smart en....God, this is insane!"

"Oh yeah, I'm awesome," I said, pleased with myself. "They should put a statue of me up in the Fraternity of Supervillains Hall of Fame."

"If you're so smart, how are we supposed to get out of here?" Cloak said, sarcastically.

"What?"

"We're in the Nothing Beyond, another dimension. You can't move through other dimensions and you just killed the power source behind the book," Cloak said. *"I'm sorry, we're stuck here."*

Looking around and seeing a whole lot of nothing, I processed that. "Son of a... okay, okay, I've got a plan."

"This I've got to hear."

"Yip! Yip!" *The Book of Midnight* showed no sign of being less active, jumping over my feet and back several times.

Cupping my hands over my mouth, I shouted at the top of my lungs. "Hey Death! A little help here!?"

"That's it? That's your big plan?"

"I didn't say it was a good plan!" I snapped at my cloak. "Listen, if all went well, then Mandy is alive. That's all I care about. I don't care if I'm trapped in the Nothing Beyond for all eternity. As long as she's alright, screw the rest of the world."

"Even if the rest of the world is going to be destroyed by Zul-Barbas and everyone's soul eaten," Cloak said. *"In about, say, forty minutes?"*

"Okay, there are a few flaws in my plan." I raised my hands in frustration. "Napoleon didn't conquer Russia in a day!"

"You're being deliberately sardonic now," Cloak said. *"It's not helping."*

"I'm sorry," I said. "I really fucked up here."

"No," I heard my wife's voice behind me speak, which was all the more unsettling because I instinctively knew it was Death's. "You didn't."

"Gah!" I said, jumping again. "God dammit! What is with you gods and sneaking up on a person?"

Death had changed out of her earlier attire and adopted the gloriously elaborate period dress of a 17th century noblewoman, complete with elaborate hairdo. Her dress was made of black fabric and positively stunning and so was she. Especially noteworthy was the cleavage exposing front; Mandy was an amply endowed woman to begin with, so Death wearing a corset in her body was eye-catching to say the least.

"Eyes up here, buster," Death said in a perfect imitation of Mandy's voice.

"Sorry!" I said, my eyes shooting up to hers. "My bad, your Grim Reaperness."

"You're my chosen, Gary. That makes *you* the Grim Reaper. I'm more the cosmological embodiment of finality."

"Pardon?"

"Never mind," Death said, popping out an ornate fan that she waved into her face. "So you were going to sell your soul to raise your wife from the dead, huh?"

Yeah, that was not the conversation topic I wanted to bring up right now. The whole Armageddon thing was topping out my agenda. Unfortunately, I couldn't think straight looking at her. Death was gorgeous in her outfit, doubly so because she was 'dressed' (for lack of a better term) as my wife. She was a visible reminder I was probably never going to see Mandy again.

"Not really," I said, trying to look away from her. "I decided to double-cross Zul-Barbas pretty early in our discussion. Being a supervillain is all about with great power coming no responsibility."

"Don't lie to me, Gary," Death said, closing up her fan and poking me with it. "I know you were willing to give yourself up to my enemy. The only thing that stopped you was being warned Mandy would be in danger otherwise."

"Please keep that to yourself. If people knew I was willing to sacrifice myself for anybody, it'd be open season on Merciless and his crew. My badass evil reputation depends on me being a complete asshole."

"*What badass reputation?*" Cloak said. "*You've killed a small number of criminals and robbed two banks with a month off.*"

I ignored Cloak, because bantering with him was the last thing the world needed right now. We both knew we had more important things to do but it was like a comedy act. I would say something funny and he'd retort and I'd do the same back and so on. It was automatic with us. In another life, I bet the two of us might have been bigger than Laurel and Hardy.

"Is Mandy going to be alright?" I asked, finally looking at Death. Her eyes were gorgeous, just like my wife's. Unlike Zul-Barbas and me, Death and Mandy had a lot of similarities in personality. For example, they loved messing with my head. "I don't care if the world burns. I just need to know if she'll be alright if I don't get back to the planet Earth or one of them."

"No," Death said. "She's won't be."

"Shit," I said, sighing. "That's no good."

"*Thirty-eight minutes.*"

"Shut up, Cloak."

"*Hurry it up. We need to get her to help us return. No matter the cost, we have to prevent Zul-Barbas's rise.*"

"She can hear you, you know."

"*Oh, right.*"

"Don't worry, Gary," Death said. "I didn't go to the trouble of subtly arranging your ancestors to get together from the Black Death onwards and manipulating events for you two to get parted by some punk dragon and a low-rent zombie apocalypse."

"Wait, what?"

"Nothing. I can't directly interfere in the mortal world. It's an agreement I made with my brothers and sisters."

What was with gods today? In the old myths Zeus and company would have struck down the Brotherhood of Infamy for impertinence by now. That's what the modern era lacked, punishments for hubris. I made a mental note to kill the gods and take their stuff someday. Eli and Death would get a pass but that was it.

"You have brothers and sisters?" I asked, surprised. "Ones who are equally unable to help?"

"My siblings Creation, Law, Chaos, Entropy, Fate, Life, and Choice. Just imagine God and chop him up into like eight people and you have us," Death explained. "There, I've just told you the secret of the universe."

"God has multiple personality disorder? Geez, I could have told you that." I snorted, sitting my elbow on my scythe's upper handle. "So, can you help me or not? By helping me, I also mean right this very second. Because, honestly, we're screwed if you don't."

"I can because we're not in the mortal world," Death popped out her fan again and gestured to her surroundings. "It's going to cost you, however."

"This deal is getting worse all the time," I muttered.

"I am altering the deal. Pray I don't alter it any further," Death said, pressing her nose against mine. "You're not the only one who can make *Star Wars* quotes around here."

"If I wasn't a married man, I'd be all over you right now," I said, unashamedly in awe of my wife's doppelganger. "We've only got like thirty-five minutes left, though, so I'd appreciate it if you could rush it along."

"*Thirty-four, actually.*"

"I know," Death said, with some disappointment. "I need something from you. Something that may result in a change within you and bring the carefully constructed house of cards you've built your psyche around tumbling down."

"Seriously, you gods need to work on your salesmanship. Can't you make something sound nice? Even the crazy fundamentalists have fluffy cloud heaven to look forward to."

"I need you to answer a question," Death said.

"Time or maybe, a man." I was getting annoyed with Death's obliqueness. "There, are we done?"

"It's not a riddle, Gary." Death looked at me, irritated.

Good, because my counter-riddle was going to be 'What's in my pocket?' I didn't need Death telling me about all the naughty pictures of Mandy I kept in my wallet, especially since they were technically naughty pictures of her now.

"I need you to tell me... why?"

"Why... what?"

"Why do all this?" She gestured at me, up and down.

"You want to know why I'm a supervillain?" I'd already answered that question once this week, month, whatever.

"I was referring to the ridiculousness of your every action. You've mocked and heckled your way through things which would break the sanity of your average mortal. You care about people, Gary. You have suppressed it but it's there. A person who genuinely doesn't feel for others can't love."

"Spare me the fantasy novel heartwarming speech," I said, annoyed Death was getting philosophical on me. Oddly, she sounded me like Mandy now than ever. "I care about one major person in my life and a handful of others to a much lesser degree. People who are going to die unless you take me back."

"We'll get there when you answer my question," Death said, undaunted. "Why?"

I was uncomfortable with this line of questioning. I also wasn't sure I could give an adequate answer. Being stumped on a point of philosophy seemed a pretty poor reason to end the universe.

"Why do you care?" I asked, finally asking.

"I get to see every mortal's final days. I've seen greedy men turn generous, good men turn evil, men abandon their faith, and atheists turn to religion. I've seen lifelong enemies embrace and families split up. I always get to know the true nature of a person by witnessing how they react to their final days but I don't know much about living. So, I often ask this question of them. Why do you live the way you do?"

"Thirty-two minutes, Gary."

I could have brushed Death off with a flippant response. After all, I'd been an asshole to her with relatively few consequences so far. Why buck the trend now? Unfortunately, I had an answer to that. Despite how much I resented having a master, Death had been relatively straightforward with me. She deserved an answer. Even if, you know, she could have asked her question *at any other time in my life.*

Thinking about answer, I wasn't sure what was the case. There were a lot of things which had motivated me over the years. Anger, greed, envy, love, and vengeance were some of my personal favorites. I was a fan of all seven deadly sins, with Pride being my favorite. Yet, what was the central guiding concept behind it all? What, at the end of the day, made Gary Karkofsky run? It then occurred to me, I knew the answer.

It was the only honest answer any mortal could give, I think.

"I have not the slightest idea," I admitted. "It's pretty much a day-to-day thing. I have no idea what the hell I'm doing nine times out of ten. I'm playing it by ear. I think we all are."

"Perfect." Death put her hands on her hips, her fan facing outwards. "Just the answer I was looking for."

"Seriously?" I said, appalled. "We're letting the world end because you wanted me to admit I have no idea what the hell I'm doing?"

"Your willingness to admit it is what makes me trust you," Death said, smiling. "Use you scythe, Gary. Use it to cut a hole to your wife and later to where you need to be. It will help you save the world and bring an end to the Brotherhood's ambitions."

"Arf?" *The Book of Midnight* jumped up in Death's arms.

"Aw, who's a good book!" Death said, making kissing noises as it yelped happily in her arms. "I'll take care of this if you don't mind."

"Make sure she gets all of her shots," I said. "Thanks, Death."

"Don't mention it."

Hoisting up my scythe, I swung it around and slashed in mid-air. The weapon tore a hole in the very fabric of reality, creating something where there was nothing. I could see the startled faces of my companions and bits and pieces of the ballroom they were located in. Having no reason to hesitate, I stepped through the hole and left the Nothing Beyond behind.

Hopefully forever.

Chapter Twenty-Seven

Where My Wife Goes Through Some Interesting Changes

The moment I stepped through the rift, I tossed my scythe aside and ran to Mandy's fallen form.

I had faith I'd managed to outsmart Zul-Barbas, confidence even. I couldn't shake the feeling that something terrible was about to happen. She was still lying on the ground, blood covering her outfit and her arms crossed over her chest.

Surrounding her like guards were Cindy and Amanda. Both had stayed at Mandy's side the entire time. Diabloman and Angel Eyes, on the other hand, were off to the side as if they'd been arguing. I couldn't have cared less. Right now, all my attention was on my wife.

"Come on," I said, clutching her wrist with both hands. "Please have worked."

I could tell her ribs were no longer crushed and *something* had happened to her, restoring her physical form. Her chest was still, however, showing no sign of breath. It was as if she had become a perfectly preserved corpse as opposed to the brutalized one she'd been before.

A far cry from resurrection.

"Mister Karkofsky... "Amanda tried to speak to me.

"Shh!" Cindy snapped at her, over my shoulder. "This is where he wakes her up with a kiss!"

I was actually thinking about trying CPR. Still, magic existed. Maybe a kiss was all that was required. "Eh, what the hell."

I leaned in to kiss my wife on the lips, imagining romantic music in the background. If this had been a movie, it'd be the big emotional climax.

It was, in a way.

Pressing my lips against hers, I felt the ice cold red ovals quiver and pulled back. I felt a stirring from my wife in return.

"Please God, work."

Mandy's eyes popped open, her canines elongated into fangs, and she leapt onto me.

"Gah!" I shouted, utterly unprepared for this.

I could feel claws growing from her fingers as they bit into my shoulders, holding me as she savagely attacked my neck. I could feel tears in the fabric of my skin, opening up to an artery as she started drinking the blood pumping from it.

"Holy shit!" Amanda shouted. "She's a vamp!"

"We knew that," Cindy said, momentarily usurping my role as our resident source of snark. Thankfully, she realized she'd made a horribly inappropriate comment and ran to assist me.

Amanda soon joined in, pulling on Cindy as she pulled on me. Soon, it was Diabloman pulling on Amanda, pulling on Cindy trying to get Mandy off me. It should tell you about how strong a vampire is by the fact all three weren't enough to pull her off. By the way, as someone with firsthand experience, the whole 'Kiss of the Vampire' thing is crap. Getting bitten on the neck by a vampire *fucking hurts*.

It didn't help that Mandy was chewing while she tried to suck my blood. If not for the fact that I was kinda, sorta, almost invulnerable she probably would have torn my throat out then and there.

"Ugh argh ack!" I shouted, trying to push Mandy off me while Cindy and Amanda pulled.

"What?" Amanda shouted.

"Get some fucking garlic!" I screamed, pushing against Mandy's face. "Mandy, it's me! You don't... want to kill me. Especially not by drinking my blood! You have no idea...what I've been eating. I had Italian a month ago!"

"Gah!" Mandy screamed, releasing me and falling backwards into a pile with the others. Blood poured out of her mouth as she coughed, her face twisted in revulsion.

"*True love wins the day, I see,*" Cloak. "*Either that or your blood tastes horrible.*"

"Not now." I applied pressure to my neck so I didn't bleed out. Blood still ran through my fingertips and I wondered if I had to go to the hospital.

Mandy stared at her clawed hands, feeling her lips. "Goddess, Gary, what the hell did you do to me?"

"What *I* did to you?" I shouted, glad she was alive but pissed as hell she'd tried to eat me.

"Vampire, Gary," Cindy chided me. "That triumphs being eaten."

Angel Eyes walked over and placed his palm on my neck, a sizzling sensation accompanied by some of the worst pain in my life. "There, I've healed the wound. I admit I did it with a bit more cauterization than was strictly necessary. You should be fine."

Falling to my knees, the agony causing tears to well up in my eyes, I coughed out. "Thank you."

"You're welcome." Angel Eyes stretched out his arms to Mandy as if to embrace her. "It's so good to see you again amongst the living, so to speak."

Mandy ignored him, instead staring at her hands and padding herself down as if she was checking out a new dress. Angel Eyes looked positively stricken when he realized she wasn't going to respond to him.

Cindy looked to him. "I wouldn't mind it too much, Angel Baby. Mandy and Gary are like gum on a shoe. Stuck together for life. Well, you know, unless Gabrielle or the Black Witch shows up. Really, they should just do the whole Biblical thing and marry each other. You know, only with more gay."

Angel Eyes rolled his eyes.

"Gary, we have less than thirty minutes until the end of the world," Cloak said, his voice becoming understandably urgent. *"We don't have time to investigate your wife's condition."*

"My wife's condition? You mean where she's now on an O-positive diet? When Zul-Barbas says there's going to be consequences, I was assuming he meant there might be loss of hearing. I wasn't expecting her to come back *wanting to eat me.*"

There was a dirty joke to be made there but, honestly, now didn't seem the time to make it.

"And he seemed like a trustworthy eldritch abomination too." Cloak sighed. *"**Just hurry it up.**"*

I wasn't sure how one *hurried up* telling your wife she was now a creature of darkness. "Mandy, you were killed by the dragon. I made a deal with the super-evil bad thing about to destroy the world but I weaseled out of the deal. Hopefully, that's not responsible for your condition. The problem is, well aside from you being a vampire is that the city is going to be destroyed in less than half an hour unless we manage to stop it. Like, pronto."

Mandy looked at me for several seconds, her stare colder than Zul-Barbas. The changes to her body were immediate and obvious. Her skin had gone from already naturally pale to milky white with her eyes taking on a peculiar cat-like shade.

Additionally, Mandy now possessed of an unnatural grace which exceeded that of her college acrobat years. There was also something missing, something which I couldn't put my finger on, but I felt she would regret losing.

"Alright," Mandy said, picking up her guns. "Let's go save the city."

Amanda seemed more than a little upset. "We can't do that. I mean, you're a vampire now!"

"So?" Mandy asked, looking at her. "What of it?"

Amanda looked about ready to object.

I shook my head. "Amanda, you're awesome but shut the hell up. Priorities."

"Such an obvious place," Angel Eyes said, sniffing the air as if smelling something foul.

"They're called the Brotherhood of Infamy, Adonis," I pointed out, thinking how it was centrally located and also the first major construction financed by Arthur Warren about the time his brother started the cult. "I don't think they're shying away from being obvious. Besides, if it's not the clock tower, we're shit out of luck because it's our only lead."

"Gary's right." Mandy licked the blood from her now ruby red lips. "Whatever concerns we may have about my condition can wait. We'll try the clock tower as well. It's the center of the city and where the barrier spell was erected. Do you have *The Book of Midnight*?"

I winced, remembering I'd left it with Death. "Uh, the book isn't to be any help."

"*Yes, yes, it would have been.*"

"*Shut up,*" I thought at Cloak. "Guys, we're just going to have to stop the ritual the old fashioned way." Which is probably what Death had wanted from the beginning. Still, I kicked myself for leaving the book behind. I'd been so focused on Mandy I hadn't realized Death was using our visit as an opportunity to steal the tome. I'd admire her if not for the fact it was potentially screwing the world.

"We'll never make it to the clock tower in time," Angel Eyes said, shaking his head.

"I've got a way." Lifting my scythe up, I spun it around and carved a rift through time and space.

This time, it opened up the Night Tower, that place which should have been my base of operations but had been permanently polluted by the smell of dead supervillain. Now, I could see it was covered in blood and mystic symbols etched in the walls.

"Yeah, I think this is the right place."

Chapter Twenty-Eight

The Final Countdown is not just a Song by Europe

The interior of the Night Tower had changed drastically in the past month. Where once it had been a beautiful monument to Lancel Warren's work as a crime fighter, now it was a shattered ruin.

Most of the Nightwalker's trophies were missing, either looted or destroyed. Every piece of his equipment was shattered to pieces across the ground or broken by other means. The furniture looked like it had been bashed repeatedly with a sledge hammer before being set on fire.

"They did not like you, did they?" I thought to Cloak.

"*No, they did not.*"

The Night Tower walls were now inscribed with runes, each crudely chiseled into stone which composed its pillars. I didn't know much about magic, the disaster with *The Book of Midnight* proved that, but I could tell this was the spot they were going to summon Zul-Barbas.

The floor was also covered in bodies, lots of bodies. All of the corpses were recognizable members of Falconcrest City's local supervillain population. There was the Watchmaker, the Ratcatcher, the Yellow Devil, Mister Sneezy, the Black Dentist, and even the KGB Commando. All of them showed severe signs of decay.

"It looks like someone took care of their supervillain zombie-guard for us." I guessed aloud, staring at them. I turned the Reaper's Scythe back into a coin for ease of movement. The weapon looked badass but was pretty difficult for anyone without super-strength to move as a practical weapon.

"Less for us to deal with." Mandy held her nose as if the already-horrible corpse smell was doubly-offensive to her. "So much blood. Almost all of it rotted. A bit of it is fresh though."

I tried not to look freaked out and failed. "That's...neat."

Three of the bodies were of special note, both elderly men wearing Reaper's Cloaks. The trio had been stabbed in the head with sun-shaped shurikens. The living capes were wrapped around their bodies, flailing as if trying to escape. I wondered why they weren't flying through the air as the other capes had, until I saw a glowing mono-filament cord wrapped around them.

"Huh. Sunlight killed these guys."

"Sometimes heroes will kill. I vowed never to do, even in the name of saving lives. Sunlight was willing to do so in the name of saving others. I wonder if that made him my moral inferior or superior."

Behind me, I could hear the rest of my group react with a mixture of surprise and disinterest to the various deceased supervillains. Only Mandy seemed unaffected by the massive number of corpses around us. Cindy, having worked for a couple of the deceased supervillains, took time to kick their corpses.

I checked the three men's men's faces. "Know these guys?"

"Yes. *Both of them were friends. All this time, they were playing me for a fool. How much of my crusade against crime was simply the Brotherhood distracting me from their affairs? I spent years battling pick pockets and drug dealers when I could have been smashing this cult to pieces."*

"Well, live and learn," I said, snapping my fingers and summoning my powers to dispose of them. "You also fought kaiju, dimension lords, and a bunch of really scary people who might have otherwise killed us."

The three cloaks burst into flames along with the corpses of the men they were tied to. The flame became a bright silver as three of the final four remaining Brotherhood owned cloaks vanished from this Earth. Now, only the Nightmaster's remained. I'd have felt a feeling of accomplishment if not for the impending destruction of the world.

"We need to get some lead-in time for the next Apocalypse," I thought to Cloak. "Any leads on what we'll be facing here? I know you haven't been a member for seventy years but, hey, necromancers. You never know."

"Keep an eye out for Lucretia."

"If I see someone wearing a Reaper's Cloak who isn't Amanda, I'll toast them. Don't worry," I muttered, finishing my search of the area. At the edge of the room, curled up in a corner and surrounded by blood, I saw the source of the zombies' defeat. A single figure clad in gold and white was lying broken amongst the corpses he'd created.

Sunlight.

"Merciful Moses," I muttered walking over to the man's side. "You've got to be kidding me."

"Mister Warren!" Amanda shouted behind me, swiftly passing me and leaning down beside the fallen sidekick.

Sunlight was wearing ammo bandoliers filled with shurikens, half of them expended and a few dozen gadgets affixed to no less than three belts around his waist. He'd gone super-equipped to the Brotherhood of Infamy and had gone down swinging. He had bled out from ten or more places, the source of all the blood around him. It looked like a couple of zombies had gotten close enough to bite him. One had stabbed Sunlight in the shoulder with a piece of metal, the piece still lodged there. The other wounds had been sustained fighting the cult. Somehow, Sunlight had managed to fight on long enough to take down his attackers. Probably right before he'd dropped. I'd say it was badass if not for the fact I hated Sunlight.

Even so, I respected what he'd accomplished.

Too bad he had to die to do it.

Amanda rushed to his side, checking for signs of life. It was useless. He was already gone. I could feel her grief from across the room and envied Sunlight in that moment. Few would mourn me that way when I passed. Perhaps that was what Keith had been trying to warn me against.

"Oh Robert..." Cloak whispered, both proud and forlorn.

"We can hold a funeral later." I snapped. "We've got a world to save." I hated myself for saying it.

That seemed to shake Amanda out of her stupor, which was good since we had about five minutes until the end of everything. I promised myself we'd deliver his body to his children. They undoubtedly knew their father was a hero already but deserved to know he died as one—silly as I may have found the old man, I felt like the final joke was on me.

"Anyone got any idea where the ritual is?" I asked, trying to figure out if we had to go down or up or if we'd missed the whole thing. I was about one hundred percent sure that the later hadn't happened but not one hundred percent, which bothered me tremendously.

Mandy herself, meanwhile, stepped over Sunlight's deceased form and took a position beside me. "The ritual is here, I can feel it, but I'm not sure we're on the right floor. We should try the rooftop."

"Yeah, I doubt Zul-Barbas is going to fit down here," I said, preparing to summon my scythe to open another portal. "Okay, everybody, prepare to engage in epic combat with a powerful sorcerer or sorceress to save the world!"

"Uh, Gary..." Mandy started to say.

"Hold on, Honey," I said, not finished with my speech. "Remember, everyone, shoot first and ask questions later. If we kill this Nightmaster psycho, we can prevent the summoning of Zul-Barbas. If we can combine our powers, the element of surprise should allow us to kill them all before they can even...."

"Gary!" Mandy shouted.

"What?" I turned my head.

Practically next to us were about twenty guys wielding futuristic guns in high tech P.H.A.N.T.O.M futureplate armor which looked straight out of *Star Wars*. Standing in front of them was a shapely woman in a long black cloak identical to my own. She was perhaps a foot taller with long black hair and skin as pale as Mandy's post-vampirism. My gaze turned between the troopers' guns and the Nightmaster. "Oh come on, the whole come up behind the guy while he's monologing is as old as Aristotle. You need to repeat that. Tell your men to leave and come back in about... ten minutes. We'll wait here for you."

"I'm sorry, Mister Karkofsky, but that's not happening," the Nightmaster said in a thick Italian accent.

"Lucretia, I presume?"

"*Indeed.*"

"Fuck." If I hadn't been run through the ringer tonight, I would have made a Sisters of Mercy reference.

"Gary, I suggest you dial back your usual flippancy. Those weapons are Venusian wave cannons. The kind used by Foundation for World Harmony agents at the United Nations. They can cut through insubstantial flesh the same as immortal," Angel Eyes said, raising his hands in surrender. "Our powers would be useless against them."

"I'm too damned stubborn to shut up." I was barely able to stand, my head hurting from all the trauma I'd endured, and yet all I could think about was this woman was responsible. She'd ruined my home city, killed tens of thousands, killed my wife (even if she'd gotten better), and all for what? To make the world more boring? To take away heroes just to get rid of the villains? Newsflash: Heroes make the world better than villains make it worse. I wanted to scream this at her but knew it was pointless. She just didn't understand.

"Allow me to speak to her." Angel Eyes flashed a pearly smile at the Nightmaster. "I'd be happy to be of service to your cult in any capacity. *Any capacity.* Why don't you delay the destruction of the world for a week or too so you can find out what I mean?"

I could feel Angel Eyes' powers wash over her. He was trying to work his mojo and I wished him luck.

There had been enough killing.

Too bad it probably wouldn't work.

"*No, it won't*," Cloak said. *Lucretia has no interest in men or women, only power.*"

The Nightmaster seemed more amused than anything. "I could kill you now, poor fools, but in a few minutes it won't matter what happens. So I'm just going to let the clock tick down unless you attack first. You will be honored above all other mortals by the arrival of the one true God."

"Already got one lady," I answered, trying to figure out how much time we had left. "Two, actually, though I'm not sure if the second is an angel or a fragment or what."

All of us stood still, unsure what to do. All of us but Mandy. She bared her fangs at the Nightmaster like an animal before launching herself forward with claws extended. It was simultaneously awesome and futile. The Nightmaster lifted a small circular disc covered in a black cross. Shadowy tendrils poured from the object, wrapping themselves around her arms and chest. Her grunts didn't fire, instead, keeping their guns aimed at us.

"You have transformed your wife into a vampire?" Lucretia asked in a thick Italian accent, one which reminded me of my mother. "I must confess, I am impressed. What I have seen with my Sight told me you were a slave to your bride."

"Mandy follows her own path." I stared at the Nightmaster. "Living or dead."

Lucretia scoffed at me.

Mandy growled the Nightmaster, her eyes turning a shade of red. "You'll die for what you've done."

Lucretia sneered, looking all too amused with herself. "Perhaps, little one, but it won't be at your hands. No undead can harm me. It is one of the powers of my Reaper's Cloak. Oh and don't think about trying to incinerate me or my troopers, Mister Karkofsky. I also know how to suppress the powers of you and Ms. Douglas' cloaks. You are as helpless as newborn babes as long as I live."

Mandy hissed, hating the fact she was helpless against the Nightmaster.

"Ouch." I winced. "Mandy, please don't divorce me for making you an unholy creature of the night. It's bad enough that it has a bunch of drawbacks but I didn't mean for you to be stopped from saving the world. Really."

Yeah, I was stalling for time. Too bad we didn't have any left to stall for.

"I'll *think* about it," Mandy said, looking outside the damaged clockface to the city outside. "Gary, the skies are turning red outside the windows. I think I see bloody rain. I think that's a bad sign. If you've got any of your tricks left, I suggest you pull them now."

"Right," I stared at her. "Absolutely."

"You've got nothing," Mandy said, looking at me with her red eyes. They slowly faded back to their natural brown.

"I'm sorry..." I took a deep breath. "Mandy... I love you."

"I love you too," Mandy whispered, the two of us reaching out to embrace as the world ended.

Cindy pulled the Typewriter's staff from her picnic basket despite the impossible difference in their sizes and shot the Nightmaster in the face with a glowing energy beam. The Nightmaster screamed as her head was seared by the high-intensity of the ray, far more powerful than I'd been hit with. Contrary to all build-up that she was a sorceress without peer, the Nightmaster was as vulnerable to high-tech beams as I had been at the start of all this. The demonic witch fell to her knees, clutching the side of her head which was still on fire but somehow not dying.

"God Almighty," Cindy said. "I'm almost ready for the world to end with sap like that."

Doing a triple-take between Mandy, Cindy, and the Nightmaster, I said, "Yeah, that was totally what I was planning. I take full credit for it and also the salvation of the world."

The soldiers, shocked by Cindy's actions, hesitated for a moment. A moment was all I needed. Drawing on the latent necromantic power in the air, I released more heat from my palms than I had ever before conjured. The flames melted through them and Lucretia on the ground as if they were nothing more than dry paper before an inferno. Seconds later, two dozen charred skeletons were spread across the floor. It was the single largest act of murder I'd committed since beginning my career as a supervillain. Once more, I found that I felt not a damn thing.

Ain't I a stinker?

The Nightmaster hissed at Cindy, her voice low and gravelly. "You pathetic worm! You stinking piece of offal. This world will burn and the whole of creation shall become nothing more than an ashen cinder! I will rule its ashes and your spirit will be nothing more than food for the Great Beasts!"

Cindy shot another blast the Nightmaster but it was absorbed against a barrier she'd erected in front of herself, now adapted to the uncertain technological properties which were arrayed against her.

"Got anything in that bag of tricks for this, Adonis?" I asked.

"No," Angel Eyes said. "But you do. The Reaper's Scythe."

I nodded and conjured it in my hands. The Nightmaster who had begun casting a spell in a language which sounded like heavy-metal monster voice, stopped dead in her tracks when she saw it and the weapon slashed through her barrier like a pin into a soap bubble. That was when Mandy leapt forward and tore out the Nightmaster's throat with her teeth, drinking all of the evil woman's blood as she struggled to cast some sort of spell.

In the end, she didn't.

We'd won.

Sort of.

"Nice shooting, Tex," I said, putting the Reaper's Scythe to the side and giving Cindy the golf clap. I tried to ignore the fact my wife was engaged in an act of decidedly unsexy liquid cannibalism in front of my eyes. It turned out vampirism was not nearly as cool as the movies made it out to be.

Cindy gave a curtsy. "Thank you, thank you. I'd like to thank the Academy, Mechani-Carl, my family, and you."

Mandy dropped the dead body of the Nightmaster, wiping her mouth off with her sleeve. "Amanda, Gary, ask your cloaks whether killing the Nightmaster stop Zul-Barbas's rise."

"Eh?"

"Is the motherfucking monster still coming!" Mandy shouted.

"I'm sorry, no. The summoning is not tied to her life-force."

"Shit," I said. "To think I killed her for nothing."

"I killed the Nightmaster!" Cindy shouted behind me. "With a cane! Do not steal my bit."

I was about to say that it was technically Mandy who finished Lucretia off when the entire tower started shaking. Cracks began forming in the walls of the clock tower with the cracks oozing out a glowing purple fluid that I likened to the plasma of an alien god.

"That's not good," Cindy said, dropping all snark.

"Okay, everybody smash the runes on the wall! Everybody try and break them with whatever you can!" I shouted, directing everyone. Grabbing the Reaper's Scythe and tossing it to Mandy, I used my powers to freeze the stone around me to such levels that it cracked and exploded underneath the runes I saw.

It was a desperation ploy, especially given the Brotherhood had potentially controlled the clock tower for a month. Still, we did our damnedest. Angel Eyes used his magic to blow runes apart while Mandy slashed through them with the scythe, leaping from wall to wall like a human spider. Amanda punched them with her super strength, Diabloman hurling rocks at them. Within seconds, we'd destroyed all of the visible runes but the place still felt like something was happening.

"Well... that didn't work," I spit out, feeling the air heat around my face. It was as hot as a sauna now and getting hotter every second.

The clock tower began to shake and I saw a crack to an alien dimension open up. It was a place of countless angles which didn't exist in this reality. Oddly, it was capable of being described by a human vocabulary; it was weird. Very weird.

"Zul-Barbas is forcing his way through this reality," Angel Eyes said. "We destroyed the runes too late."

"It's the end of the world," Diabloman said, pulling out his cellphone. "I must call my daughter to let her know I love her."

Cindy looked between me and Mandy. "I suppose now is too late to reveal I was always horrifically jealous of you two."

"Yeah, we got that," Mandy said.

"We did?" I asked.

Angel Eyes' likely last seconds on Earth were spent looking horrified.

"Well, I'll have you know—" Amanda was interrupted by the sound of an unearthly wail which shattered the windows of the clock tower.

A small black tendril started slinking over the side of the crack in the floor. From there emerged the true form of Zul-Barbas, a ball of tentacles and orifices every bit as disgusting as I remember. The only difference was in scale.

It was six-inches-tall.

I stared down at the tiny Great Beast. "Huh. That was unexpected."

Chapter Twenty-Nine

So Long and Thanks for all the Fish

I was standing in the middle of a ruined clock tower, its shattered face open to Falcocrest City's skyline. My henchmen stood still, stunned expressions on their faces. Before us was a Lovecraftian abomination bent on destroying the world.

And he was kind of adorable in an ugly-cute sort of way.

I can't explain it better than that. You'll have to take my word for it. The Great Beast was slithering towards us at a snail's pace, perhaps trying to grab our face like the hatchling form of *Alien*'s monster. Seriously, though, tentacles are not the fastest means of travel outside of an ocean environment.

"Okay, what the hell is that?" I asked, pointing at the nightmarish but pint-sized creature.

"Well, you and the others did disrupt the ritual towards the end. Not to mention, much to my personal delight, the majority of residents were smart enough to evacuate. It's not like the whole of Falconcrest City's population was sacrificed as the ritual probably requires."

"Huh, no wonder the world didn't end. The cultists in charge of this thing were morons. With so many of them tied to the government, I should have expected this!"

"You have to be an idiot in order to want to bring about the end of everything," Amanda said, looking over my shoulder at the horror. "So, what do we do with it? Donate it to a zoo or something?"

"Fuck no," I said, snapping at her. "We're killing this thing dead while we still can. For all we know, it could end up eating its Wheaties and return to kill us in five or ten centuries. Then wouldn't we look like assholes."

"I think that ship has sailed," Cindy said.

"Hush, you," I snapped back.

"A wise decision," Angel Eyes said, removed his ruined jacket and undershirt. This exposed his magnificent washboard abs and spectacular chest. I proceeded to look away and blush. He was really starting to annoy me when he did that.

"I am the beginning and end of all life in the universe. All souls exist to be consumed by me. "The miniature Zul-Barbas shouted in a cry of a hundred alien voices, louder than you'd expect from such a small frame.

I looked down at the little ball of evil. "You know, I liked the emotionless alien thing you appeared to me in my dreams as. If this is the cultist's view of what you were like, it sucks."

The eldritch monster responded by leaping through the air and attaching itself to my face. Its tentacles wrapped around the back of my head, its hundreds of mouths bit into my face, and it tried to shove something down my throat. I would have made an *Alien* reference but I was kind of busy having my face assaulted.

"Blargh klarfg muaf blarg!" I shouted, waving my hands around like a madman and dancing around the room in a stunned panic.

"What did he say?" Amanda asked, looking to Mandy who'd been staring at the sight in stunned silence.

Mandy then burst into action. Her voice a low growl, sounding more annoyed than concerned. "He said to get it off him."

Mandy rushed up to me and grabbed hold of Zul-Barbas' miniature frame and started pulling.

"Mmmph!" I shouted, pushing against the abomination. For those of you wondering what I was saying, it could best be summarized as 'try not to rip my face off in the process.' I think. It's all a bit fuzzy now, mercifully so.

Amanda and Mandy were strong enough together to pull Zul-Barbas off. Apparently, the Great Beast had left its world-crushing power back in its home dimension. Zul-Barbas sailed through the air, the thing flying back toward the rift it'd come through.

"Oh no you don't!" Mandy shouted. With superhuman speed, she hefted the Reaper's Scythe and used it to slice through the creature in mid-air. Zul-Barbas split in half, its two sides landing three feet apart.

With that, the threat of Zul-Barbas ended. The walls stopped oozing and the crack in reality became nothing more than a hole in the floor. Outside, the downpour of blood was replaced with good old-fashioned acid rain. Even the air lost its crackle, becoming no more ionized than it would be after a common electrical storm.

"*Well, that was anticlimactic. I confess, I was hoping for something a trifle more traditional. An epic confrontation between good and evil where everyone combines their powers to drive back the evil monster. Maybe a heroic sacrifice or two. This is almost subversive.*"

"Blargh!" I responded, coughing up the goop Zul-Barbas had oozed from its appendages. "Blargh!"

"I can see you're busy now, so I'll wait until you're done to talk to you about it."

"Gary, are you okay?" Mandy asked, using her vampire speed to return to my side in an instant.

"I'll pretend you didn't ask that." I wiped off my mouth with my sleeve, partially to annoy Cloak. "Congratulations, Mandy, you saved the world. You're a superhero now."

"At the mere cost of my soul," Mandy said, showing her fangs. Her eyes glowed red too. I thought she was adorable.

"I wouldn't believe in any God or Goddess who didn't consider you his favorite child." I moved to embrace her.

Mandy stopped me before I could, putting a hand against my chest. "You smell like alien goop. Also, I want you to brush your teeth." She paused. "For a month."

There was something odd about her posture, as if she was expecting to feel something but didn't.

I put my palm in front of my mouth and breathed in the smell. The stench was enough to make my eyes roll back into the back of my head. "Maybe I'll mix bleach in with my mouth-wash. God, what the hell are Lovecraftian abominations made of, anyway?"

"You did a good thing here, today, Gary. For once, I'm proud to be joined with you."

"Don't get too sentimental there, Pops. Don't forget this is all your fault."

"I see we're not going to be having one of those 'start of a beautiful friendship' moments."

"I preferred *The Maltese Falcon* myself," I said, wiping my tongue down and trying to spit up any remaining goop.

"It didn't like, lay any eggs inside you, did it, Mister Karkofsky?" Amanda asked, walking up behind me and giving me a hug. "You're not going to have any alien demon babies, are you?"

"Please, never ever say that again." I said, giving her a pat on the shoulder. "Don't you have high school classes to attend or something?"

"I'm twenty-five."

"Don't worry. You still have plenty of time for the bitterness and hate of adulthood to set in."

I vowed to help Amanda with her superheroics. A staggering number of Falconcrest City's supervillains had been killed during this nightmare but not all by any stretch of the imagination. She'd need all the help she could get. Besides, I wanted to buy her evil castle as a potential lair. I was going need a new one now that the Brotherhood had wrecked the clock tower.

Diabloman looked up from where the pieces of Zul-Barbas had fallen. "Boss, how do you want me to report this? Many of the city's ganglords and master criminals will want an explanation for recent events."

I thought about how they would react to my almost getting eaten by a six-inch-tall monster. "Say I beat it up with my bare hands and it was two-hundred-feet-tall."

"Very good, Boss."

Amanda tapped me on the shoulder. "What's going to happen with the zombies?"

"Cloak?"

"Without Zul-Barbas to animate them, I imagine they're all going to return to the grave within the next hour or so."

"Huh, that wraps everything up in a neat and tidy package, doesn't it?"

"It's hard to believe it's over. For nearly a century, the Brotherhood has been preparing for Zul-Barbas' rise. In the span of a month, you've wrecked their plans and left their god dead. There's no chance of recovering from this, they're finished."

"Oh please," I snorted, finding his optimism idiotic. "They'll be planning to resurrect Zul-Barbas or finding themselves a new evil god to worship in a month, tops."

"Probably." Cloak sighed. *"It's the endless dance of our world. Supervillains commit crimes, superheroes arrest them, and then supervillains escape to commit more crimes. In Zul-Barbas' case, there's no end of fools like Chief Watkins who will be look for a way to bring him back. I bet there's already a line of criminals forming to take over the Typewriter and Ice Cream Man's identities too."*

"Eh, I wouldn't worry about it. If this is the best they can do, we'll be able to stop them easy."

"Be careful, you're sounding dangerously close to an antihero."

"Perish the thought."

"It's a never-ending battle between good and evil." Mandy hefted my scythe over her shoulder. "It gives us something to do."

"But we're evil," I said, before realizing the implications of her words. "Wait, you can hear him now?"

"Thank God, I couldn't imagine speaking to you alone for all eternity."

"Yeah," Mandy said. "It makes you sound marginally less like a crazy person."

"Marginally," I said, looking around the ruined Night Tower for my henchmen. "Okay, head count people, who's still alive?"

I knew everyone had gotten through this alright. Cindy was standing there looking exultant, still smiling the cane in her hand. Angel Eyes was looking bored, probably annoyed he hadn't had a chance to seize the spotlight. Either that or realizing Mandy preferred me over him.

"No accounting for taste."

"Ha-ha, very funny. Even if I agree with you."

Diabloman looked shell-shocked by everything which had happened. I'd have to take my Number Two on my next couple of heists. He hadn't had much chance to shine during our final battle and I wanted to give him that option. Maybe I could arrange a 'Take Your Daughter to Work Day' when I incorporated my evil empire. I bet he'd appreciate that. Mandy and Amanda, the resident non-evil members of my team, were beside me. Both looked worn-out yet triumphant. I couldn't blame them. They'd contributed the most to seeing the world saved. Yes, even more so than me. I'm not afraid to say it.

Amanda, despite everything, had weathered the storm of her first real crisis successfully. Despite my teasing, I was starting to see her as a worthy heir to the Nightwalker legacy. If I could come to believe her as the next one, I'm sure the average citizen of Falconcrest City would do the same. In a few years' time, I suspected she'd be tough enough to take me down. I'd have to make sure I was tougher too by then.

Mandy, on the other hand, had a lot more on her plate now with the whole 'transformation into a creature of the night' thing. She looked *hungry* now, more than anything else. I wasn't sure I was going to be able to provide all the blood she needed, especially if it involved chewing me up. Still, a woman like her came twice in a millennium and I was willing to work through whatever problems life (and un-life) had to offer us. After all, if a marriage outlasted 'til death do us part' then it was worth saving.

Angel Eyes spoke up. "This is not what I signed up for, Merciless, but I will say you've rid the city of competition. A staggering number of my rivals are dead along with most of the city government. We will have little difficulty taking over the city."

"Yay," I said, without enthusiasm. I was just glad the city was safe, which I never expected to say.

Cindy, meanwhile, waved around her cane, looking armed and irritable. "Is anyone going to comment on the fact I shot the main villain? Or are we going to ignore that because Mandy killed the little octopus-gerbil thing?"

"Yes, Cindy, you're awesome. You are a special snowflake princess who rules over all other snowflakes."

"And don't you forget it." Cindy put the weapon back into her picnic basket. "I'm expecting a bigger cut of the billions we'll be extorting from the city over this."

"I'll see if I can work something out with the city fathers," I said, imagining they'd do anything to get the city's tourism trade back on track. I was already thinking of Planet Merciless, Merciless Supervillain Rap Records, and a dozen other franchises to rebuild the city on. I'd have to work out the details with Diabloman.

Speaking of which, Diabloman stood on the edge of the shattered clock face, gazing out onto the city below. "In a moment like this, all of a person's sins are erased. By saving the world, we could abandon our paths as supervillains and embrace the light. We would be accepted as superheroes and the world would laud us as champions."

"Why the hell would we want to do that?" I asked, walking up beside my Number Two.

"You have no regrets?" Diabloman asked.

"Why should I? As far as I'm concerned, I have learned nothing from this little adventure except how to do evil more efficiently. Oh and never try to summon horrible monsters from another reality. That never works out."

It wasn't true. I regretted what happened with Mandy. I regretted what happened with Sunlight. I also regretted not getting the chance to kick Amanda's father's ass for what he did to his wife and child. Overall, though, I was pretty satisfied with how things had turned out. After all, the world wasn't primordial chaos or a place without superpowers. I think I'd go mad in such a banal and colorless place.

"You are truly a great supervillain," Diabloman said, bowing his head. "One we are all honored to follow."

"Speak for yourself," Angel Eyes said.

"I'm thinking of actually demanding a full partnership," Cindy said.

"He follows, I lead," Mandy said.

"I'm not a supervillain. I'm more just not arresting you guys." Amanda clarified. "Which won't happen the next time we meet."

I smiled. "I wouldn't dream of it, Nightwalker."

Diabloman didn't notice. Instead, he just laughed. "What next?"

I looked out onto Falconcrest City, taking in all its breathtaking glory. It was a whole city ripe for the taking. Seeing Ultragoddess' light move through the air, I pushed aside those thoughts. "I'm not feeling very supervillainy right now. If you won't tell anyone, I think I'm going down there to take care of any remaining zombies to get this place back on its feet."

Angel Eyes said, "I won't tell."

Cindy and Diabloman laughed.

Mandy was silent.

Epilogue

I worked until the better part of the morning, only stopping when it was clear I was running out of power. My compact with Death had given me massively expanded energy reserves, far more than the Nightwalker ever had, plus the city was a walking negative reservoir but my experience with channeling was limited. The others helped, though, and with the Shadow Seven's help we'd made the city absent several thousand more zombies.

Now the city was freed from its dome prison, hopefully the government would be able to send relief or allow superheroes in. If not, we'd probably be able to cleanse the city ourselves in a week. Falconcrest City had suffered a terrible blow but my city would recover, I guaranteed it.

It helped that I intended to extort the government into sending a massive amount of relief money and, if not, would steal however many billions necessary to get it fixed. The fact the Brotherhood of Infamy was no longer present to the corrupt the city or outright working for me would help.

Angel Eyes, Cindy, and Diabloman went off on their own after I decided to retire with Mandy. Angel Eyes was fascinated at the prospect of being a hero and my suggestion he use the camera equipment at WFCB to address the city and nation. If nothing else, social media would let the world outside know who had saved them. I certainly didn't want them to know it was me and Gabrielle's team was, at present, still a secret.

I hoped I hadn't created a monster.

Mandy was conspicuously silent on the way home, giving one word answers or staring out the window of the Nightmaster's car I'd stolen. I wasn't sure how our marriage would adjust to the fact she was a vampire now, but I was willing to try. Pulling the car to a stop, I opened the door for her to get out and walked beside her to the porch.

"I think we'll focus on finding you blood stores which won't offend your moral sensibilities," I said, smiling.

"That would be best, yes." Mandy's voice was cold, colder than I expected.

Entering through the front door with my wife by my side, I was already trying to figure out how to introduce our dogs to their newly changed mother when Mandy grabbed me by the arm.

"Is something wrong?" I asked, looking at her.

Mandy shut the door behind us. Her gaze was empty. "I don't know who you are."

I stared at her, a sudden sense of overwhelming terror filling my belly. "What?"

"I know your name, I know our past together, and I remember the emotions associated to them. But you are a stranger to me."

I shook my head. "Don't joke around like this, Mandy."

Mandy closed her eyes. She then spoke, her voice absent of all emotion, "Such a strange thing, a name. Only two people in her life ever spoken it with that much unreserved affection. Selena Darkchylde and you. I remember feeling so terribly proud of you, willing to do whatever you could to save this city. My sister, her sister, and the city she grew up in. Then I remembered dying at the dragon's hands. The pain, the crunching sensation, a sense I was being picked up by loving hands. Then an emptiness of neurons dying without a spark to guide them."

"You're back now, though." I reached over to touch her, only for her to take a step back.

Mandy shook her head. "I was born in the fires of your spell. A moment of agonizing pain followed by immense hunger and strange, alien emotions. She could have prevented my return to existence, forbidden my body from rising from the grave, so strong was her heroic willpower and purity of spirit. Yet, she did not. So great was her desire to protect this city."

I stared at her in abject horror. "You're not Mandy?"

A sense of cold, terrible dread, went up and down my spine.

Mandy lowered her gaze then looked up to me and I saw the emptiness in her eyes. "No. I am something new."

"*Soulless*," Cloak whispered, his voice filled with terrible sadness. "*A husk animated by the Ka and Sheut but absent the Ba. She's missing the part of her soul which makes her, her. Oh God, Gary, I'm sorry.*"

"Shut up! Shut the hell up! Get the hell out! You're lying!" I shouted, screaming at my Cloak from every direction my neck could manage.

Mandy looked to one side. "I cannot feel sympathy for you. I do not feel that emotion. Only pain, pleasure, appetite, and need. Yet, the memories which distinguish this body from the past carry a shade of great feeling. She would not want you to blame yourself, Gary. You did not lead her down this path. If not for you, this world would be destroyed."

"I should have fucking let them destroy it!" I shouted, falling to my knees and clutching my head.

This couldn't be happening.

I'd fix it.

Somehow.

I'd make another deal with Death.

I'd sell my soul.

I'd sell anybody's soul!

Silence greeted my call into the spirit world.

Not-Mandy as I came to view her, removed our wedding ring, looking at it. "I am enough of her to know what I must do with my life. This city needs a protector and the bloody revenge you have wrecked upon the Brotherhood of Infamy will not be enough to keep the citizenry safe in this land, especially when the people start to return. She was a great heroine as Nighthuntress and I will try and follow in her footsteps."

"You are not worthy," I said, looking through the fingers pressed against my face. "What made Mandy a hero was her compassion and love."

"Yes." Not-Mandy placed the wedding ring on the ground. "But you act as if she did not know what the risks were. That this is about you. Better than you, she became a superheroine knowing it would perhaps lead to her death. You treated it like a game but to her it was a calling. A chance to rise up above the mundanity of this world and become a protector. It is not an uncommon choice. The firemen, policemen, ambulance drivers, doctors, priests, and soldiers of the world often follow a similar challenge. To be willing to give of yourself. Which she did, both to save this city and save your friend Cindy."

I held back saying saving Cindy was not worth my wife's death. I wanted to say it but I wasn't going to profane my wife's dying act. "She didn't *have* to sacrifice herself."

The Not-Mandy's voice softened, to the point of becoming near-identical to my wife's. "But she was willing."

Tears streamed down my eyes as I heard our dogs growl loudly at Not-Mandy, treating her as a stranger in their home. "You say you can feel the emotions of the past and her memories? We can awaken these emotions in your current ones. You've gone through a traumatic experience. An even more traumatic transformation. Maybe you just need an adjustment period. Further treatments of magic to—"

Not-Mandy shook her head. She then stepped to one side.

I saw a shimmering silver-white figure staring at me from behind her.

It was Mandy's ghost.

"No," I whispered. "Please no."

In that moment, I broke.

Mandy's ghost walked over to me and placed her hand on my shoulder, leaned down, and gave my lips one last kiss. "I'm going onto a new life, Gary. The Goddess watches over me and will watch over you to in my absence."

I placed my hand on her face. "Is there anything I can do for you?"

Mandy smiled and whispered in my ear. "Live."

And then she was gone.

Later, I would come to wonder if Death had sent that an illusion to bring her servant comfort in a time of great sorrow or whether or not I'd hallucinated the entire thing. A memory I'd conjured in order to deal with the immense amount of grief. I could not bring myself to completely belief it was real, the doubt gnawing at me like rats on a piece of cheese.

But I willed myself to believe.

It was the only way to go on.

The Not-Mandy, Nighthuntress, walked to the window of our house rather than the door. Something about thresh-holds not agreeing with them even when being invited in. Opening it up, she spoke. "I will watch over you, too, Gary Karkofsky. Merciless—"

"Don't call me that," I snapped.

I wasn't in the mood to play dress-up.

Nighthuntress' voice softened again. "As you wish. I am grateful for the life you have given me and the memories which provide me a greater context for this existence than most vampires ever get to know. I will try and make it count for something. Mandy believed that life and death were part of an eternal wheel which gave rise to on another. Do not be ashamed of who you are or what you have done. Know only that, this is not the end."

She then disappeared through the window at a speed so fast I couldn't see her vanish.

And I was alone.

The dogs yowled, sensing their mistresses passing.

I went to the window and shut it tightly before locking it.

"No words can express my sympathy, Gary," Cloak said, trying to comfort me. *"Know I, too, have suffered loss and will be there if you need me. My...friend."*

I wiped away the tears on my face, pushing down the emotions afflicting me. Blinking rapidly, I took several deep breaths and went to go let the dogs out. They'd probably piddled in the floor but there wasn't much you could do about that during the zombie apocalypse.

"Thank you, Cloak. I mean that. Don't worry, though, I'll be fine."

"What?" Cloak asked, surprised.

I spoke with more resolve than I'd ever had in my entire life. "I am going to *fix this*."

***

Fear not! Merciless will return in *The Secrets of Supervillainy*. Coming in 2016!

About the Author

C.T. Phipps is a lifelong student of horror, science fiction, and fantasy. An avid tabletop gamer, he discovered this passion led him to write and turned him into a lifelong geek. He is the author of The Rules of Supervillainy and the Red Room series. C.T. lives in Ashland, Ky with his wife and their four dogs. You can find out more about him and his work by reading his blog, The United Federation of Charles, (http://unitedfederationofcharles.blogspot.com/)

Made in the USA
Charleston, SC
14 January 2016